MW00944802

The TAMING of the LOON

Discover the Blurry Line Between Right and Wrong

A Novel

PAUL FRANKS & S.P. STAMATIS

XULON PRESS

In Loving Memory

of

Christopher Franks

Xulon Press
2301 Lucien Way #415
Maitland, FL 32751
407.339.4217
www.xulonpress.com

Unless otherwise indicated, Scripture quotations taken from the King James Version (KJV)–*public domain.*

Paperback ISBN-13: 978-1-6628-3677-0
eBook ISBN-13: 978-1-6628-3678-7

ACKNOWLEDGEMENTS

Jim Frankiewicz

Dr. Susan Anderson-Khleif

Betty Stamatis

Ernesto Chivilo

Alexander Rassogianis

Perrin Stamatis

Dr. Paul Kachoris

Rev. John Artemas

Jay Stamatis

Nia Toloken

Anna Toloken

TABLE OF CONTENTS

Part 1

Part 2

Part 3

Part 4

PREFACE

The Danish writer Janne Teller once wrote "From the moment we're born, we begin to die." That statement has the makings of an unchangeable universal truth. Also, mostly everybody agrees that the sun rises in the East and sets in the West. So, Universal Truth has not totally disappeared yet.

A closer look in this area reveals that the terms "Relativism" and "Post-Modernism" are fancy academic labels that have reshaped universal principles of human behavior. Terms like Right and Wrong, Good and Evil haven't vanished; they are merely redefined and applied to today's acceptable norms.

Clearly, when released into society, we're not given an instruction manual on how to live. We rely on parents and family to cultivate our values and build character; although in recent years, this custom has given way prematurely to individual choice. Broadly speaking, Relativism is the belief that there is no Universal Truth—only the truth that characterizes a particular person, society or culture. Hence, people around the world have different ideas about what's right and wrong.

For example, it was socially acceptable to practice cannibalism in Papua New Guinea as late as 2012. In our own country, just 200 years ago, slavery was an acceptable practice in the Southern states. Thankfully, a loud cry for human rights echoed across the civilized world to reject these and other dehumanizing practices.

The Taming of the Loon is a work of fiction which focuses on the rise of Relativism in our 21st Century culture where Good and Evil, Right and Wrong have become flexible and are continually reshaped and redefined until they fit a specific social construct. And they reside there until the next paradigm shift. We can thank the post-modernist movement which began in the 1950s that celebrates skepticism, sub-jectivism, diversity, an appeal to feelings and a growing suspicion of faith-based principles, even reason itself.

In the absence of permanent values, everything is subject to self-re-flective interpretation where a path of wrong-doing can be sugar-coated with layers of rationalization and/or justification to appear normal. Clearly, we are left without a moral standard—stranded, without a compass or a map; very much like Moses coming down Mt. Sinai with two blank tablets and imploring the people to scribe their own values.

This "To Each His (or Her) Own" thinking has gained notoriety, expanding into a herd format. It has settled into our schools, institu-tions, companies and our politics. As a result, we're watching Relativism replace traditional principles grounded on the Judeo-Christian foun-dations of our country. Even the Bible is looked upon as just another book, on a shelf with other books, rather than on a nearby table for daily access.

Now, God is slowly being evicted from our culture. A secular, social godhead, is poised to replace Him and regulate how we should live. Worse, our leaders are urging us to feel good about it because…it's the "New Normal."

Authors' Note

The following story is a work of fiction. It may reflect current conditions in the United States and Middle East. Names, characters and organizations in the story are not intended to represent any real persons or entities. The story may also reflect events and documented news stories. However, any resemblance to actual persons living or dead is unintended and coincidental.

This story is intended to evoke an awareness to the perils inherent in the subjective interpretation of long-held moral standards of human behavior. Terms such as rationalization, justification and intellectualization are used to describe this trend.

Many kudos to those who observe and hold dear inherited values of a well-balanced life, for whom Right and Wrong, Good and Evil never have to be explained.

We are discussing no small matter,
but how we ought to live

Socrates, in Plato's *Republic* (390 B.C.)

Part 1

Chapter 1

THE GREATER GOOD

On a cool autumn morning, Father Stan Rybak enters his office at All Saints Church in Sycamore, Illinois. He hangs his blazer on the coat rack and wakes up the computer to check on his reservation at Saul's Fishing Resort. He notices his confirmation for several days in late October just as the door chimes ring. He looks out the office window. It's Jim Winters, the attorney from nearby Hampshire.

"Jim! Nice surprise! I just got here myself. How are you?"

"Hello, Father. I'm headed for a meeting in Beloit, thought I'd come by for a few minutes."

"Great. I'm happy to see you—I'll get some coffee. How are things at the oil company?"

Jim unbuttons the coat of his 3-piece suit and sits nearby showing off his Italian shoes.

"Well, that's what the meeting's about," he says softly. "Company's being sued by multiple plaintiffs regarding the Rockstone Pipeline..."

"Sorry to hear that, Jim—what's going to happen?"

"I'm not sure. We have to discuss it today and clarify our position for a hearing scheduled just a few months away. The boss will be there and he'll want to hear from me and my team that we will be ready to present evidence to dismiss our culpability. How about you? You must be busy with all your programs starting now."

"Yes! All start at the same time—choir, Sunday school, Bible study, community outreach."

After volunteering details about his company's careless record in a subdued tone, Jim checks his watch and stands. "I think I better go, Father. Thanks for the coffee. I'll keep you posted on developments."

"Thanks for stopping by. I know you'll do the right thing. I'm here for you, Jim."

Jim Winters steps out onto the small courtyard. His 6-foot, 38-year-old frame pauses a few moments deep in thought while fumbling to find his keys. Suddenly, he snaps out if it and slips gracefully into his Volvo 2-door coup. His brown hair with hints of grey and a bronze tan give him that Gentleman's Quarterly cover look.

* * * *

Jim and his team of four lawyers representing The Continental Petroleum Co. march into a conference room at the Goodwin Hotel in Beloit, Wisconsin to address multiple suits filed against the company. These allege violation of several EPA statutes concerning the Rockstone Pipeline. The lawyers are to appear at a hearing early in 2020 at U.S. Federal Court in Madison.

Several environmental groups, including Green Peace, have also joined a long list of residents claiming the company polluted land and great lakes waterways with toxins and gasses. The allegations have attracted the attention of the attorney general of Wisconsin and U.S. attorneys. In particular, suits have been filed for pipeline leaks that have polluted ground, rivers and streams in the state.

A graduate of Harvard Law School, Jim Winters is chief attorney earning well into six figures. His focus is to render existing evidence inconclusive and thereby weaken the state's case for a trial. He opens his laptop with authority and begins.

"Good morning, everyone. As you know, the hearing in Madison will establish if the allegations levelled at our company by the U. S. Attorney in fact warrant a trial. We must avoid a trial at all costs. It would delay completion of 600 miles of pipeline to Northern Indiana refineries. Before we start, please welcome our CEO Joe Morrison."

Mr. Morrison, a short, stocky man in his 50s stands sporting a head-full of grey hair pressed tightly, resolving in a tiny pony tail. He leans on the mahogany table displaying his glossy fingernails, takes a deep breath and looks up.

"I'm glad to see everyone here," he begins softly, forcing the legal staff to lean forward slightly, "and I hope you all did your homework. Jim is right! We began servicing Minnesota and Wisconsin with natural gas barely four years and we're months away from Gary refineries. Once there, we can establish refining capacity and begin the next leg south toward the Louisiana coast. We have to do the right thing here. We must show these allegations to be spurious and misdirected.

"Look people, we have spent close to $500 million so far and are just beginning to create a revenue stream now. The suits we can deal with, string them out several years and settle them one at a time. But a trial, with subsequent damages awarded if we lose? No way! Thousands of jobs are at stake! I leave you to do the right thing."

He looks at his Rolex, waves to everyone and leaves the room. Jim Winters stands and asks for opening arguments designed to refute allegations and evidence that would necessitate a trial. Lawyers and legal researchers take the floor one at a time to reveal cogent reasoning in defense of the company. And Carol Stempke, a secretary, is there to record minutes, a copy of which will reach the desk of Mr. Morrison.

The presentations all merge into droning background noise for Jim as his attention drifts to personal issues regarding the case against Continental. He visited Fond du Lac last month where most of the class action litigation originated. He went incognito in an unofficial capacity and discovered information about violations his company committed that would be difficult to defend.

Further on-line research revealed numerous deaths and illnesses due to cancer, leukemia and respiratory complications. And the pipeline has only been in service for four years. A closer examination of case files alarmed him. He located more than 165 injuries, 43 fatalities, more than 180 fires and 38 explosions in the thousand-mile pipeline. The explosions and fires (typical occurrences in pipelines) can be dealt with, but for the rest of it, he felt a knot in his throat. His company was responsible for ruining people's lives not to mention 1,200 residents that had to be evacuated near Fond du Lac.

He knows that Joe regrets accidents, illness and loss of life, "...but it's not like they're done on purpose," he heard him plead once. "Those things happen," he recalls him saying in a meeting. "It's unavoidable collateral damage that comes with running an energy company."

Jim's attention quickly returns to the meeting as he listens in on Howard's presentation.

"...Look, we received a clean bill of health from the PHMSA (Pipeline & Hazardous Materials Safety Administration) last year. We all know there are millions of miles of pipe out there and that they can't check every mile; fact is, only about 5% of pipelines are currently subject to safety regulations. So, most of the lines are unregulated which allows companies like ours to cut corners and risk accidents while moving product to market.

"We have one defense: our lines have the seal of approval from PHMSA even though my research shows that on average, any pipeline catches fire every week, ends in an explosion every two weeks, creates an injury every five days and a fatality every month. That's a matter of record."

At this point Jim is looking for an iron clad defense to take to the hearing. He knows he can get a couple continuances with some fancy legal showmanship. But for the sake of the company he needs something better.

"Does anyone have an argument that can deflect attention away from Continental and avoid a trial?" Pat Mackey, a young lawyer out of Notre Dame just a year ago, raises her hand and stands.

"What do you have, Pat?" Jim probes mechanically, not expecting a whole lot.

"Well, gentlemen, I took the liberty of investigating the nature of the complaints from pipeline leaks or line breaches. The main problem happens to be toxic chemical exposure. If a leak occurs in a pipeline, toxic chemical exposure puts at risk nearby residents. This exposure can lead to migraines, painful rashes, breathing irregularities, nausea and cancer..."

"We know all this," Roger Kirby, another lawyer interrupts. "What we need..."

"Please, Roger! Give me a minute," Pat raises her voice while still focused on her notes.

"The main culprit behind 95% of all the cases involving illness and death is methane gas."

She opens her laptop and activates the screen on the wall. Everyone sees a map of Wisconsin. Pat walks over to the map and points to two large paper mills around Lake Winnebago.

"Gentlemen, I draw your attention to Intercostal Paper Co. here and Chippewa Paper Products here. You notice they're near the lake. That's because a fresh water supply is required to make paper. Now, these mills have been here for decades and have supposedly filtered out their contaminants before the waste water spills back into rivers and streams.

"Curiously, the medical problems have afflicted people around Fond du Lac long before our pipeline was constructed. Guess what the main demon is in their waste? You got it! Methane gas! So, it's not just us causing environmental problems."

Pat now has everyone's attention and all eyes are riveted on the screen. Even Roger is nodding with a sense of sudden awareness.

"Look, when paper rots," Pat continues in a professional manner, "it emits methane, a greenhouse gas which is 25 times more toxic than

CO_2. Also, the chlorine-based bleaches used in paper machines are toxic and ultimately end up in the water supply, the air and soil.

"Mills were required to install pollution prevention devices in their paper-making machines many years ago at great expense. Because of this EPA requirement, some small mills were forced to close. So, except for yearly inspections, they are expected to maintain standards of pollution control on their own. And you know how that goes! Gentlemen, I rest my case."

Silence falls over the room for a few moments as everyone sits in a daze. Finally one of the lawyers stands and begins to clap slowly. Moments later, all stand and add to a thunderous applause for this rookie lawyer who stole the show. Jim is also pleased that now the company has some sort of defense that can distribute blame for the health issues around the lake and take the focus away from Continental. Just what Mr. Morrison expects! But deep in his gut, Jim can't avoid the gathering guilt associated with the terrible cost of life and property. And nobody else in the company is losing any sleep over it.

Chapter 2

Tony's Dilemma

T ony Cassata, CFO of Temple Graphic & Publishing, just finishes talking to a customer on the phone when Marta comes into his office to drop the mail on his desk. He's been on the phone all morning trying to collect over $55,000 that's 60 days and more overdue. Just as he's opening some envelopes, Gus, the president, walks in.

"Any mail yet, Tony?"

"Yeah, it just came in."

"Let me know if we can collect some of that old money in the next couple days. When do we have to pay quarterly taxes?"

"Has to be in the mail by Friday!"

"What the hell is it with people? Thirty-day terms isn't enough time? When you call the Rockford customers, tell them not to mail their check, we'll send someone to pick it up!"

"I don't know what's going on, boss, I'll let you know how it goes."

Tony knows very well what's going on. Gus watched the industry turn digital 20 years ago, but he was in no mood to re-tool and keep up with changes—he had just paid off the equipment. Meantime his competitors went high tech and were able to produce better work quicker and cheaper. He paid off a 2-color Heidelberg press when competitors were acquiring 4-color digital equipment.

He opens the rest of the mail: three utility bills, a paper bill, a bunch of junk mail and four out-of-state checks totaling $4,200. The 40-year-old finance chief takes his John Lennon glasses off, leans back and shuts his eyes. His degree in Economics from DePaul University has earned him the CFO position at Temple for the past six years. But he's concerned about the company as sales have fallen more than 12% this year.

At least a dozen major clients have either merged or were acquired by bigger fish, moved out of state or just closed their doors. This is what he told Gus. But Tony knows the real reason: customers opted for better product, quicker delivery and cheaper prices. And the sales department wasn't picking up the slack. There were no reviews in a year, so nobody gets a raise, not even Tony.

Besides the company problems, Tony worries a lot more about his own financial condition. His two sons, Chris and John will be entering college soon and wife Rita, was laid off from Ace Hardware last month. She was chief cashier, but the manager replaced her with a part-time college student.

He knows he needs to earn more money and he can't afford to lose this job. He checks the receivable file on Quick Books, marks the outstanding invoices paid and prepares a bank deposit. He usually stops to make deposits by Bank of America on the way home.

"Marta, I'm leaving early today, taking a deposit to the bank and picking up Chris from football practice. If Gus comes back, tell him I went to the bank and will check with him tomorrow morning."

"Will do, Tony, have a good night!"

"Thanks, you too."

Gus has shown great trust and confidence in all his employees. And they in turn love working for Temple. They have seen him change into work clothes many times and join the crew in the plant to help move the work out during busy cycles.

On many occasions he asked pressmen to stay late to finish projects. He rewarded them by ordering food and beverages as well as overtime pay. His wife, Penney, and two sons, also come in to help at the bindery department, especially during production of customer annual reports around the first quarter each year.

But the cash flow has not been streaming recently. The plant has been busy even though sales have tapered. But receivables in recent months have been lagging, some of them over 90-120 days. That represents over $45,000 of uncollected money, from overdue accounts normally turned over to collection after 60 days. He knows too well this is money sorely needed for inventories, payroll and taxes; and he is determined to find out why these good customers are not paying even though Tony has been on the phone with them all week.

So, on this cold and windy November Saturday, while the phones are quiet and the plant is down, Gus sits at his desk logging onto Quick Books to flag bills and review new orders for production. He also checks paper stock inventories to service the new orders and marks the tickets accordingly. He then fills out a requisition for paper stock to order since certain needed grades are not on hand.

Now, on to the receivables account. He opens a spreadsheet of paid customer invoices for the past several months and everything seems in order. He checks current invoices outstanding particularly those over 60 days and notices unpaid accounts totaling $58,000. "They are our best customers—why are they so late?" he can't help saying out loud.

Gus reviews the last bank statement and realizes that part of the outstanding balance has been paid but not reflected in the accounts receivable ledger; also he sees payments to another account: Temple Graphic & Publishing R & D Account at the same bank.

In addition, a quick mental calculation reveals there is not enough money to cover the bills scheduled to go out on Monday. He pulls copies of all invoices over 60 days and walks them over to Tony's desk and picks up the phone. He tries to pull a file drawer in his desk, but it's locked. He doesn't understand why Tony hasn't brought this cash squeeze to his attention. Gus begins to fume! He punches Tony's number and a lady's voice answers.

"Hello, Rita? This is Gus from the company. Is Tony available?"

"Yes, he's in the garage. I'll get him for you."

In a few minutes Gus hears some static followed by a nervous voice. "Hi Gus, what's up?"

"Look Tony," he says, trying to stay calm. "Do you know we're going to be short at the bank next week? Have you followed up on past due money owed us?"

"Yes I have! I've been on the phone last few days and I'll find out when we can get our money on Monday. Everybody is slow in paying lately. I wanted to give you an update yesterday, but you left early..."

"Listen, Tony, get on the horn and collect this money. If necessary, send Frankie to pick up from Rockford customers. We need to order supplies for in-house projects and we're cutting it close. Jesus, Tony! The checks you cut puts us in negative balance. We need that money in the next few days. We don't have the time to turn them over to collection. Besides these are our best customers!"

"I know, I told Marta to hold those checks a few days. Meantime I'll follow-up on Monday and take care of it."

"Okay, Tony," Gus says in a more conciliar tone, "We'll talk on Monday."

Tony has been great in juggling accounts, playing the float with checks and other questionable activities for the benefit of the company. However, Gus begins to suspect something, but needs more assurance on the financial condition of the company.

Although knowledgeable in business, accounting is not his strong suit. Does he engage his CPA accounting firm to examine the books in a thorough audit and risk offending Tony? He even wonders if he's over-reacting and conditions will stabilize. They certainly faced other financial problems in the past and worked them out. Then there's this other R & D account that he and Tony discussed. But they haven't agreed to actually do it!

Gus meets with his close friend Harry Callas who is in the exterminating business and would know about these matters more. He also has an in-house person that deals with financial matters. Gus shares his concerns and asks for his opinion. Following a few minutes of reflection, Harry lights a cigarette.

"Look, Gus, we know each other over 25 years and I won't pretend to tell you how to run your business..."

"I know Harry, but you're the only one I can turn to right now. What would you do in this situation?"

Harry turns away for a moment, then he faces Gus with a look of resolve.

"Why don't you just talk to him?"

"You mean my accountant?"

"No! Tony! Talk to Tony! Just have a face-to-face and put it to him! Ask him to explain the discrepancies to your satisfaction."

Gus doesn't like what he hears, but he knows it's the right thing to do.

"Thanks for your input, Harry. You're right. That's the right thing to do!"

Monday morning quickly arrives and everything seems normal at the plant. The drone and rumble of equipment fill the pressroom, music to an owner's ears. But there hangs a dark cloud of silence over the front office. Marta is busy with order entry, Tony's on the phone, salesmen are preparing to leave while Gus reclines in his plush chair, stares at his computer screen, deep in thought.

Chapter 3

North Woods Resort

The October setting sun splashes its orange light across the horizon leaving a fiery glow over Long Lake at Saul's fishing resort. The weary fireball settles on the surface for a while alerting man and animal life that another day is about to end in the Northern Wisconsin woods. The yodel of a loon in the distance passes on the message as an eagle soars across the lake playing with the wind currents. He's heading home high up on a tall pine, the catch of the day in tow.

The green pines along the shoreline darken as the scattered maples around them acquire deeper hues of yellow, orange and red. Dusk also settles softly over the long pier as well. Father Stan Rybak is drawn there while his wife, Stacey, stays at the cabin to unpack and get settled. He stretches his legs on a bench and savors nature's brilliant setting while following a young buck out of the brush toward the shore. It scans the area carefully before lowering its lips into the water. Stan (as he prefers to be called) jumps to his feet and stretches his 5' 10" stocky frame toward the sunset with eyes closed and hands lifted in an appeal position; a familiar pose for him before the altar table at All Saints Church.

The waning twilight bathes him into a Robert Redford-like profile showcasing his fine-honed physique and chiseled facial features. Barely 35, he looks upon his ministry as an opportunity to help people and to make a difference in their lives. For him, ritual, doctrine and church protocols have taken a back seat to more engaging real life connections. He believes he's more effective in counseling when he has a relationship with parish members. He also knows that being too close to others, even getting personal, may not be in harmony with ministry expectations; that one day he will have to account for this practice to his bishop.

His attention quickly turns to his surroundings. Each time he arrives at Saul's, his first task after settling in the assigned cabin, has been to walk out on the pier at Long Lake for his second check-in. It had become a habit to sit there and absorb the magnificent surroundings. And he would remain in a pensive state until he becomes one with nature and believes that his presence is accepted.

Stan watches a familiar buoy, a few yards from the pier, bounce to a sudden rush of wind. Anglers refer to the marker as "Stan's Buoy," because two years ago, the young priest snagged his first musky near that very spot. He recalls wrestling with the 40-inch beauty for a good twenty minutes before it finally surrendered into his capable hands. He pulled out the lure and noticed to his surprise that the large predator lay quietly in the netting. He was tired and forced to submit to a higher authority after a painful struggle. Stan felt the fish was undergoing a life's reset, a sort of death and rebirth cycle. That image continues to occupy a special space in his psyche. He wishes this would happen more often to people—an experience very few ever encounter.

He remembers after measuring and taking a picture, he lifted the enormous net and placed it in the water with the opening facing out. Soon, the musky's gills began to pump and pelvic fins fanned the water. Then the tail swayed back and forth. He watched his catch slip out gracefully into familiar waters, renewed. He relived the experience over and over again and considered it an unofficial sacrament in the altar of nature. Later that evening at dinner, other anglers congratulated him after seeing his name on the Musky Record Board. Since then he achieved recognition and part time guide duties for younger anglers hoping to catch the "Big one."

"Father, you're not only a fisher of men," one of them yelled, followed by laughter and slaps on the back. However, in Stan's mind, that experience represented an epiphany for him and for the fish as well. In his ministry in Sycamore, Illinois, he had often witnessed a similar scenario with some parishioners. Following strong resistance and struggle over seemingly irreconcilable issues, many sessions ended with a sense of renewal and liberation. And the setting for these sessions rarely occurred in the church confines. Most played out in the churchyard, a person's home, on a boat at Saul's, even at TJ's Tavern.

His focus returns to the buoy and recalls the pile of rocks beneath the surface that cascaded down into a deep drop. The spot was a haven for walleye, small mouth bass and an occasional musky. He came to know every inch, even used an underwater viewer to actually see the 20-foot drop off through the clear water. So, each time he returned, he always began by casting toward the buoy. It had become a ritual. But not today. The first day is always a time of adjustment, a time to reach out and connect with God's creation—in a landscape where the only man-made contributions are cabins, piers and boats.

The next morning, Stacey is deep in reading mode with William Bennett's *Book of Virtues* while looking out for Stan's parents who planned to visit them at the resort. She watches Stan go out on the lake with two young beginners. She began reading the book last week and realized the urgency to build good character in children. She loves it because it includes these essential building blocks, an area of education that's been neglected in schools. She believes qualities like courage, honesty, compassion, faith, persistence and friendship are essential components in developing good character in young people.

While deep in thought and taking notes, she watches Stan position his boat about 25 feet from the buoy. She marvels at his ability to instruct and gesture so the two teen-age boys understand exactly what to do. He shows his companions where and how to cast near the site and allow the bait to sink along the steep drop-off. They're excited to be in the same boat with a master fisherman, a well-earned reputation.

"Listen, guys," Stan breaks the silence, "reeling in a fish can invite a cruising musky to follow and latch onto an easy meal. That kind of action would surely accelerate your heart rate. This is the excitement that makes for great fish stories, believable or fabricated.

"We've been casting here over 15 minutes without any bites," says Stan in a pastoral tone. "This doesn't mean there are no fish here. It could be that they're not desperate enough to go after our offer. Instead of changing bait and insisting on our way, let's try working the shoreline. Don't forget, we're not in charge here!"

The 10-horse-power motor slowly guides the boat to the next fishing spot about 20 feet from shore. Stan is always careful to avoid a wake that may disturb the fish below. As they cast to drop-off points off shore, Stan's thoughts suddenly turn to the Matthew 4:19 citation of Jesus when he challenged simple fishermen nearby: "Come, follow me, and I will make you fishers...of men." This command makes him think of upcoming winter programs. He's wondering how he can fulfill the spiritual needs of his parish. A deep thinker, this young clergyman might have been a university professor of Philosophy or Literature had the Church not attracted him to a nobler calling.

Unlike other priests who consider their ministry a "profession," he looks upon his calling as a personal quest to help people visualize and achieve spiritual growth. Of course, he must perform the various services, sacraments and hospital visits. He realizes these acts are part of the ministry, but for him there is so much more to be done. During the seminary years while working summers at a Target back home, he recalled discussing religious matters with an agnostic co-worker. One day the skeptic asked him about his faith:

"Tell me, Stan, what's the difference between a Christian and a moral person?"

Stan struggled with the question then and it still haunts him today. Like most literate people, lingering doubts still surface to annoy his spiritual complacency. He believes that faithful from all religions confront similar doubts, even agnostics and atheists. He has come to understand that only through an internal struggle can a person grow spiritually. He often repeats to himself his own recurring admonition to stay focused:

"You have to work at it, all of it!—meditation, giving, acts of kindness! And you have to feel good about doing those things." This command fell from his lips in a loud whisper, attracting quizzical glances from the young anglers.

A loud dinner bell jars Stan to the present state of affairs. He guides the boat back to the dock. His fishing companions scatter back to their rustic cabin as he walks uphill toward his. He's wondering if his parents have come, driving up from Rockford. He warned them not to get too dressed up, that the cabins are "rustic" because for one, there is no heat and certainly no A/C; no TV or radio either. There is light, however, powered by propane. Candlelight was used in the early days, but the insurance company later considered it too hazardous.

What he wanted to tell them was the customary conveniences of the world are left behind and considered distractions from the real purpose at Saul's: to clear the mind and calm the soul. But something inside him felt they would not understand.

"Hi, honey," Stacey beams as she stands placing her book on the chair. "How are things down at the pier?"

"Beautiful, the same scene just as we left it last year—Say, where's mom and dad? I saw their car outside."

"Oh, they arrived about 10 minutes ago. I told them you were down by the pier checking things out. They just went to the mess hall. I think they're hungry and a bit tired. I told them to go ahead, that I'll wait for you."

Stan notices the bags and luggage by the door. They stroll uphill to a large wooden building for supper. They find his parents seated at an assigned table with an old, worn-out "Rybak" name tag on a small stand. They wave to one another as they approach, then hug, exchange greetings and finally sit next to a large window facing Long Lake.

The setting sun now directs its orange glow obliquely against the window to form strong shafts of light across tables and people. A column of light forms a smile on Stan's face while Edith Rybak shades her eyes with an open hand, fumbling in her bag for her sun glasses. She appears visibly uncomfortable. They hadn't seen one another for a couple months, so there's a lot of catching up to do. Edith leans forward and looks at Stan directly with concern.

"How is your ministry coming along, son?" she pries while adjusting her glasses. "Are you happy at that small church in Sycamore?"

"I'm doing well, mom," he quips, no longer able to see her eyes. "This is my second assignment. It was a small parish of barely 40 families when I was assigned there four years ago. Now, it's grown to over 100!"

"Are they paying you enough in that small church?" his father, Bill, probes impatiently. "Damn shame you didn't accept the position at St. Andrew in Boston."

"Dad, don't worry. With what I make and with Stacey teaching, we're doing fine."

A few moments of silence descends over the table as they wait for the food to arrive. Stan tries to ignore the irrelevant concerns of his parents.

They just don't appreciate the bigger picture, he thinks. *I know dad has done very well in the restaurant supply business, becoming a formidable competitor to the corporate giants of Illinois. But life has to be more than about status and material success!*

Dinnertime is usually a quiet time at Saul's where guests exchange fish stories and other adventures. The dinner menu includes an entrée designed to satisfy a lumberjack's palate. The interior walls showcase mounted trophy fish as well as some deer heads. They've been up there for years, though recently, taxidermy has given way to "catch and release" except for hunters. At the end of the dining area, a painting of a loon hangs over the soft-serve machine with the caption "Great Lakes Loon: symbol of wilderness."

Conversations across the tables vary from the tranquil, life-enhancing fishing yarns to other topics of the world including sports, economics or politics. But for the most part, after the first day, fishing talk dominates. Concerns center on: "what shall we go for tomorrow, what lake should we fish and what kind of bait or lures should we use?" In short, a few days here sure gets your mind off the madness of the world and allows many opportunities to sort out dilemmas, personal issues and enjoy the peace and tranquility. It's water and nature therapy at no extra charge!

Suddenly, loud cheers follow the birthday song at the next table. A server brings a cake all lit up for one of the regulars celebrating his 70th year. Stan looks over and raises his glass. "Happy birthday, Charlie," he shouts. While still smiling, he sees his dad lean over to announce something important. At the same time, the server arrives with the evening's fare served family style.

"Stan," his father fires over the potatoes, "your mom and I have decided to move south, you know, we often talked about Florida? Well, we're finally doing it!"

"That's great, dad, I understand, you two have to get away from these winters, the shoveling, driving on icy roads and braving the bitter cold—it would be great, and we can drive down and visit when we can. When are you doing this?"

"We're flying there next week to look at some properties," his mom added softly. "We'll let you know the details once we decide. Thanks for inviting us here, such a beautiful facility! When dad brought you here many years ago, you really took to this place, didn't you?"

"I sure did, mom, more than you know. Saul told us the story last year about this place. It dates back to the early 1890s, originally built to accommodate lumberjacks who worked the forests and the nearby mill. He said in those days there was a thriving lumber industry in this area. But as the immediate forest thinned out, the owners decided to remake the property into a resort to attract more people from the surrounding towns and counties.

"The Haddad family," he continues, "moved here from Lebanon in 1975 to flee from the civil war that began between Christians and Palestinian militants. He preferred the wooded area over big cities, bought the resort and added more cabins. Unfortunately, Emil passed away over ten years ago and his son, Saul, took over the resort. His friendly disposition attracted more guests and Saul's became a popular fishing resort.

"Just look at these grounds! The 3,000 acre property consists of five closely-knit lakes and five cabins. In addition, as you can see, this resort offers clean air, water, abundant wildlife and most of all, serenity and a slower, more deliberate pace of living. What else can I say, mom, we just love coming here."

A loud call of a loon added an exclamation point to Stan's last statement. He feels the need to explain the magical wildlife, but saves it for another time.

Chapter 4

SEEKING A MENTOR

F r. Stan waves goodbye to his parents and Stacey after three days at the resort. His wife joined them to resume her teaching schedule. He listens to the crackle of the gravel driveway as they inch their way to an inner drive that leads to the main highway. Stan believes they enjoyed their stay mainly because they were with him and their daughter-in-law.

It's clear the environment didn't add any memorable experiences even though Mr. Rybak tried his hand at fishing for bass near the pier. A nearby loon looked his way, then dove and appeared about 50 yards away. After nearly twenty minutes of casting, he called it quits, picked up a coffee from the cafeteria and spent the rest of the afternoon in the cabin.

During this run, Stan decides to fish by himself. His pursuit now is the illusive and mysterious musky, the fish of ten thousand casts. He ponders Thoreau's words "Many men fish all their lives and find out it's not the fish they're really after." As he casts a 12-inch floater lure toward the lily pads in Monet's Bay, Stan wonders about his own motives.

"What am I after if it isn't the fish?" he says quietly as he's determined to answer that question much sooner than a lifetime.

About 50 yards away a lone loon lets loose a variety of sounds while facing Stan. It even swims a little closer and continues its repertoire. *What do the sounds mean?* he wonders. Is the loon bonding or communicating with him? Perhaps it recognizes Stan as a friend of nature who considers this habitat as sacred; or maybe it's tracked him many times when he was sitting on the pier and while fishing.

He quietly takes an oar and draws nearer to the loon. He's expecting it to dive from threat or fear and surface somewhere else safely. But not this one and not at this time. For a few seconds they both stare at each other as though a connection is forming. Stan pulls away gently to show no ill intent. The loon does not dive; it just follows as the boat drifts away. He turns towards it and names his friend, "Adviser," convinced the last call he heard is one of outreach. His thoughts now turn toward other churches and faiths.

I wonder if the loon would behave the same with other religious leaders. They too, are men of peace, deep thinkers and friendly to the environment and animal life. The ministries we all serve include a wide range of people from all walks of life: single, married, religious, agnostic, widowed, straight or gay, wise or illiterate, with varying levels of spiritual growth.

Stan feels a sudden wake rock his boat, disturbing the calm surface of the water. Another boat arrives nearby with eager anglers looking for the big catch. At that moment the loon disappears below the surface. Stan scans the lake to see where he will surface but cannot locate him. He makes a mental note that the Adviser has a white heart-shaped crown and a zebra collar. Even though they all may have these markings, Stan is confident he will be able to recognize his new friend.

He looks around and savors the beauty of his surroundings. The virgin pines stand upright and proud like the Swiss guards at the Vatican. As the autumn wind whips around through the pines and hardwoods, he hears the howl of a coyote. A large fish near his boat breaks water, takes a look around and rolls back down. For a moment he feels like an unwelcome intruder, but seconds later, he recognizes a friendly environment conducive to self-examination and sorting out his ministry.

Whenever doubts about his calling and ministry disturb his conscience, in addition to meditation and prayer, he looks to this scene for additional inspiration that clarifies his purpose and spiritual agenda.

He finds a crystal clear vision on how to help people navigate through troubling times.

Soon the surface gets choppy from stronger winds passing through as nature flexes muscle. Stan captures the scene in his mind's eye and is able to recall it during those moments of stress and challenge in the untamed wilds of society.

A Mentor for Stacey

Stronger winds also sweep through Thomas A. Edison School back home in DeKalb. Stacey wishes she stayed at Saul's with Stan. Her 3rd grade class was especially unruly yesterday. Students were throwing paper airplanes and gum at one another and she saw an obscenity on the whiteboard. She had to discipline the students with limited recess and she gave them a long lecture on behavior and respect. That's why she's at the principal's office this morning.

"Ms. Rybak, I got a handful of calls yesterday afternoon from upset parents. They complained that you shouted at their children and took away their recess time. What happened in your class?"

"Ms. Daily, I stepped out of the class for a moment to talk to a parent whose child has been sick. And when I returned, there was anarchy in the room. So, I had to restore order. I did not call Ms. Wagner at work to complain that her son was throwing papers across the room. I did not call Ms. Rediki to complain about her son scribbling obscenities on my whiteboard. No, Ms. Daily, I did my job and restored order. Are we not supposed to have order in the classroom?"

"Look, Stacey, I understand, it's just they said you frightened the children and they're concerned that shouting at them makes them feel less valued. See if you can tone it down next time."

"Okay, talk about feeling less valued, what they did in my class devalued me as a teacher—do you ever support your teachers in these issues?"

"Of course, I do. I just don't want these parents showing up in school board meetings complaining about my teachers. It reflects on my value as an administrator. These complaints are recorded. You have two. One more and I have to inform the superintendent, okay?"

"Okay, I get it. Thank you."

At home, Stacey thinks about Stan and how he finds revitalization in the wilderness. She finds herself in the unforgiving wilderness of a supposed civilized society, one where traditional values are shrinking; a culture where you have to teach decency and social skills to generations of amoral young people through no fault of our own. She had been convinced years ago during undergraduate work that critical thinking skills, character-building values, even spiritual intelligence ought to be part of learning packages in schools—especially these days.

She realized that long ago, these values were taught at home by caring and loving parents who drove a hard line when it came to discipline and responsibility. Right and wrong, good and evil were part of the moral development of children. She's looking forward to sharing her experience with Stan when he comes back home. Stacey is amused at the level of respect he gets because of who he is. Her phone plays a jingle.

"Hi, Stacey, it's me. I'll be coming back tomorrow. How are things at school?

"Okay, I guess. I had a problem last couple days. I'll tell you about it when I see you. When do you plan on getting here tomorrow?"

"About four o'clock. Tell me about what happened."

"Some parents complained about my yelling at their little darlings. I had a whiteboard jungle in my classroom couple days ago. And when I finally restored order, I bruised their sensitive feelings...Look, it's the same old story, where everybody's covering their backside. No one really cares about education of children. I miss you, Stan. I'll make your favorite meal. Don't eat on the way, okay?"

"Okay, see you tomorrow. Love you!"

"Love you, too!"

Chapter 5

RELUCTANT DEPARTURE

F ollowing a few days of "water therapy," Father Stan Rybak feels the need to transition back to land since he's set to leave the next morning. He decides to venture out for an afternoon walk around the area of the resort. He begins a 2-mile hike toward the main highway noticing details along the road that one misses when driving. He hears his every step as he crunches along the quiet gravel road, that bridge between the soft contours of grassy knolls and water, and the unyielding hardness of the world. He feels that he's being watched by a thousand eyes.

Further down the road, Stan spots a mama bear with three lively cubs. He pauses and allows them to cross into the brush. Mama bear casts a friendly stare at him as they scamper across. Soon, Stan arrives under a large shingle with a message painted on it.

> *As you leave Saul's you're re-entering the world you escaped from only a few days ago. Please take with you the gift of Peace. The transition can be painful. Good luck, we expect you back soon*
> *—SAUL HADDAD*

Just passed the exit shingle, the gravel road ends in front of a 2-lane paved highway. He turns and starts walking about a quarter mile toward the 9-Mile Bar, a favorite stop for locals and visitors alike. It acquired that name many years ago because the bar happened to be nine miles from the nearest town of 300 residents. He heads toward it walking on the side of the road. A gust of wind forces him to zip his jacket.

Soon, the bar is within sight and he's visualizing a 7-ounce glass of draft, a favorite at 9-Mile. He rarely drinks beer except on special occasions of fellowship or on days like this. His stride feels more labored walking on solid pavement. The thought comes to him that floating on water takes away some of gravity's authority, that on land we feel the weight of the world more.

He pushes a screen door in and enters a tavern scene of 75 years ago. He notices a pinball machine to the left and a small knobby pool table. Everything here is 1950s, even the electronic Hamm's beer sign at the end of the bar. The lights flicker to create a cascading waterfall effect and a recorded jingle that follows. Quite a technical electronic feat at the time. This is the place where time has stood still, where the owners, Herb and Sally, remember tales of horse-drawn farm wagons holding up traffic many years ago.

A no-frills, establishment, this bar caters to fishermen, hunters and nature lovers. And if you're not old enough to reminisce, you're not welcome here. Herb always enjoys opening up to stool warmers about the old days when a few Native Americans in the area would come in for a shot 'n beer.

"Hey Fatha," Herb shouts, "remember when this taxidermy guy opened up a shop a few years ago down the road where the bait shop is?"

"Yeah, you mean Harvey the animal stuffer?

"Yeah, that's him. What a character! He always come in here for a few beers and kept a half-pint in his pocket. Six months ago he drink one too many while mounting a deer head—he even smelled like a deer that day!"

As he's nodding between sips to Herb's story, Stan's attention is drawn to a lady several stools away wearing a sleeveless blouse. Her shapely figure wrapped in tight jeans with ornamental belt is a sight he's unable to ignore.

"...Well," Herb continues, "as he was walking back, he wanders onto the road and gets wacked by a log truck coming 'round the turn—threw him a good 20 yards into the brush...poor son-of-a-b...gun!"

Next to the bar a large abandoned building still stands. And behind both properties there's a forest with a virgin river running through it.

"Hey Sally," Stan yells as she's going by, "what's with the building next door, anyone buy it yet?"

"No, it's been vacant for a couple years now," Herb fires back. "Why don't you buy it Fatha? Would make a great retreat center for your church!"

"I would if I knew you were coming," is his quick reply.

Herb laughs hysterically showing some black teeth with large spaces between.

"I don't think you want me around your people, Fatha."

"Look Herb, my people as you call them, are just like you. Yes, we grow up and live in different settings, but we're all made from the same cloth, you know and desire the same things."

Stan places $5 on the bar and stands to leave.

"Thanks, Herb, Sally. I'll be leaving tomorrow. I know I'll sure miss this place. I'd like to come back in spring. When does the ice go out here?"

"By the end of May we should have our water back. Always good to see you Fatha. Have a good trip back."

It's time to walk back to Saul's. The changing fall colors, a calmer breeze and the two beers make him think about a pre-dinner nap. It seems the walk back is quicker. He finally ambles into the compound and waves to Frankie at the guardhouse. He settles in his cabin and collapses in bed. The bird noises filter through the screen window lull him to sleep inviting the mystical workings of the subconscious to play out.

* * * *

Stan finds himself walking toward that building next to 9-Mile Bar. He notices a sign over the entry: "All Saints Retreat Center." He walks to the door feeling dizzy and confused. He can't remember ever acting on the purchase of this building. He's curious to enter and find out for sure. How did he forget developing a retreat in Wisconsin?

He rushes in to see a well-furnished facility: a kitchen off to one side, a library and reading room, a huge hall with tables and chairs. There's a small riser, a podium with microphone.

A staircase leads to a second level. About a dozen locals are sitting as though waiting for something to begin. He sees himself at the podium facing the people. On the side on a chair by itself, the cute lady from the bar sits holding a bottle of beer while next to her, a loon observes. It has a white heart-shaped crown and a red ring around its neck.

Suddenly the attendees get up and walk forward facing the podium. They take turns speaking..

> *"I lie a lot, mainly to protect myself and my family. Doesn't everyone? It doesn't hurt anyone, does it?"*

> *"I stole two pumpkins for my kids for Halloween. With a receipt from another store in hand, I drove up to the stack and loaded them in my car. Look, I promised my kids! I just lost my job, nobody cares about that!"*

*"At the grocery checkout I had to pay over $84 for about three bags
of food. I put a couple candy bars in my pocket for the kids. I figure
I had something coming paying all that money."*

*"I watched the lady in front of me leave money at the ATM
machine. It was about $50. I kept it as a gift from God for all the
bad luck I had this week. I figure I had it coming."*

*"I take home paper clips, writing pads and pens from the office.
The company won't miss them—my kids can use them for school."*

*Five more people step forward with similar confessions and none of them
express any remorse or regret. He looks at a banner on the wall that reads:
<u>Any act can be justified with rationalization</u>. Stan is about to respond but
he is jarred by a loud dinner bell.*

* * * *

He jumps to his feet rubbing his face and eyes and looks around to
get his bearings, still thinking about the string of confessions he heard.
Big deal! A few simple lies and trivial theft, he muses...*But that's how
it starts! Harmless little lies that can be fiercely defended. Then the door
opens to more serious misdeeds.*

He takes off his T-shirt and changes into a long sleeve tan fishing
shirt with colorful flies over the pocket. He notices the "Dry Clean
Only" tag. He also grabs his hat and rushes out. Stan can't believe how
hungry he is. As he's the only one left in his group, he decides to sit at
another table with friends. With a glass of Merlot in hand, he begins
to talk about his shirt.

"See this shirt guys? Stacey gave it to me last year. It says on the tag
Dry Clean Only. Do any of you know of a dry cleaner around here? So,
I had to wash it. Pretty good job, no?"

"I don't think so, Father," one of the regulars asserts. "If it says *Dry Clean Only*, it means dry clean only! Look at all the wrinkles. And the cuffs look kind of tight. She won't be pleased when you bring it home."

Everyone breaks out in laughter except Stan. He is quietly thinking about the dream he had and doesn't know what to make of it. At this time the server brings the food in platters: ham steak with sweet potatoes and beans. Apple pie and ice cream follow. There is no talk of fishing on this the last night for Stan. Tonight it is all about the Bears/Packers game next week.

As darkness falls over the resort, Stan is invited to Leo's cabin to play cards. Leo starts up a fire to get the chill out as four of them sit at a table. Father checks his cell phone and sees several messages. Tony Cassata and Jim Winters called the same afternoon and want to meet with him when he gets back. Stan plays cards for a while and excuses himself to pack and get ready.

"See you all at breakfast."

"Good night, Father."

After a Paul Bunyan breakfast the next morning, Stan loads his gear in the car and heads to the bait shop/office to pay. Along the way uphill, a young deer follows him and actually sticks his snout in his side pocket. Startled, but amused by the encounter, he catches his balance, pets the deer and walks inside.

"Everyone seems to be searching for something...for food, nourishment, security, but most of all, love and acceptance." he whispers out loud. He writes a check, gets a hand written receipt from Wanda, waves goodbye to all and he's finally on his way. As he's heading out, he hears his Adviser's echo resonate in the distance.

Hmm! Tony Cassata and Jim Winters? I wonder what's up with them!

He makes a mental note to call Tony first when he gets back; also to leave word with Jim that he's back in Sycamore. He also plans to remind them about attending the conference in December.

During the 6-hour trip back home, all he can think about is his dream. He remembers the Adviser sitting on the side watching, waiting for him to respond to all the confessions. Of course, he didn't get the chance.

And that lady! What was she doing there?

Chapter 6

THE ART OF LYING…
AND OTHER MISDEEDS

"It happened many years ago in summer, during a period of infatuation with cars. I must have been 14 years old when my father showed me the basics of driving, only because I pestered him into it. It wasn't because I was ready to drive; I just had a fascination of pretending to be in charge of moving such a big machine."

Stan pours more coffee in Tony's cup and leans back in his office chair.

"Well," he continues "several days later, I sat behind the controls while Dad worked in the back yard. It felt great! With my foot on the gas, I enjoyed a vicarious journey speeding all over town."

"What happened then? You really didn't drive, just playing around, right?"

"That's right! But he found out that I had been toying with the car."

"How did he know?"

"For one thing, he noticed the seat had been adjusted all the way forward. Mom never touches the seat. Then, he couldn't start the car and realized the engine was flooded with gas."

"So, what happened then?" Tony now leans forward, anxious to learn where he's taking this story.

"I got busted, that's what happened! But that wasn't the worst of it. I denied that I had anything to do with it! I mean, when he asked me if I played with the controls and stepped on the gas pedal, I actually said absolutely not!—I was adamant, almost indignant.

"Tony, I felt as if I had given up control of myself and given into an irresistible urge to defend my actions...my very honor! Well, after a few moments of silence, I calmed down and owned up to it...sort of. Believe me, it was painful to actually finally admit it. Dad didn't push or scold me, he just smiled and said nothing. Meantime, a battle raged inside me until the forces of deception and darkness surrendered and the truth emerged.

"With a grin still across his face, he pressed my shoulders and told me something I've never forgotten.

Son, many people keep a little closet deep in their psyche where they hide misdeeds protected by lies. They hold them very private, so no one ever knows. But the more you conceal, the more lies you have to remember to keep your stories straight. One day you will slip up and be exposed. So, learn to tell the truth, no matter how much it may hurt. You will be a better person and you won't have to remember anything.

Tony is impressed with the story and believes it to be a valuable lesson for youngsters, but he understands the real world is more dangerous and less forgiving. He feels Father Stan is someone he can talk to freely about ethical issues. And he's always come away each time more enlightened.

"Wise words, Father. But don't you think that lying in the adult world is kind of a given? I mean, everybody lies in varying degrees for personal advantage. You just have to remember what you say to different people..."

"That's the point," Stan interrupts, "look at all the things you must remember to maintain credibility! What if the people you lie to talk to one another and your name comes up? See, here's the thing. Your reputation is shaped by others, not by you. You can look in the mirror and see one person, but others you come in contact with may see quite a different person."

Tony is about to rebut, but his argument would receive no traction after what he just heard. He looks down as he reviews his situation with Gus and the company. He realizes there is no case to defend his actions at Temple. For the moment, Tony is not prepared to discuss his situation at the company, mainly because he won't be able to act on Stan's advice; for sure, not now.

He's confident that whatever he does is necessary; and the company will also benefit from his special skills in the long run. This rationale will keep his agenda on course and mitigate any guilt that may accumulate. Stan can tell there are issues that weigh heavily on Tony during moments of silence where he looks down or away. But, for now, he decides it's best to move the conversation and stay on point.

"Take politicians, for example," Stan continues. "By definition, they all must lie with reasoning that defies logic; but at the time it makes all the sense to those in need. And it's interesting that in most cases, crafty politicians get away with it. I believe that's because people have a critical need to trust someone who promises to make their lives better. It never fails! And when they are betrayed in the end, they kick the rascal out and look for someone else to trust. It happens every time. But whoever replaces them, is destined to suffer the same fate."

As he's talking, Stan walks over to a table and brings a plate of cinnamon cookies. He bites into one and lays the plate in front of Tony.

"Case in point," he continues, "Senator Billy Joe Summer, from Georgia. His first term is coming to an end and to retain his seat, he's fabricating promises he knows won't be possible to deliver; and they even defy the truth. He was on TV the other day. Look, Billy Joe is a tall southern gentleman with a body of a line-backer. He represents the quintessential image of a southern senator. His hair is neatly combed, slightly graying around the ears, with a touch of facial make-up.

Recently divorced, rumor mills peg him as a womanizer. And, clearly, his over-riding obsession is power, wealth accumulation..."

Unexpectedly, his phone plays the spiritual hymn "We gather together..." and Stan checks the caller I.D. and quickly picks up. He motions to Tony to stand by—that he had to take the call. For the first few minutes it's a one-way call where Stan does the listening. Tony can hear the residue of a stern voice escaping from the periphery. Finally, he gets the chance to respond and end the call with "Very well, Your Grace, I can come tomorrow to discuss. Have a good afternoon." Stan writes some notes and returns to the conversation.

"Okay, where were we? Ah, Billy Joe! He's aware that the American people want equal rights regardless of race or creed. So, his platform on race relations, human rights, social reforms and equal pay for equal work assures the voters he deeply cares for them. But in reality, his voting record cancels any progress in these areas.

"Another concern is law enforcement and crime. He claims to support gun control, yet senate bills forbidding sale of automatic weapons and enforcing tighter background checks never reached the floor for a vote. Obviously, the gun lobby (NRA) contributes generously to his campaign. In addition, he assures voters that environmental concerns are high on the list. Yet, he votes to relax restrictions on fossil fuels, off shore drilling and fracking.

"Finally, politicians often promise to lower taxes to secure votes. But behind closed doors, when tax reform bills are presented, they languish and are ultimately tabled. Billy Joe promised to lower drug costs, but big pharma greased his re-election fund to maintain the status quo...I can go on, Tony, but the point is, people like him lie and use the system to enrich themselves.

"The irony is they, themselves, really believe what they're saying at first. That's why they sound so genuine. But, it's not only politicians; those in industry and business, retail, even advertising! All lies and deception! They all play the same dangerous games without realizing the unintended consequences that can follow."

Astonished on hearing about the collective moral corruption that has conquered our culture and way of life, Tony feels a low grade wave of fear and guilt gather inside him. He glances at the wall, fixes his eyes on a photograph of Fr. Stan with an angelic smile holding a large fish.

"What consequences, Father? What happens next?"

"It starts with insignificant, seemingly harmless lies that curl up into a little ball held together with justifiable arguments to support words said and deeds done. The ball of lies starts rolling slowly down-hill adding more misdeeds as it grows in size. Unchecked, it gathers speed and before long, it rolls over, conquers and defines the host. In short, you forfeit your higher calling—and everyone is given a higher calling. We are charged by our Creator to find what it is, nurture it and develop it at the expense of our worldly self."

"So, how does all this affect your life?"

"Tony, my hill is steeper than yours and I have to be more vigilant to prevent a ball from ever taking shape!"

"So, what do you do?"

"First of all, I try to give more than I take. I meditate to clear the mind and I pray to clear my conscience. Then I seek a level field..."

"How do you get away from the hill?"

"I go to water. There are no hills in water. That's as horizontal as you can get! There, I meditate, pray, try to outsmart a fish and become one with nature."

"And what does that do for you?"

"Regeneration, Tony. And renewal, just like a tree that drops its weary leaves and returns renewed; just like a snake that sheds its skin many times; just like a fish in shock that's placed back in the water; just like Jonah who was cast overboard to drown; but was saved by a whale and spat out at the nearest island."

"You mean like having an A-Ha moment?

"More than that! An epiphany! A re-birth, a new awareness that shifts your focus to more noble pursuits—like an old shirt that's been dry-cleaned to appear like new!" Stan finishes the thought as he stands checking his watch.

"Tony, ethics and morality are traded daily in the marketplace; and lies, deception and half-truths are often tools that advance material success. These people who are so focused wouldn't recognize the high ground if they fell on it. However you cut it, Tony, when you build a case on lies, deceit with creative rationalization, any conclusion you arrive at can never pass the test of truth."

Stan reaches out and hugs Tony, thanks him for his visit and looks forward to talking with him again. "I can see you're struggling," he tells him "and that's good to recognize that a conflict is going on. Most people don't even notice and before they realize what's going on, they're conquered! Just know that I'm here for you. By the way, make sure you register for the conference in Green Lake. It's coming up in less than two months. And we'll have a workshop to discuss a lot of this."

"I will. Thanks again, Father."

Tony walks away knowing full well that Stan is right in everything he said. But he also realizes to do the right thing is not always possible. He wonders what demons Stan has to deal with and the moral concessions he has to make. Maybe his self-righteous position is necessary to remind himself that he, too, must continue to reach for higher ground.

At this time in his life, Tony's first duty is to family and children. In spite of Stan's advice to clear the conscience, he feels comfortable with his actions at the company, for now. He also believes that indiscretions and misdeeds can be short-lived and have a reckoning sometime in the future. In any case, he reserves this dialogue only with Stan.

Chapter 7

MEETING WITH THE BISHOP

Although many church hierarchs live in different quarters than their office, Bishop Mark's office is, in fact, his residence. Rockton is a fashionable suburb of Rockford, Illinois. At the end of a winding driveway through trees and brush, Father Stan finally sees the stone mansion nestled among enormous honey locust trees. The building is surrounded by a tall wrought iron fence showcasing an ornamental electric gate. He drives close to the gate and leans into a call box, presses the button.

"Bishop Mark's residence, do you have an appointment?

"Yes, this is Father Stan Rybak to see the bishop."

"One moment, please," a man's voice replies.

Following a few moments, the gate swings open emitting an initial squeak. Stan drives through and watches it close in his mirror. He parks, reaches for a small bag and begins a 30-yard walk through several levels of steps toward an arched portico leading to a double door entry. He pauses to gaze at the limestone header. In the center he notices a pair of chiseled angel heads, one of joy and the other of sorrow, reminiscent of the happy/sad theatrical masks.

Stan rings the bell and waits. Except for co-celebrating a service with him on All Saints Day last year, he hasn't seen his bishop since his ordination four years ago. And today, he's here to explain and clarify some of his actions. The door finally opens.

"Hello, Father, I'm Deacon John, please come in and have a seat. His Grace will be with you shortly. May I have the bag please?"

Stan watches the deacon search through the bag, examine the contents; only a box of mints, there was no time for anything personalized. As a seminarian, he was urged by an adviser to always keep in touch with the area bishop.

You need to get to know him, after all, he's your boss, he recalls Father Gregory saying. *When you visit, always bring something. They love receiving gifts, however small.* Stan is already feeling nervous since this is not a social visit. The bishop summoned him.

The opulence of the reception room surprises Stan, especially the high coffered ceiling. He can't help but be impressed by walnut-paneled walls with recessed shelves of books surrounding the room; and period furnishings with area Persian rugs over parquet floor.

"This is quite a facility, I feel like I'm in an embassy or a palace in Europe."

"I know, Father," the deacon asserts with a tinge of guilt. "I felt the same way when His Grace selected this place. But he believes it adds importance to his position, especially when he receives the archbishop, heads of state and others from business and industry who feel at home in such surroundings. In the past year, we've received many wonderful comments about this diocese. They say it ranks at the top.

"This mansion once belonged to Andrew Wagner, an immigrant from Germany who settled here in 1849 and formed Wagoner Tool & Machinery Co. in Rockford. In 1917 the factory transitioned into munitions and weapons production for the war effort."

Stan stares at a painting of a reclining angel on the wall behind Deacon John's desk.

"Interesting painting, is it an angel?"

"Yes, it's called *Fallen Angel,* a work by the French painter Alexandre Cabanel—a copy, of course. The ornate frame cost 10 times more than the print; gives it an authentic look, doesn't it? Cabanel introduced it to the art scene in 1849, the same year of Wagoner's arrival in America.

Strange coincidence, don't you think? Anyway, the original hangs in the Musee d'Orsay in Paris."

A light blinks on the deacon's desk. "Father, his Grace will see you now. I've already submitted your bag on your behalf. He knows of your gift. I apologize, we can't be too careful these days!"

Deacon John escorts Stan into another room and leaves, closing the door. Stan is astonished at several things at once, but now he must focus his attention on the bishop. His office is just as impressive. A classic chandelier hangs over a marble table with French legs. Bishop Mark sits behind a mahogany desk with angel head carvings in the corners. Behind him is a fireplace with decorative brass bi-fold doors. Just above on the mantle, a dwarf grandfather clock sits on one end and a mosaic cross on stand at the other. Just above on the wall, a portrait of Archbishop Philip looks out over the room.

Stan's curious concentration is interrupted when the bishop walks around his desk to welcome him. He sports a 3-piece black silk suit with a stunning gold chain leading to a vest pocket.

"Greetings Father Stan," he declares loudly through the thick thatch around his mouth. "Thank you for coming on such short notice." He offers his hand. Stan holds it, bends down slightly to kiss his sizeable ruby ring. Lifting away, he notices his soft manicured hand, wrap-around gold cuff link and glossy finger nails.

"The pleasure is mine, Your Grace. I can't help but admire your beautiful residence..."

Miriam, the bishop's secretary, draws his attention as she approaches with a note, Bishop Mark missing Stan's last comment. He quickly scans the note and places it on his desk.

"Please have a seat, Father, I just want to review a few things with you. I see that stewardship is up substantially at All Saints and I commend you for attracting more to the parish. You obviously add a meaningful message to your ministry that connects with the faithful. It's clear you're doing a great job. But I want to clear up a couple other things that have come to my attention, simple things really, but ones that can be problematic."

The bishop pauses and looks at Stan for a reaction but Stan says nothing, just waits for the other shoe to fall. "Is it true," he continues while turning away, "that on many occasions you do not wear prescribed clerical attire, especially during Bible study and other church activities? Is it also true that when shopping at local stores, you dress casually like a layman? Father, people see you and call me with their concerns."

"Yes, Your Grace, correct on both counts; however, it doesn't happen all the time. At All Saints, I've developed an interactive relationship with my congregation and I believe they know me and appreciate me as I am."

"My dear Father Stan! You should know we have to maintain our protocols. You've been blessed with the Holy Spirit upon your ordination and our church dictates you wear appropriate attire..."

"But isn't everyone blessed with the Holy Spirit?"

"Yes, but we're different. God expects us to be more and do more—become community examples. I can't have my priests walking around wearing backyard work clothes. We must retain the image of what we represent or what would people think of us? In short, appearances are very important to people. They form a first impression—and first impressions are difficult to alter. Do we understand each other, Father?"

"Yes we do, Your Grace. Thank you."

"Thank you, Father. And keep up the good work!"

Stan leans and kisses his red ruby, backs away slowly and leaves the room. He is brimming with conflicted emotions demanding clarity.

"Oh! By the way, Father," the bishop interrupts Stan's internal turmoil, "I trust you will be attending the conference on Ethics next month at Green Lake?"

"Yes, a group of us is going. As a matter of fact, Your Grace, I will be a presenter for the Christian community."

"Really! I won't be attending, but I'd like to get a report."

"Your Grace, the program will be recorded and you can view it on U-Tube."

"I know, Father, what I mean, I'd like to get your assessment of the event. You could have informed me you are attending...and also presenting!"

"My apologies, I'll be back to discuss it with you."

On his way out, he feels a quizzical stare burn between his shoulders. He realizes that he should have informed his bishop of his participation—another one of Stan's oversights which feeds the need for hierarchical scrutiny into his behavior. He pauses by the deacon's desk. He stares at the *Fallen Angel* painting once more for a few moments while trying to tame the gathering turbulence building inside him.

"John," he says casually, "even though the frame is classic and showcases the painting as an original, I can still tell it's only a print! And by the way, the outside gate squeaks. Someone needs to oil the hinges. Have a great afternoon!"

Chapter 8

JOURNEY TOWARD UNDERSTANDING

Tony and Rita arrive at All Saints on Friday afternoon December 6, 2019. Tony offered his van for the trip up to Green Lake since Father's car could not accommodate six people. They walk inside the church office to meet everyone.

"Hi, Stacey," Rita shouts "Father, Rich. How's everyone?" Stan shakes hands with Rich as they exchange a few hugs and comment on the conference.

"So, Rich, how many do we have going?"

"Besides us, there are another nine, maybe ten attending from the parish."

"Pretty good turnout don't you think?" boasts Stan. "Hey, everybody, say hello to Rich, our newest board member. And I'd like you to meet a dear friend, Famir, a Middle Eastern Christian I met at an ecumenical conference in Chicago several years ago. I remember the topic promoted peace and hope."

"Yes," asserts Famir, swiping at his long black hair that keeps falling forward. Though his hair is pitch black, his skin seems too light to suggest he's from the Middle East.

"It was three years ago, after an attack at Jerusalem's Holy Sanctuary. That's what the Christians call it. It's a common worship site for the different faiths of the area. The Jews call it Temple Mount while the Muslims call it Noble Sanctuary. And because of this common claim, incidents occur there all the time."

Everyone is quickly jolted into the dangerous realities in that part of the world. They look upon Famir with admiration as a modern warrior for peace among diverse people and realize that conflict among belief systems continue to fill the front pages and flat screens with violence and loss of life.

"Anyway," Stan continues, "Famir is the former director of the Arab-Christian Cultural Center in Haifa, Israel. Sadly, he had to flee his birthplace of Nazareth and the area for fear of his life, leaving wife and two children behind. His peace initiatives raised suspicions with the Palestinian radicals who were less tolerant of Christians. Famir shares with us many common qualities that define peace-loving people."

This is one relationship Stan has not shared with his bishop as his church is not keen on co-mingling with other cultures and faiths. Stan's ecumenical approach makes Bishop Mark uncomfortable as the latter is focused on an exclusive ministry for his own people.

"I noticed some snow flurries in the air," Rita cautions Tony. "I think we better get going! It's a good 3-hour drive, maybe more if there is snow up there. We don't want to be late for the welcome."

"You're right," Tony asserts, "Come on everybody, let's hit the road." All agree and begin walking out. They pause to look at the conference poster on a tri-pod near the door. Stan takes a picture of it and everyone hurries into the van. He passes his phone around to show the details of the event.

MIDWEST INTER-FAITH FORUM

Multi-Faith Conference on

ETHICS

Subjective Relativism in Our Modern Culture

Green Lake Conference Center
Green Lake, Wisconsin
Friday and Saturday, December 6-7, 2019

Guest Speakers

ISLAMIC ETHICS: **Mohammed Ali Nusreth**

A BUDDHIST VIEW: **Bodhi Samsara**

VALUES & JUDGMENT: **Rabbi Lester Abrams**

THE ETHICS OF CARE: **Dr. Chunhua Lee**
National Psychology Association

REBIRTH & RENEWAL: **Fr. Stan Rybak**

Your Host: Jonathan Connors

For Reservations call (920) 239-3432 before December 1
www.greenlakeethics.org
$200 per person
Includes 2 Days & Nights, Meeting Rooms, All Meals

Stan hurries into the office for some last minute instructions to George Nicholas, a seminarian in town for the holidays who offered to help at the parish.

"George, we're leaving for Wisconsin, you have the keys to the church. Take down any messages and tell whoever calls I'll be back on Sunday evening. I told you Father Dimitri from Janesville will officiate in my absence. So, you know what to do, help him out at the altar."

"Not to worry, Father, I'll take care of things. Enjoy the conference and have a safe trip. See you when you get back."

Tony's Suburban merges onto Interstate 90 North toward Wisconsin. There's more snow in the air now and some is beginning to stick. Tony checks the dash clock: 2:20. He's thinking they should arrive around six o'clock if all goes well.

"Anybody ever been to this center before?" He yells out.

"I have," Famir pipes in, "about five years ago for a symposium with Muslims, Christians and Jews. I remember the event was wrought with endless arguments regarding the value of each faith. The Muslims were very rigid in their faith with fierce fidelity to the Koran which justified their resistance to continuing Israeli settlements on their lands.

"The Christians too, echoed their own beliefs to be correct, but showed flexibility and tolerance toward other faiths. The Jews, although unyielding to some traditional customs on fasting and condemnation of enemies of Israel, allowed for compassion to play a role in trying to avoid judging others. At any rate, on the second day tempers flared where security arrived to calm tensions.

"In spite of a spiritual impasse, I recall the facilities were superb. You are all going to like the amenities and the food. They have several good-sized meeting rooms and guests are assigned according to their numbers. The plenaries are held in these larger halls. For breakout meetings they have what they call Veranda Rooms for smaller groups. I'm also looking forward to their Tea House on the grounds which faces Green Lake."

"By the way, everyone," Stan adds, "Green Lake happens to be the deepest lake in Wisconsin. Its depth mirrors the depth of the human psyche."

"Now Father," Famir says, "that's a very deep thought." Everyone enjoys the humor except Stan who didn't think it was funny.

Stacey, sitting in the middle row of the van leans forward toward Famir with some concern. "What do you think of the roster of speakers for this event? Do you think this group would be more conciliar with their inter-faith rhetoric?"

"Don't be alarmed, Stacey. Every year the most extreme ideologies become a little more tolerant and understanding. It's hard to say what will happen this week-end, I don't know the Buddhist Mr. Samsara, but I have listened to presentations by Ali and Rabbi Abrams before and I can assure you, they are sensitive and understanding gentlemen who appreciate the basic tenets of all faiths.

"Look, my friends," Famir continues in a calmer tone, "last year, I attended the world famous Parliament of World's Religions gathering in Toronto. Just think, over 2,000 guests came from 80 countries to listen to over 100 spiritual traditions. The theme of the event was *The Promise of Inclusion, the Power of Love: Pursuing Global Understanding.* It was wonderful!"

"Wow," exclaims Stan, 'That's quite a mouthful! When you think about it, isn't that exactly what we're going to do? I'd be happy if we made some strides toward local understanding first."

Minutes away from the center, Tony is driving slower as the snow accumulation has now grown beyond a couple inches. It's falling softly over the freeway covering the grassy knolls and some trees that refuse to release their leaves. He can see swirling flakes up around the highway lights as he passes a sign on Rte. 23: Green Lake Conference Center Half Mile.

Turning into the center, the van comes to a stop until a snow plow clears more parking spaces. Tony finally parks and they're all happy to get out. Stacey reaches down and squeezes some snow into a ball and throws it at a post missing it widely and laughing. The others, too, join in the fun.

Famir looks down and turns serious as recurring thoughts of home and homeland revisit his consciousness. This happens every time he's surrounded by cheerful activities. After several years away, he longs to reunite with his wife and children and to live long enough to see a real Palestinian home in peace.

"I love this time of the year," Famir snaps out of it. "This is one feature that doesn't exist at the Holy Lands." He looks up and savors the falling flakes around his face like a child. He scoops up some snow with bare hands and tosses in the air. Tony lifts up the rear gate and starts taking luggage out. They all grab their own and head for the registration desk.

Chapter 9

In Search of Harmony

A well-dressed man in his 40s, the host of the event, steps up to the riser in Stoughton Hall, faces a wall-to-wall group of attendees and approaches the microphone. Seated behind him are the five speakers. He looks around for a moment and is pleased to hear cacophonous sounds of fellowship, people greeting one another, fixing on name tags, introductions across the seats, shaking of hands, touching and hugging.

"Good evening, ladies and gentlemen," his voice rings out to quell the noisy hall. "Can I have your attention, please? I'm Jonathan Connors. On behalf of the Midwest Inter-Faith Forum, welcome to the First Multi-Faith Conference on 'Ethics.' We're pleased to see so many of you here—and many younger faces. That's wonderful! We hope you will enjoy fellowship and dinner tonight and meet our presenters.

"First, a few ground rules for tomorrow's program. Following my opening remarks, these five distinguished speakers have planned to inspire and challenge you with their views on the rise of Relativism and the need for a moral reset not only in the American scene but a beacon of light around the world.

"We all realize this topic can be complex and often confusing. So, in the packet you received you'll find a copy of each presentation which you can read in advance and follow along when presented. As you'll notice, the content is short and to the point. We have advised our speakers to deliver a difficult topic in understandable English with little ambiguity. In this manner discussions can be more substantive.

"The presenters will speak in the morning session beginning at nine o'clock. Then we break for lunch where we return here for the Q & A until three o'clock. The last two hours will be reserved for breakout sessions with your group at Verandas A, B and C on the grounds. The buildings are so marked and have round tables for discussions. Please check with your group for your breakout location. We look forward to a robust feedback from everyone. Thank you! If there are no questions, kindly proceed to the dining room. Enjoy the evening!"

* * * *

Stan brings his tray of selections from the buffet bar and joins his group at a round table.

"So, what do you all think so far," he asks Rich.

A man in his 50s, owner of several dry-cleaning stores in the DeKalb-Sycamore area, Rich has a look of wonder about him. "All I can think of right now is, what a great turnout! This isn't exactly a favorite topic over lunch, is it? I mean, we're not here to learn how to make money in real estate, or buy into a time share. Several hundred people came to hear why we feel okay about our ethical violations."

"That's a good way to put it, Rich," adds Tony.

While everyone is busy eating and making comments about the place and all the accommodations, a young man comes around the table and places his hand on Stan's shoulder.

"Father Stan!" shouts Jim Winters. "I'm so glad to finally see you. I wanted to talk to you, left you a message and then I realized you were up at the resort..."

Stan looks back to see a gentleman dressed in business casual with silk scarf around his neck. "Yes, I received it, Jim. I was going to call you when I got back, but became involved with the conference—so glad you could make it! Let's talk early in the morning at the coffee bar, say seven o'clock?"

"Sounds good. Looking forward to it!" Jim walks off to his table. Stan notices Rita has her packet with her. "Rita, did you have a chance to check the presentations for tomorrow?"

Rita opens her binder and pulls out the five speeches." Yes Father, they're all about a page each and very focused, even yours!"

"Well, in our talk, we will add a little more narrative and explain our position in greater detail. Because of the subject matter, Jonathan did not want long academic presentations. *Make it short and focused and get people talking,* he emphasized. Those pages are a digest of our presentation for you to follow along—excuse me everyone, I have to circulate."

Just as Stan wanders off to the next table, a tall, thin brown man in a black suit and grey turtleneck, with a white embroidered topi on his head, approaches the table. He introduces himself as "Ali" and reaches out his very large hands to everyone and thanks them for coming.

"Mr. Ali, I'm curious about your speech," says Stacey in a soft, courteous manner. "I've read a lot about Islam—and I know about all the violence in recent years. But I never heard any Muslim ever say anything bad about his faith..."

"Oh, nice lady, nothing wrong with faith! Every society has very excellent people and among them there will always be a few bad people I call troublemakers. We cannot ignore the big tiger in the room! I believe mostly 99% of all people are ethical and moral people. So, it is those few who create problems and give a bad name to the good people and the faith...I will have more to say about it tomorrow..."

"That is so true!" asserts Famir. "Growing up in Israel many years ago, Muslims, Jews and Christians lived in peace and respected one another's way of life. Violence reared its head when a few outsiders—agitators, provoked incidents and created unrest and hostility among the people."

"You are right, sir," Ali responds. "I remember those days too! I wish you all a very wonderful evening." He cups his hands, bows respectfully and moves to another table extending his large hands to greet others.

On the other side of the hall near the bay window, Stan and Bodhi Samsara, the Buddhist, are deep in conversation. Stan listens as the sandal-footed monk appears to be articulating an important point while gesturing with his hands in sweeping motion. With shaven head and wrapped with a black fold-over cassock, the towering figure looks down at Stan who appears confident and unshaken by the encounter.

"Venerable sir," Stan looks up, "It is true, that Buddhism and Christianity are truly two distinctly different faiths drawing their inspiration from different traditions. Although Buddhism does not acknowledge a supreme God, you must agree with respect to ethics and morality, they intersect more often than not and share similar teachings and values.

"It almost seems like they are trying very hard to be different, perhaps to secure a distinct following; but a close examination reveals the eternal truths on how we are supposed to live, to be similar. We have God we answer to while you hold yourself accountable for achieving inner peace or falling short. You have *Karma* and we have *Salvation*; you have *Nirvana* and we have *Theosis* or becoming God-like."

"My dear Father Stan, you are correct, but your path to understanding 'right and wrong, good and evil' has been too difficult for people to follow. We view those principles as simply *Kusala* for Good or Right and *Akusala* for Evil or Wrong. Those who have *Kusala* live a righteous life and enjoy the gifts or talents to improve and ultimately purify themselves. But those who have *Akusala* suffer pain and turmoil because of their immoral behavior and ignorance. It is simply a moral cause and effect principle!

"It is such a pleasure talking with you Father Stan," the monk quickly shifts gears. "I shall speak more about this tomorrow and I look forward to hearing your presentation. What a wonderful place this is! Until tomorrow."

"The pleasure is mine, sir. Until tomorrow then."

In the middle of the dining room, Rabbi Abrams, 50-ish and a bit plump, makes his way toward a table of ladies. He sports a beard and wears a dark suit with a yellow tie.

"Ah, it is my good fortune to be in the company of such fine ladies. I am Rabbi Lester. Where are you all from?" he asks looking over his rimless glasses.

"Hello, Rabbi, it is our pleasure!" the woman closest to him responds as she lays down her fork next to the carrot cake. "We are from Holy Trinity Cathedral in Chicago, the Women's Auxiliary. I'm Helen Cunningham, the president, and these ladies are our board members. Great to meet you! Forgive me but we were expecting to see you in a more Hasidic attire."

"Ha! Sorry to disappoint you! Actually, I'm from the Reform Branch of Judaism although we often share experiences with our Conservative and Orthodox brothers and sisters. We hold a high level of respect for them and as a result, Jews have a choice on how to worship and rules to live by. Actually the Reform Branch was formed in late 18th century in Germany. It was a way to introduce more modernist practices while observing tradition."

"So, you really believe the same things?" asks another lady.

"My dear ladies," he leans toward them, almost in a whisper, "we ALL believe in the same things. We are all created in the image of God, so we are equally important. We have free will to choose good or evil... and...you'll like this one: we are committed to the equality of women. Actually, we were the first movement to ordain women rabbis, a practice the Catholic Church avoids even discussing its merits."

At that point, Helen digs her fork in for another morsel of carrot cake.

"No offense intended ladies. Another tenet of our faith is we don't judge others, whether it's how they worship, how they live or the values they hold dear. I will talk more about this tomorrow."

"No offense taken," Helen responds. It's a pleasure to talk with you. Thank you."

"For me as well, ladies."

Seated at a table by the end of the room near the doors, is Dr. Chunhua Lee. She's conversing with a group of late arrivals who don't know one another as they were assigned this last table.

"Dr. Lee," a man in his 60s draws her attention. "My name is Charles Reilly; I'm a professor of comparative Religions at DePaul University. It seems difficult to discuss ethical behavior and moral living without a connection to religion or a body of belief. What has social science to say about this issue?"

"Not necessarily, Mr. Reilly. Religion may provide a moral framework or punch list to maintain a balance in life, but generally speaking, those who behave morally or immorally need not be adherents to a particular faith."

"You mean ethics has nothing to do with religion?" asks a woman next to Prof. Reilley with some trepidation.

"I didn't mean that Ms.?"

"Mary, Mary Vaughn."

"What I said, Mary, was that a person who is not religious can be ethical and live a moral life. Studies have been done on the justification of wrong-doing that is so prevalent in our culture. The findings show that the rationalization process settles into character during early human experiences that gets organized in the psyche or character building blocks. This happens between ages four and eight.

"More important is the *Ethic of Care* subject I shall explain more tomorrow. Feminism is not only about equal rights, equal work for equal pay and other social demands. Feminist values and female moral development form attitudes like caring and sensitivity to the human condition; sensitivity that most men do not develop because of their duty to principle and absolutes of right and wrong. Generally speaking, the value of care and empathy are passed on from the mother figure in the family, a learned capacity that is not inculcated in boys. There are, of course, exceptions."

"That's very interesting," exclaims an elderly woman. "I always knew I was special! You explain it so well." All enjoy a hearty laugh.

"Indeed you are! Have a nice evening everyone; we'll continue tomorrow."

Chapter 10

A Rude Awakening

Συβηλλα, τι θελεις; Αποθανειν θελω
(Sibyl, what do you want? I want to die!)

T he next morning, a brilliant sun reflects off a shiny finish from last night's snowfall. Everything sparkles! The verandas sport a crystalline frost toping, spilling off the ends like layer cakes. Water droplets drip from rooftops as a balmy winter morning gets under way with early temperature in the upper-30s.

Guests awaken to the sound of snow-blowers clearing the paths throughout the grounds. The snow-laden sculpture of children dancing in a "Circle of Peace" near the entrance offers a continuous warm welcome to all who pass, snow, rain or shine.

The coffee shop door opens for the early risers who need their morning cup. Stan walks in with a binder under his arm and sits at a table near the window. This is the day he presents, so, to straddle between the clerical and lay worlds and look as close to a priest as possible, he's wearing a white turtleneck under a grey blazer.

Just as he opens his binder to check the schedule, he spots Jim Winters holding a coffee mug and waves him over. They shake hands and embrace, Jim sits across the table. The morning sun casts a column of light across Jim's face and rests comfortably on Stan.

"So, how are things going, Jim? Last time we talked your company was involved in some litigation regarding the pipeline. What's the latest?"

Jim cradles his mug looking down searching for the words to begin. He lifts up, shields his eyes from the outside glare, fixes on Stan.

"Well, Father," he says in a reflective tone with wrinkled forehead, "we had a hearing back in October and we presented an iron-clad argument to dismiss the case."

"What happened?" asks Stan, as he lifts a mug to his lips.

"Plaintiff's attorneys represent hundreds of people whose rights have been affected by the allegations. They've interviewed a lot of residents around the Fond du Lac area and further south along the pipeline path who have contracted severe respiratory conditions and filed complaints. The pipeline is destined for Northern Indiana refineries near Gary. Father, we can't even go through one state without disasters!"

"What's the next step?"

"Well, without getting too technical, the presiding judge will most likely certify the case as a 'Class Action' case. We'll know in a couple months if it goes to trial. Meantime, the company decided to offer a settlement. But if I know Morrison, his offer will be rejected outright.

"Who's Morrison?"

"The CEO. He's really peeved the case has gone this far. Although we were able to cite other polluting companies in the same area, the judge ruled there were too many claims against us specifically."

He jerks his chair away from the window's glare and leans toward Stan.

"This may delay completion of the pipeline and if we go to trial and lose the case, damages can be awarded which means heads will roll, even mine. The company may even go broke! But if my team wins the case, I could be in line for a serious bonus. But, Father, that's not my big concern...yes, I don't want to lose my job; but a bigger problem is keeping me up nights."

"What do you mean, Jim?"

"Look, when I graduated from law school, I married and was ready to fight for justice and try to help those in jeopardy and make things right, you know? I began as a public defender and I loved it, but you know, I had to move on...we were building a home and planning to raise a family."

Jim now, looks around and lowers his voice. The sun finally moved away from the window.

"But I didn't foresee that I would be in court defending illegal and immoral actions of my company in the name of profit. I never realized I would be expected to ignore and even deny hundreds of illnesses and deaths resulting from my company's negligence. You know what he called all those casualties? Collateral damage!"

Both sip more coffee and remain silent for a few minutes. Stan realizes after many years, that Jim is comfortable sharing his feelings not only with a clergyman but, more important, a trusted friend. He knows Jim's equipped with the gifts of argument and rationalization to justify company operations, but he also suspects that Jim may be planning to lose the case and witness just compensation for survivors—company be damned! Stan suddenly looks up with resolve.

"Look, Jim, you accepted a position in the legal team of a major oil company and you moved up to lead counsel. What did you expect you'd be doing, defending the company from only zoning issues or property rights? The way I see it, your allegiance is to the company right now and to do the best job possible."

"What happened to doing the right thing?"

"Look, you still have time to do the right thing, a hundred times over! But right now, you're getting paid the big bucks and you have an obligation to your company. You must do your best in your job and when the trial is over, however it turns out, you can make a career change and feel better about yourself. Then you can do the right thing the rest of your life. What do you think?"

"Thanks," he says, surprised at the unexpected advice. "You've given me some things to think about."

"Good! Say! I think it's time for breakfast! I'm hungry."

"So am I, let's go." Jim stands weighing in on Stan's enigmatic advice.

Morning Session

Jonathan Connors steps up to the riser at Stoughton Hall, checks his watch and approaches the podium.

"Welcome back everyone, please take your seats so we can begin."

Guests are slow to return. They hesitate terminating meaningful discussions that began during breakfast. The host is pleased with the interactivity and fellowship among the guests, but at the same time, he has a program to move along.

Jim is thinking about Stan's advice and wonders if there is a little hint of Relativism where you postpone doing the right thing for a more convenient time. He suspects the human condition requires adjustments to objective truths, that we cannot escape subjective morality totally.

"Good morning, ladies and gentlemen," Jonathan continues. "It's presentation time! So, what is Ethical Relativism? Perhaps we can examine what it isn't! This social doctrine has no absolute truth, no right and wrong and what one person or society celebrates, another may condemn. In other words, one person's meat can be another's poison.

"Expressed in another way, Ethical Relativism is a concept that all points of view are equally valid and a person decides what is true and relative for him or her. So, black and white, right and wrong have been subtly removed from the lexicon of moral behavior. Clearly, Relativism dictates that no principle is true for all people in all places and at all times. For example, in ancient times to the 19th Century, slavery was an acceptable practice globally. Of course, today it is not.

"So, I ask you, is this the society we're living in now? I'd like you all to think about this as we listen to our speakers who will shed more light on this social phenomenon. You have their presentations in your packet and you'll be able to follow as they clarify their positions.

"Mohammed Ali Nusreth is an Imam at Islamic Cultural Center in St. Paul, Minnesota. I hope most of you had a chance to meet and talk to him last night. He's been an advocate of peace and harmony all his life. In recent years he has reached out to religious communities in the St. Paul-Minneapolis area with the spirit of co-existence and peace. Currently, he is director of the Islamic-Christian Coalition in Minneapolis. Please give a warm welcome to Mohammed Ali Nusreth."

A ripple of applause resonates through the hall, then calms to a dead silence.

"Good morning my good people! You brave the winter snow, spend your money and time to travel to this beautiful place, for what? To hear strange people talk about Ethics and Morality! I truly commend you. You have my presentation, so I will just provide some additional comments.

"When you hear the word 'Muslim,' how many of you feel a little fear, perhaps some apprehension? Come on, be open." A few hands go up slowly across the hall and then retracted.

"But when you hear the word "Islam" you don't have the same reaction, right? Well, that's because Muslims are people and Islam is a faith. People have flaws, they err and make mistakes just like in other faiths. But Islam, the faith, stands as an unshakable beacon to guide the faithful toward an ethical life under the eyes of God.

"With respect to the man-made condition of Relativism, Islam rejects this concept. Ethical behavior and morals are not relative, they are absolute and universal. A Muslim's actions are either moral or immoral, right or wrong, black or white—there is no middle ground in which to relax and feel comfortable. This social trend is a western idea that gained traction in recent years, perhaps because of the diminishing importance of other religious beliefs.

"My good friends, the practice of Relativism enables one to lessen the severity of wrong-doing and make unacceptable behavior appear acceptable. I'm quite sure that this practice is condemned by most religions, not just Islam. Thank you so much for your attention, I look forward to active discussion later. May the same Godhead that governs everything and everyone bless this conference and all the guests."

Following a lengthy applause, the host returns to the podium.

"Ladies and gentlemen, it's my pleasure to present Bodhi Samsara from the Deer Park Buddhist Center in Oregon, Wisconsin. He is resident monk responsible for education of Buddhist teachings at the center. Please welcome the Venerable Bodhi Samsara."

The monk, dressed in orange and red robes raises his arms to subdue the applause as he stands behind the podium.

"Forgive me for not basking in your praise, for if I am to grow spiritually to a *No-Self* level, I have to resist praises and expressions of vanity. You understand I must resist the idea of self or the *Ego* as you would call it. The Buddhist way of life is one of balance, similar to Aristotle's view of avoiding extremes of over-indulgence or deprivation.

"The Great Buddha warned his people about self-punishment and physical sacrifice. He taught that satisfying the necessities of life is not evil; that to keep the body in good health is a duty. Otherwise, we shall not be able to keep our mind strong and clear.

"The great teachings of our faith understand the human flaws and weaknesses that we as mortals must endure. For this reason absolute right and wrong must yield to a more broad meaning rather than being an absolute truth. For example, if a Christian were to commit theft, murder, or even anger or disrespect, he would be a sinner. To enter the realm of heaven he would have to repent for his sins and seek redemption. Without this act, he would be separated from God and face an eternity in hell.

"In Buddhism, any of these serious actions would deprive an individual a level of enlightenment and cause him great unhappiness and distress. This condition would push him further away from the path to *Nirvana*. So, you see, it's a case of cause and effect brought about by the individual. Living the *Middle Way* clarifies the difference between desire and need. So, my friends, the middle way urges us to live a life of balance and harmony and work toward cultivating character. Thank you so much for your attention."

He cups his hands, bows slightly and walks back to his seat. With great respect and consideration, the audience does not applaud. Jonathan comes to the podium quietly, turns toward the monk and acknowledges him.

"We thank you for your wise counsel, Venerable Samsara.

"From the Congregation Shalom in Milwaukee, I have the pleasure of introducing Rabbi Lester Abrams. I hope you already met him last night. As a disciple of the Reform Branch, he's been serving Synagogues in Wisconsin for the last 15 years. Please welcome Rabbi Abrams."

"Thank you, John," he says softly as the shortest speaker on the dais takes the podium. He's wearing a dark blue suit, off-white shirt, blue tie and no head cover. To see this man out of context, you could mistake him for a lawyer or doctor, a stock broker, even a salesman.

"Hello, again, everyone. Please read my presentation. I'll just add some remarks to my position. Judaic researchers ascribe the concept of Monotheism to a band of nomads who made that claim more than 5,000 years ago. Indeed, it was a revolutionary idea that far back. It must not have gotten much traction since polytheism and paganism reigned until the advent of Christianity and Islam, both raising a banner with the words *God is One.*

"As for Moral Relativism, Judaism definitely celebrates objective morality, right and wrong, good or evil and all the Judeo-Christian legacy we inherited. Ladies and gentlemen, for the modern Jew, Relativism and Judaism are total opposites. The former is an abomination as it insults the Torah, even God himself.

"The Ten Commandments are absolute, but this new ideology years in the making, has made them obsolete. It has brought disaster upon our society and western civilization. Lying, cheating, extortion, bribery, theft, embezzlement, betrayal and a host of other transgressions, appear to have become a way of life. And there are so many of them that they are grouped in a category called *Corruption*.

"This unethical behavior has infiltrated education, sports, media, government, business not only here but also around the world. In Politics, an immoral act is justified if it is legal. Finally, the practice of and submitting to moral relativism is simply WRONG! And no justification, rationalization, logic and reason can ever make it right."

At this point, the good Rabbi receives a thunderous round of applause which surprises even him. While still clapping, Jonathan walks to the podium.

"Wow! Rabbi, you must have hit a nerve out there! By the way, how is everyone enjoying this so far?"

Shouts echo throughout: *Excellent! Great! Educational! Very Uplifting!*

"Now, from the National Psychology Association, I call to the podium Dr. Chunhua Lee. She is professor of Clinical Psychology at University of Wisconsin, Madison."

A tall, statuesque lady in her 40s approaches the microphone with a pleasant smile, wearing a charcoal pants suit and silver shawl.

"Good morning everyone. I am very happy to be among my learned colleagues who have inspired us all with their knowledge and wisdom. I shall discuss the role of Feminism in our society from a different perspective, one of sensitivity and care more prominent in the female species. Generally speaking, women have a 6th sense that drives the *Ethic of Care* inspired by their ability to seek out options for resolution of moral issues.

"I bring this topic to you to demonstrate that there is no right and wrong in the absolute sense; there never was! And Relativism is not a modern phenomenon. The 5th century BC historian Herodotus spoke about Ethical Relativism when he noticed different customs and standards in societies; and each person and society regards their own as the best. Of course, the wise historian knew no set of social customs that was better than any other.

"Through the millennia and into post-modernism, we've evolved into a diverse society and adopted an ethic of tolerance with a variety of options. My good friends, we all know that Man is a flawed creature and studies have proven people simply cannot live up to a strict absolute standard of behavior. They do have the capacity to reach admirable levels of behavior and enjoy temporary bliss, but it soon fades into a fleeting memory. Religious institutions are on hand to mitigate the guilt that follows and offer a path to higher ground through meditation and prayer.

"With the focus on *Diversity* in recent years, we've been taught to adopt a mantra of tolerance for society's diverse beliefs. This has led western societies to adopt a system of subjective beliefs, distancing away from one of absolute truths.

"Regarding the Ethic of Care provision of subjective morality, I'd like to end with a personal story if I may. Many years ago when my brother Tom earned his driving license, I, my mother and my dad rode in the car as he was showing us his driving skills. Well, several blocks from the house, Tom drove passed a stop sign without stopping. Sure enough, a police car followed us with all its colorful lights.

'You missed a stop sign, Tom,' shouted Dad. 'Now you have to pay the price for your mistake. He's coming to write you a ticket.'

"I remember Tom was very upset being stopped by police with the family in the car. The policeman asked for his license, told him what he did and began writing a ticket. Just then, when we all thought that judgment was inescapable, my mother, sitting next to Tom, not well versed in English, leaned over toward the window and began an emotional defense for her son.

*Please, mister policeman, Tom just get license, is a good boy and
safe driver. Maybe we talk too much and he not see stop sign.
Please, give him another chance, he not do this again.*

"This impassioned plea comes from a woman's moral platform,
much different from a man's. My dad was a man of universal principles and prepared Tom to face the consequence of his action. But my
mother found other options with which to negotiate. The policeman
looked at Tom, tore up the ticket and warned him to be more careful.
Ladies and gentlemen, thank you so much for listening and have a
wonderful day."

Jonathan hops onto the riser. "Thank you Dr. Lee for a most infor-
mative presentation. Don't forget folks, take notes and prepare questions for discussion following the presentations. Now, I'd like to call
on Father Stan Rybak. He's pastor at All Saints Church in Sycamore,
Illinois, serving that parish for the last four years. His distinct, interactive ministry has energized his community and doubled the stewardship pledges. Please let's welcome Father Stan."

The audience applauds as Stan approaches the podium, pauses and
scans the large hall.

"Hello, everyone, it's certainly exciting to share with you this conundrum called *Moral Relativism*. I think by now we have a good idea
what it is and we can agree that it has changed the landscape of human
behavior. But we haven't addressed any remedy for it or if, indeed, we
need one. Can we turn it back? Can we live in a world of right and
wrong absolutes, or are we destined to languish in this dead zone of
moral compromise?

"I like to fish in the north woods of Wisconsin, an activity that has
reset my balance and view of life. You should all try it sometime—and
it doesn't matter if you catch fish or not!

"So, am I saying that in order to reset your moral compass, you
have to go fishing? Well, not exactly. You must open yourself up to an

enlightening experience other than what happens to you daily. It could be fishing, maybe beholding a sunset or being moved by the innocent giggle of a child.

"For me, in addition to my strong faith, I also connect with nature. Each time I come away renewed. Couple months ago my family and I spent a few days at a favorite northern resort. That's where I met a new friend: a loon. The thing about loons is you can't get near them; the moment they feel fear or danger, they dive underwater and resurface some distance away. They do this every time, except for me.

"Just last October my boat came close to one, but it didn't leave, just stared at me. I maintained my composure and just looked back. It shook its wings and cried out a loud yelp. I had just made a new friend. It took four years of struggle and reaching out to finally connect with one.

"So, in order to tame the loon YOU encounter, (it could be an animal, or a person) it must trust and feel safe near you. It must feel secure, that you're a caring and loving person, the real deal. This is where renewal and regeneration is born and developed; and these life-enhancing feelings are then passed on to others without effort.

"Regarding the need for renewal, let me tell you a quick story from Greek mythology. There lived a lady called Sibyl, a prophet and fortune teller. She enjoyed an almost perfect record of prognostications and drew the attention of Apollo. As a reward, he asked her to make a wish and it would be granted."

'I want eternal life,' she shouted.

"And eternal life, she was granted. All was well for decades and millennia, even though she was getting older and her beauty had faded. When she reached 1000 years old she had shriveled to a tiny wrinkled creature living in a jar hanging in the marketplace. She was actually decomposing and because of her continuous pain and suffering, she kept screaming out for help. Passersby would often ask her,

'Sibyl, what do you want?'

And her reply was always,

'I want to die.'

"You see, Sibyl neglected to clarify her wish to include staying young along with eternal life. Several takeaways from this story: first be careful what you wish for…and second, a reset and renewal of our persona is necessary for personal happiness and spiritual growth. Sibyl did not renew, was not enlightened and did not experience transformation and rebirth; she just grew old.

"The physical limitations of old age which brings about death in mortals, did not happen to her, so she was destined to suffer forever. My point is you are challenged to renew while still living, not to wait for the grand transformation upon death. This will require commitment, struggle, even suffering. But, once you locate and attach to your higher self, you will be renewed!

"So, my good friends, it's important to "tame the loon" so to speak. For this to happen you must secure peace at heart and sincerity in intent. You must be trusted and radiate empathy and understanding. Once the loon feels secure and safe in your presence, you are on your way to renewal. What is your loon? Thank you."

"Ladies and gentlemen," Stan adds, "Jonathan asked me to announce a short 15 minute break. Then we'll continue with the Q & A portion of the program."

Stan draws a robust applause as guests stand to stretch and talk amongst themselves.

Chapter 11

APPRAISAL AT THE VERANDA

Following a lengthy Q & A session after lunch, Stan's team from Illinois is assigned Veranda B for their breakout at three o'clock. The distance from Stoughton Hall is barely a 100-yard leisurely walk. Most of the snow has melted, leaving behind heavy, wet clumps that weigh down smaller evergreens in the grassy areas and knolls. Stan notices some bushes have lost their manicured shape but realizes it's only a temporary burden. They leave the hall in groups of three or four discussing their exchange with the speakers.

Veranda B is situated in the middle of a long and narrow building. Stan motions to his group to meet inside in ten minutes. Famir draws closer to Stan and lights up his pipe.

"Father, it seems to me that Moral Relativism is securely entrenched in our way of life and absolute principles may be noble and look good on paper—but impossible to live up to."

"I know what you mean. If I were judging this event as a contest, I'm afraid I would have to declare Relativism the winner. But absolute truths are necessary for us to aspire to. Famir, the struggle to reach that higher level is a sacred quality of human life—a continuous attempt to reach beyond and discover our higher purpose."

Famir takes a couple drags from his pipe and watches the smoke diffuse into the afternoon frigid air. "Look, Father, higher purpose? I understand we are given one, but how many of us recognize we even have one let alone aspire to connect to it? I feel life's become too complex and people devote their time to just get by with their worldly self and hope for the best."

As the sun retreats far off into the horizon, the afternoon air begins to bite also. Stan realizes many cannot recognize a higher purpose. And this is the main reason he became a priest: to help people discover it.

They decide to go inside and assemble their group. The room can accommodate enough tables for several groups and there's a bar against the wall with coffee, drinks, ice, cheese, chips and crackers. Most of the fifteen attendees from Sycamore line up for a snack.

"Okay, everyone," Stan announces, "now that we're all here, please appoint a chair at your table to run the discussions. Each table has a discussion report as a guide. The chair will be responsible to pilot the discussions and fill out the report. When you finish, please give me the report so I can assess our group's response to today's proceedings. Good luck."

Stan walks over his table and sits with his group: Stacey, Tony, Rita, Famir and Rich.

"Here's the broad question for us: Do we no longer have good and evil, right and wrong in our society today? And what are some take-aways from the speeches and the Q & A?"

"I think our faith in God," Rita bursts out, "is related to our changing attitudes."

"What do you mean?" asks Rich.

"Well, think about it! Through many religions, mankind has demonstrated strong faith in a higher power. Across the millennia, thousands of belief systems were created to glorify God. Tens of thousands of houses of worship were erected in His name. Even wars have been fought in His name with untold human sacrifices.

"My point is, after all this display of abiding faith, God has not gestured or given any sign of acknowledgement. Isn't this enough reason to begin refashioning absolute systems of right and wrong? So, my question is if God responded with some visible and unquestionable sign that people can trust, wouldn't that slight gesture guide mankind back toward discovery and purpose? Even launch a new renaissance toward faith itself?"

Famir hangs on her every word. "Interesting points you make, Rita. I remember when you asked the Rabbi about man maintaining these objective truths, he remained adamant about watering down God's commandments. He said we're not to wait for divine proof to act, that our strong faith should be enough. What do you think, Rich? You got into it with Ali about the Koran."

"That's the point! Our faith has weakened through the millennia. And it needs to be revitalized. Regarding the Koran, I recall bringing up one of the Hadis that says "Do not kill a person, except by legal right, or if the faith is threatened. The sixth Commandment of the Old Testament states 'Thou shalt not kill,' period! There are no conditions attached. So, I suggested that Islam may be using relativist reasoning when attaching conditions. For example, what constitutes a threat to the faith? Also, are not legal provisions man-made? His response merely repeated previous statements."

Tony is busy writing. When he completes his thought, he looks up.

"The question I'm left with is, can a person live up to strict standard of moral behavior? The evolution of mankind through the ages, has created a world of thousands of interpretations and options—especially in the absence of any visible Divine hint. Look, we don't live in a time warp. We get separated from traditional standards and...kind of swept up in generational waves of change, through no fault of our own. No, I don't think we can live up to a rigid traditional standard!

"I agree with Rita. Follow me on this! If the hand of God were to descend before a slab on a mountain and carve His message on how we should live—and TV cameras are there to record it, can you imagine what that could mean? This event alone would help reconnect mankind to their creator and secure many generations of allegiance to universal truths we can live by."

Stan notices Stacey raising her hand and asks her to give her views.

"...Tony, that's a great thought and we all wish that could happen. But it's too simplistic—an unreasonable expectation that removes the discovery, struggle and mystery necessary for achieving personal renewal. I've been thinking a lot about today's talks. What sticks in my mind is Samsara's position which pretty much legitimizes a relativist view of moral behavior. If you recall, he spoke about avoiding extremes, about moderation in all actions. He led us to a *Middle Way* satisfying both need and desire, toward a life of balance and harmony. But values like honesty, faith, compassion can get lost in the process, don't you think, Father?"

"Very interesting point, Stacey. The Buddhist allows the individual the freedom and will to seek a proper balance and grow spiritually at his own pace. The Christian concept of individual will, along with meditation and prayer, will guide a person towards renewal and rebirth. So, when reaching toward a higher level of growth and awareness, balance and harmony follow.

"It's the *Admitting* to wrong doing that's the most difficult to do. Once one admits to it, he's on his way to redemption. The denial leads to lying and cover-up; and the lying leads to having to remember many details. This is true whether it involves stealing a watermelon, or massive fraud involving a national scandal.

"Now, Dr. Lee's position is another example of *Guided Relativism* where a woman's intuition and ethic of care can guide one to acceptable options of solving a moral problem than a rigid black and white position as expressed by her dad. I put great emphasis on the word 'Guided' because one can exploit various options for negative and harmful intent."

The two chairmen of the other tables and Rich hand in their written report to Stan. He exchanges discussion with them for a few minutes as they head on to the dining room. Stan puts away the papers and joins everyone to dinner.

Chapter 12

A Reluctant Return

Less than a dozen guests around them at the non-denominational chapel, Stan and Stacey sit quietly in front of a candle stand. He fixes on the red glass vessels with dancing flames. There is no real altar, except a recessed cove with an all-seeing eye painted in the arch. Stained glass windows direct the strong morning sunlight through prisms to form shafts of blues and reds throughout the small chapel.

When he inquired about the chapel on the grounds, he was told there are no services per se, guests are welcome any time to meditate, pray or even just sit, wonder and breathe in the silence. And there is no lock on the door. After ten minutes, they stand and begin to walk out quietly; Stan stuffs a couple dollars in the donations container near the door.

They enter a dining hall full of guests enjoying breakfast and lively conversation before heading home. Stan returns waves of hand from his group as they walk over to claim a couple chairs. Stacey wanders to the buffet while Stan sits near Famir.

"Father Stan, I forgot to ask you," says Famir. "When you get a chance I'd like to come and see you for a lunch or coffee after we get back. I want to discuss something important and get your opinion."

"Of course! Anything serious?"

"Regarding my homeland. Not an emergency. I'll give you a call first of the year and we'll get together. Thanks."

"Great! Anytime in January would be good. By the way, thank you for your contribution to our discussions. Your diverse experience here and abroad in many matters of human behavior is sure appreciated."

"My pleasure, Father."

Stacey returns to the table with two plates including eggs, bacon, potatoes and French toast.

"Oh, thanks honey! You read my mind," Stan shouts. "Just what I was thinking to get for myself."

"This is for me dear," she smiles. "Get your own!"

All burst out in laughter at the look on Stan's face. Moments later, he begins to laugh as well—a spontaneous response he can't control. It's as though he was ready for a hearty laugh, a part of the human condition he sometimes ignores. After such serious discussions for several days, everyone is ready to just interact and enjoy.

Soon, this episode with Father and Stacey cascades into a humorous segment of silly anecdotes and funny tales that lift everyone's spirits with less energy than required for serious revelations. While still laughing, Famir feels his phone vibrate and moves away to answer it. He sees a Middle East area code and quickly assumes it's his wife, Amira.

"Hello, Amira?"

"Sorry to disappoint you, Famir. It's Mohammad Najjar!"

"How did you get my...?"

"Don't worry, Famir. Amira and children are fine. We don't bother them. Famir, the Christian!—always looking to make peace with people who don't want peace. But deep down, we know you are first, a patriot. I am just keeping in touch. We miss you and more important, we need you and hope to see you soon. You have been away too long." Mohammad hangs up leaving Famir with feelings of mixed loyalties to a Palestinian cause that continues to haunt him.

Following a sumptuous meal and great camaraderie, Stan settles the account for his group at the desk while Stacey inspects the gift shop.

He loads up their bags in the Suburban, checks the room a last time and joins the rest of the group.

On their way out of the compound, they pause to look at the ice-covered sculpture of the circle of children dancing. All marvel at the perpetual joy in their faces, frozen in time. In a similar way, Stan feels everyone in the conference formed a circle of peace, a verbal attempt to reach out and help heal old wounds and grievances.

While driving, Tony's thoughts default to earning more money.

Riding alongside Tony, Famir is consumed with the difficulty in accepting injustice by those who have been abused and wronged by history and are powerless to affect change.

"You're awfully quiet," Stacey whispers softly.

"Thinking about all that must be done by the end of the month. If you recall, you organized the Christmas pageant last year when I had difficulty getting the right people to run it."

"Remember," she says, "you were apprehensive about tapping into the leadership qualities of our young people—a valuable option I explored that worked out perfectly."

"If you can help with that again, it would be great. I have to finish a report for the bishop and the food bank for the homeless."

"Okay, Stan, I'll do it on one condition!" she declares.

"What's that?"

"If you take us to downtown Rockford to see the lights?"

"Of course. We'll go for ice cream too!"

"Deal!"

Chapter 13

TONY CASSATA BARES ALL

Stan arrives for the third basketball game of the season on Saturday, December 14, 2019 at St. Andrew's gym in Belvidere, Illinois. Stacey stayed back to work on the Sunday School Pageant. He invited Tony to the game hoping to get him to open up in a different venue.

The high school church conference league has a 12-game season that will run through March of next year. His team, All Saints Loons, lost the first two games. Stan walks up the stands and sits just behind the team as family and friends begin pouring in for the game.

Two referees walk on the floor and begin talking as they check the scoreboard. They motion for the coaches to approach. Stan notices Tony on the other side of the gym. He waves and whistles until he gets his attention. Tony walks around to the other side.

"Hi, Father, thanks for inviting me. I didn't know we had a basketball team! The Loons? Why the Loons? Sounds loony or crazy."

"No, Tony, the loon is a bird of the wilderness. But once you get to know one, you experience tranquility, peace and a reawakening of hopes and dreams; and if we pay close attention, loons help us identify our destiny and pursue our dreams. Isn't that what we talked about before?"

"Yeah, I know. Look, Father, when can I talk to you? I got some problems I need to fix..."

"Well, we're both here now. Last time we spoke, I noticed there were things you just couldn't unwrap. What's going on? Talk to me!"

The stands are now filled and a loud horn just sounded for the game to start. The two centers step into center court, the referee tosses the ball and the game is underway. The Belvidere Eagles bring the ball down the court as a foul is called.

"I don't feel good about what I've been doing at the company. My boss, Gus, is a good man and he's been generous to me and the other employees. I did something that I can't undo and I think he suspects something is wrong with the books..."

The home team just scored and the Loons are bringing the ball down our way. The guard gets a pass, cuts and scores on a jump shot. Stan nudges Tony and applauds.

"I remember you telling me about rebirth and regeneration and why that must happen often to focus on noble acts, things you can be proud of...Christmas is coming, Father and I feel terrible."

"Tony, you're providing more suspense than this game! For God's sake, what have you done?"

An Eagle guard stands on the foul line for two shots. He makes them and the score is Home team 18, Loons 12. Now, Stan twists toward Tony, looks in his eyes and waits.

"Father...last year I opened another account at the same bank," forcing his voice to rise above the nearby crowd "...and I've been diverting money into it. At the time I set it up, I felt okay about it...a side fund to help with my son John's college expenses next year. I'm just not earning enough to support this—and his brother's a year behind!

"I began last year, just depositing a small portion of the receivables... to slowly build the account and not draw attention to it...I mean, I didn't see a problem, the company was doing well. A part of me felt it was the right thing to do. But, when business slowed down along with cash flow and some customers were not paying us at the same time, Gus felt the pinch and wanted to know why. Anyway, since last month, I've been depositing all money in the regular account..."

A piercing horn signals the end of the quarter and stops Tony's narrative cold. Home team: 26, Loons 20. They concentrate on the game for a while and allow time to digest the quick morsels of information Stan has been able to extract. He can feel Tony's burden is too heavy for him to manage. With a serious, but empathetic demeanor, he looks at Tony's eyes again and connects.

"Do you think Gus knows?"

"I think he knows something's not right...he's been going to the office on weekends and I'm sure he's examining the books."

"Tony, have you pulled out any of that extra money for anything?"

"A couple weeks ago I paid the company's corporate franchise fee."

"How much was it?"

"Just $100. Since cash flow was drying up, I thought of conserving..."

Suddenly, all around them stand and join in a thunderous blast as the Loons score a 3-pointer just in front of halftime. Home: 39, Loons 41. Then the crowd settles down.

"You thought of what?" Stan yelled.

"I said I paid that fee from the extra fund trying to conserve the account."

They decide to head for the refreshment stand outside the gym before the rush at halftime. Stan gets a couple hot dogs and some pop and secures a high table.

"How much is in the account now?"

"About $8,400."

A loud horn signals halftime and the people start jamming the lobby. Tony unwraps the hot dog and starts eating as Stan stops a passerby.

"Say, what's the score?"

"43/41 Eagles."

"Thanks."

Stan takes a bite and sends it down with a deep drag from a drink.

"Tony, if you feel bad about what you did and regret it—and you want to make it right, there's a simple path to fix this and maybe you can't see it!"

"What are you saying, Father? In a couple days I may get fired. Gus is onto me!"

"Tony, calm down. You're not thinking straight. Look, you have to take care of this immediately—first thing on Monday! Here's what I see. You created a slush fund for yourself to help defray future college costs, right?"

"Yeah, that's right."

"You are paid well, but you need more. Your intent was wrong and dishonest and legally, you are liable for mismanagement and intent to defraud. So, your intent is wrong, immoral and illegal. But, BUT! You haven't exercised it yet! You can't be held to account for an act you haven't committed yet. The company's funds are still secured in bank accounts save the $100 fee you paid—and that's a company expense!"

"But, I opened another account and I'm the only signer."

"Okay. Why can't you explain that you did this to have money available, outside the operating account, for taxes...and insurance? It seems like a good idea to me! Of course, you have to abandon your original intent and figure out another way to finance college costs."

"Father, I...I didn't think of that!"

"I told you, you're not thinking clearly. You're too focused on the original intent, and guilt is clouding your business sense. The morality of the intent is something you and I can work on. All Gus needs to hear is that everything is still okay—that you planned to tell him and it slipped your mind; that a separate account is in place to take care of other than day-to-day business expenses. And any audit will show all moneys are accounted for. It's a no-brainer! Dah!"

A big smile slides across Tony's face. They finish eating and quietly walk back to the gym where play is under way. Minutes before the 4th quarter, the score is close: 56-50 Eagles. Stan and Tony are quiet, their attention on the game. Suddenly, Tony turns toward Stan.

"Would you say I'm about to experience an epiphany?"

"Only if you do the right thing on Monday."

They stay to the end to watch the Loons bring home a victory: 62/59.

"You know, this is the best basketball game ever! But aren't we applying Relativism to my problem, Father?"

"Not admitting to what you might have done does not hurt anybody except yourself, because you didn't do it! It's more a *Guided Relativism,* don't you think?"

Chapter 14

RECONCILIATION WITH THE BISHOP

S tan carries a potted Basil plant wrapped in red foil up the multiple tiered stairs of the diocese. Bishop Mark's secretary Miriam, comes to the door. In her early 60s, she wears a white satin top with a navy blue skirt and low heels. Large glasses balance on her nose secured with ornate chain around her neck.

"Hi, Father Stan, what a sweet-smelling plant! His Grace will love it! I'll take it right into his office. Have a seat, I believe he's expecting you."

"Thanks. Miriam. By the way, this is Basil, named after Basil the Great whom we celebrate in just a few days."

"Oh, that's right!"

"Yes, this plant is associated with purification, nature's attempt to cleanse and renew us. I'm sure the Bishop understands. By the way, where's Deacon John?"

"He left yesterday, went home to South Bend for Christmas. I'll be right back."

He sits in an antique French chair wondering why Miriam didn't inspect the potted plant for possible explosives. He opens his binder to review the conference report while admiring the colorful lights in the chandeliers and the huge Christmas tree near the fireplace. Then he looks over the deacon's desk and notices the fake Fallen Angel painting still hangs on the wall only now, it's between two ornate sconces to flood artificial light on it.

Miriam returns and sits by Stan. "He's on the phone, Father. He'll come out to see you when he's finished."

"Okay, thanks. Where is your home, Miriam?"

"Oh, I live in Rockford."

"Really! That's where my parents live."

"Oh? Where about?"

"On West Alpine Street. How about you?"

"I live with my husband and daughter on East Riverside. That's the area that the governor is going to declare a..."

At that point, the bishop comes out of his office to interrupt Miriam from going on about her classy address. He walks over with a gentleman in grey slacks and charcoal blazer, holding a trench coat and hat.

"Father Stan, good to see you again, Merry Christmas!"

"Merry Christmas to you, Your Grace," he responds while bending to kiss his ring.

"I'd like you to meet Greg Elliot, chairman of the Diocesan Council and attache to the Catholic Archdiocese. He is also head pharmacologist at *Lab-Rinth Pharmaceuticals* in Hartford. Actually, Greg's a neighbor of yours, lives in Sycamore."

The bishop looks at Greg, then at Stan.

"Greg, Father Stan is one of our most ecumenical priests—perhaps too ecumenical at times"—they laugh. "And has some ideas about reaching out to our Christian brothers and others. He's just returned from a multi-faith conference in Wisconsin."

They shake hands and Greg gives Stan a card.

"Call me after the holidays, Father, let's meet and discuss a challenging turning point facing our church." Stan gives him his card also.

"Great to meet you, Mr. Elliot, looking forward to talking with you."

While Miriam sees Mr. Elliot out, the bishop grabs Stan by the elbow and leads him to the office. Stan gives him the report he expected and the bishop lays it on his desk turning without looking at it or referring to it. Stan's troubled by Greg's enigmatic comment. *What turning point?* he wonders.

"Father, when I saw you two side by side just minutes ago, I visualized a special alliance that could launch common initiatives. This is what we were talking about when you came. We've been too rigid, too 'Black and White' with this whole thing."

"What do you mean, Your Grace?"

"We always expect too much and in the end nothing ever happens. Too many jurisdictional and ecclesiastic obstacles with other leaders. Now we're adopting a more tolerant position with other jurisdictions. Instead of unity and consolidation, we now look for harmony and cooperation as a first step; and I suspect this will yield more fruitful results. What do you think?"

"I'm impressed with your vision! I would be humbled and proud at the same time to be part of a program that seeks out our common qualities that bring peace among us."

"Thanks for coming, Father, and thank you for the Basil plant. My blessings to you and your wife, have a wonderful Christmas."

Stan kisses his ring and leaves the office. He walks over to Miriam's desk, gives her a prolonged hug and then a kiss on the cheek.

"Merry Christmas, Miriam!" he shouts, triumphantly.

Her glasses fall off her nose as she sits there in shock and Stan saunters off walking on air. Expecting to be reprimanded for his lack of proper church protocols, instead he is congratulated. He wonders if *Guided* Relativism is at play here as well.

Is Greg Elliot assigned to keep an eye on me? Stan wonders.

For Stan, one thing is certain: absolutes are not working in efforts to bring church leaders closer. They are grasping for defensive positions to protect their turf, jurisdiction and control of the status quo. He recalls many attempts by Christian denominations to join forces throughout the years, but initiatives were always tabled for future consideration. He's come to understand the biggest unexpressed concern leaders worry about in a union, is who will be in charge? And this question is so sensitive, nobody dares to ask it as talks never progress that far.

Part 2

Chapter 15

2011—Graduation, Nuptials and Ordination

S tan had been dating Stacey Russos during his last two years at Holy Cross Divinity School in Boston. Having grown weary of the day-to-day obedience culture, he would see her every weekend he was allowed to leave campus. Stan was drawn to her quick wit and sharp analytical mind. She was also very attractive with light brown hair and hazel eyes. Though she stood an inch taller than him, he didn't mind, he felt secure and confident building a relationship with a girl much smarter than most.

During his last year of study, he enjoyed greater liberties and they met more often. She would drive up to campus, pick him up and visit their favorite restaurant in Jamaica Plain for lunch or for just a frappe.

On occasion, she would secure tickets for the Huntington Theatre in Boston for an opera or play. By spring, 2011, their relationship grew serious and they began talking about marriage. For Stan, there was no bended knee plea for her hand, as their intimacy blossomed and was ready for harvest without the ritual.

"What does your family say about marrying a priest?" he asked her one day.

"Well, Dad is close to the church and he considers having a priest in the family a feather in his hat, so to speak—Stan! Dad lunches with the bishop often!"

"More important, Stacey," he probed, "how do you feel about being a priest's wife? It's going to happen this fall, you know. I know you realized what you were getting into when we started going out, that it is a different life—you know, people talk and you're always being judged..."

"Look, Stan! I'm a teacher and in many ways, so are you! I focus on children and you teach everyone. I have a mind of my own and can stand my ground. The rumor mill doesn't concern me. Besides, I love you. Isn't that why people get married?"

Her family was in the dairy business serving Boston and surrounding suburbs for three generations. It was started by her dad's grandfather and successfully managed by an uncle. When the uncle died, the company fell into the capable hands of Michael Russos.

When Stacey grew up she favored academics and earned a degree in Primary Education at Boston College; clearly a disappointment to her father who had expected her to major in Management or Accounting and be part of the family business. Regrettably, Stacey had no interest in Shoreline Dairy Company, especially having to work under a controlling patriarchal figure. She tried to explain she's not a business type and would not be an asset to the company; that her interests lie in education of children.

The Russos insisted the wedding take place in Boston and that was fine with Stan's parents, since the New Englanders were paying for it. The date was set for Saturday, September 10. Michael was well connected with the cathedral and the diocese and he would begin planning for the wedding following Stan's graduation in June. He and his wife, Anne, had a couple months to coordinate all the details and to make it into a big gala event, sparing no expense.

Ceremonies, Rituals & Receptions

The year 2011 was indeed, a time when all the components came together to seal Stan's career and life—all in four months. First on the calendar, was graduation, followed by a lavish wedding several months later. Then came time for ordination into the priesthood. And Stan took everything in stride knowing that it was time to set his life's course.

* * * *

Graduation at Holy Cross in June is always a premier event. New England hierarchy, family and friends all attend the outdoor ceremony. This year, it begins with the school chorus marching out toward the reviewing stand singing a triumphant hymn reminiscent of the "Battle Hymn of the Republic."

Following behind, the faculty wearing black robes with purple facings, head to the front seating area. The chorus now sings church hymns as the graduates march out, all eighteen of them. They stand facing the faculty and guests while the Dean arrives with an aide to hand out degrees. Graduates also bow slightly to receive a chain with school cross.

Right Reverend William Pharris, the Dean, congratulates the graduates and welcomes guests to the annual ceremony.

"Ladies and gentlemen, we offer you," he squints facing the afternoon sun, "another handful of inspired stewards to continue our spiritual legacy in a changing world. Remember, Jesus began His ministry with but a handful of followers who made all the difference! Let's give them a round of applause, they certainly deserve it!"

Among the graduates, the valedictorian, Philip Stevens, stands and approaches the podium. He's the precocious and ever popular son of Theodore Stevens, vice-president of Staples. Philip delivers a passionate speech about morality and justice culminating in a challenge to his colleagues to face not only a changing society, but an evolving culture desperately seeking to define itself.

Following a robust round of applause, the Dean invites everyone to the hall for a reception. All enjoy punch and hors d'oeuvres and surround the graduates with talk of ordination and community assignments. Parents, Stacey and family circle around Stan with pats on the back, hugs and kisses. Stan's parents interface with the future in-laws and begin talking about the up-coming wedding. Stan spots Philip nearby.

"Hey, Phil," he shouts. "Nice job!"

"Thanks, Stan. So, what are your plans?"

"I'm getting married in September...to a girl I met several years ago. How about you? Are you staying in New England?"

"Yes I am. My father is with Staples. I was introduced to the daughter of one of the board members last month. She's wonderful! Dad is talking to Bishop Anthony about a position at the Cathedral, right here in Boston. How about you?"

"Well, my girlfriend's dad owns Shoreline Dairy, and he also knows the bishop well!—but don't worry, Phil, I think I'm going back to the mid-west, closer to home. Bishop Mark is eager to discuss a parish for me when I get back."

"Good for you! Good luck then," Phil adds warmly.

"The same to you, Phil. Let's keep in touch."

"You got it!"

It sounded good to say it, but deep down, Stan knows they would not communicate or cross paths unless by accident or at a clergy-laity conference. Phil's family is a lifetime member of the Eastern blue-blood establishment where career paths and opportunities rarely intersect with average people, especially from the Midwest.

* * * *

September arrived quickly and the Rybaks find themselves at the Marriott Boston lobby, checking in for a memorable weekend. Since the church is only several miles away, Michael advised against renting a car because of parking issues; he said that cabs are always around the hotel, especially in the morning.

While at the lobby, they decide to check out the Grand Ballroom where the reception is to take place. They walk in while the hall is being prepared and are impressed with the modern art-deco spacious room with soft grey and blue patterns that adorn the ceiling and carpeting. Judging from the guest list Michael gave them, it looks like this reception may test the limits of 1500 guests.

"Edie, look at the size of this hall! They must have invited half of Boston. Do you know what this evening's festivities cost with the hotel, music, food & bar, flowers, photographer, etc.?"

"I don't know, dear. Stacey is...his only child!"

"Over $80,000, just for a few hours! You believe that?"

"How do you know?"

"He told me." She turns, gives him a stern look. "Oh, I never asked him," he quickly adds. "Why would he tell me?"

"He's just bragging, dear."

The next morning, Bill turns on the TV. "Good morning, everyone," says the announcer, "on this cloudy Saturday morning. There is a 30% chance of rain..."

Bill lowers the volume and looks out the window on Huntington Avenue to see dry conditions, but no sun.

"What time is it?" Edith mumbles.

"Just after nine. We should go downstairs for breakfast and then get ready for church. Wedding ceremony starts at one o'clock. It's finally happening, Edie! Our son is getting married! He'll be on his own now."

"Bill, he's been on his own since high school!"

Just as Michael told him, cabs are lined up in front of the hotel, the ride to church, barely 15 minutes away. Before they realized, the imposing cathedral stands before them. A blend of neo-classical and basilica architecture, Annunciation Cathedral dominates the area with its center dome reaching for the heavens.

Guests begin to file into the sanctuary and take their seats under the spacious air space. Some, not familiar with the faith, survey the iconography and stain glass arched windows and point to the Jesus icon in the dome; much like tourists inspired by the Michelangelo fresco of the Last Judgment at the Sistine Chapel.

"This is beautiful," Edie whispers, "isn't it, Bill? Look at the gold leaf art around the windows. I hope Stan gets a church like this, don't you?"

"You may need a few years of experience before you're assigned to a cathedral like this. I think Stan will probably start with a small parish first—unless, of course you exercise some pull or influence."

"Well, Michael has strong connections with this diocese, doesn't he?"

"You're right, Edie, he does. We'll see what happens."

The Rybaks know a typical wedding ceremony normally takes about an hour, but this one is special. The presence of the hierarchy and additional priests co-celebrating, the extra chants, hymns and congratulatory speeches, draw it out to almost two hours.

Later in the evening, a gala reception is on the way. Stan feels a little uncomfortable with the opulence of the celebration. He will soon become a priest, preaching the simple, moral life of the sandal-footed Galilean. But his concern over the glaring hedonism of the evening is mitigated for now.

After all, he muses, *we didn't plan any of this. Besides, it's my wedding!*

Even Stacey thinks it's a bit overdone, with the cascading champagne pyramids and two $1,000 five-tiered glazed wedding cakes. But the Russos are basking in it like children in a candy store.

A waiter arrives to take drink orders at the dais. He comes before Archbishop Philip and asks what drink he would like.

"What Scotch do you have?" he asks confidentially.

"Your Eminence, we have Johnnie Walker, Founders Reserve, Woodford Reserve and Buchanan."

"How about Glenlivet 18 or 25?"

"I will have to check to be sure. How would you like it?"

The archbishop leans toward the waiter.

"A double, straight up—in a coffee cup!"

He sits back, glances at Bishop Anthony next to him and smiles.

"I love your amulet," he confesses—"and the chain, very stylish! Where did you get it?"

"Your Eminence, it's the work of a gemologist monk, Gabriel, from Lazarus of Bethany monastery near Nazareth. You don't know him?"

"I know of him. E-mail me his contact information."

"Of course, Your Eminence."

A few minutes later, the waiter returns with a tray of drinks to distribute on the dais. When he faces the archbishop, he lays a cup and saucer with spoon in front of him.

"What did you find out," the hierarch inquires.

"It's a '25' Your Eminence."

The archbishop smiles and nods his approval.

The portable food warmers are rolled out near the dais and among the 150 tables throughout the hall. Large elegant gold-bordered plates are placed before guests with white gloves at great efficiency and speed. The clinking of china and conversations raise the noise level where one has to almost shout to be heard. And to add to the din, members of the band appear on the stage and start tuning up for dinner and dance music.

As Bishop Anthony leans over to the Archbishop, he gets a whiff of the aged scotch.

"I've been talking with Stan's father-in-law, Michael Russos. He's in the dairy business. He's sitting at the end with his wife, Anne, on your left."

"Yes I know them. I met Michael in New York when he made a donation to the orphanage last year."

"Anyway, he was asking what I can do for Stan."

"When is he getting ordained?"

"He's scheduling it sometime in October, but I don't know where. He hasn't talked to me yet. By the way, Your Eminence, that is some vintage coffee!" They both enjoy a hearty laugh.

Defining Moment of 2011

For Stan, Sunday, October 20, came faster than graduation and the wedding, completing the triad of whirlwind events for the year. A week earlier, in a private ceremony, he was ordained into the diaconate level by Bishop Mark, the first level of the priesthood.

But today is the culminating moment where his spiritual readiness is laid bare as he faces the altar of Holy Trinity Cathedral in Rockford. He stands in a white baptismal robe and begins his petitions for the blessing of God and Church. He endures over 90 minutes of ritual and ceremony while the service is in progress; and is periodically vested with clerical garments one at a time as the service progresses until he's fully vested.

Finally, Bishop Mark lays his hands on Stan's head, turns toward the faithful and proclaims: "AXIOS!" (Worthy). The congregation returns the proclamation: AXIOS! This is repeated three times and marks the end of the service. Stan is now a priest and takes his place among the clergy; and he shall be addressed as Father Stan from now on.

Later at the reception, Father Stan fulfills his first priestly duty, a prayer of Grace. Following a short petition, Stan is still standing, remaining silent for a minute.

"That was a well-thought-out prayer, Stan," Stacey said. "Where did you find it?"

He gives her a saintly look and points to his heart.

"Why did you stay standing and silent after the prayer?" she asked quizzically. "Was there more you wanted to say?"

"No, honey. I've always had a problem with priests saying Grace. The moment they get to the 'Amen' everyone sits and starts eating."

"And...your point is...?"

"Well, look at all the things we're asking God to give us in the prayer! And we assume they're all automatically bestowed. I just like to give God a few seconds to assess our petitions and make sure we're worthy to receive His blessings. It's like an employee asking his boss to take the afternoon off and leaving without hearing the response. What's the point of asking for something if you don't wait for the reply?"

At first, this explanation confused Stacey; she looked at him to see if he was joking. But thinking through it several times, it made sense to her. She realized then that Stan was an unusual person with special gifts that one day will make a difference on how those he touches choose to live.

Chapter 16

MORAL HAZARDS AHEAD

Following a busy and eventful holiday season, Stan enters his office, takes off his parka and hangs it on a rack near the window. He looks out at the snow-covered churchyard where a handful of monuments have collected about four inches of snow overnight. Then he replaces the wall calendar with the 2020 one that arrived from the archdiocese. Flipping open his laptop, he signs on to emails and opens one from Tony.

> *Hello, Father, happy New Year! Just want you to know, had long talk with Gus—glad I went to him first. Explained my actions about the account, told him not to worry, nothing's changed. All the money is there—All is well. Thanks so much for your help. When is next game with the Loons? —Tony.*

He smiles and notices a message from Saul's Resort—kind of unusual. The resort usually sends out a newsletter during winter. It's a questionnaire to find out if guests are interested in winter activities so they stay open year-round. Included would be snowmobiling, cross-country skiing, ice skating and ice fishing.

Stan imagines sitting in a shanty on Long Lake near the buoy cutting a hole through the 2-foot thick ice with a power auger and dropping a line into familiar waters. He's also wondering how the loons are doing in sunny gulf coast Florida where they spend the winter. As he's savoring the vicarious experience, the phone plays the hymn to bring him back.

"Hello, Father Stan? This is Greg Elliot. Remember, we met at the bishop's office?"

"Oh, yes! You're with the Bishop's Council. How have you been?"

"I'm well, thanks. Listen! Bishop Mark suggested I contact you. We live in Sycamore, you know and right now I'm driving my daughter to school. Do you have time to see me this morning?"

"Yes, that's right! You're a neighbor! Greg, I don't have any appointments today, so come on over and we'll catch up."

"Great! See you in an hour. Don't go to any trouble. I'm bringing coffee and croissants."

"Okay. I'll be here. Use the side door. It leads into the office."

Stan searches in his desk drawer for Greg's card. It's an engraved corporate card with the company name *Lab-Rinth Pharmaceuticals* and his name in the corner as Head Pharmacologist. The card has a Hartford, Connecticut address.

Suddenly, George Nicholas comes into the office holding a duffle bag.

"Is there anything else you need, Father? I'll be going back to the seminary now."

"Thanks for all your help this month, George. We could not have done it all without you. I will be sending a letter to the bishop about your service while in town. How are you going back to campus?"

"I'm catching the Am-track tomorrow night. It's an overnight ride, cheaper."

"Don't forget to go by the diocese and say goodbye to the bishop."

"Yes, tomorrow morning."

"You have anything to take to him?"

"No, not really...I didn't have a chance..."

"That's fine, don't worry. See that holiday box of candy on the table? Take it to him. Just add a tag with your name on it. George, listen, this is important! Stopping for a few minutes to see the bishop when you're in town and taking a gift, shows respect and decorum—and he likes that. Trust me, you'll earn a lot of points that way. You do that a few times and he'll remember you when you need him. Have a good trip."

"Thanks, Father."

At the same time George is leaving, Greg brushes passed him holding a box and a bag. He lays the box on the table and takes out two coffees from the bag. They greet each other warmly and Stan takes his coat to the rack. They take their coffee and move to a more comfortable table near the window. Stan opens the box and takes out a croissant.

"Thank you, this is so light and tasty!"

"My pleasure, Father," he says biting into one himself. "Say, Father, how long have you been out of school?"

"Has to be over eight years now. My first assignment was up in Duluth. I served Holy Apostles Church for three years, almost on the banks of Lake Superior. It was a small parish, but it was great being near water. I got used to the rural landscape, mainly a Germanic territory with rugged, but simple, kind-hearted people."

Greg wears a serious demeanor, lowering his large frame unto a chair. "Even though the bishop encouraged me to share an on-going issue with you, today I'm here on my own."

"It sounds serious."

"It is," Greg adds. "We have an alarming problem which has led to a crisis condition in our church. We had a meeting with the archbishop and members of the Archdiocesan Council in New York last week."

"So, what's the crisis? What's going on?" Stan takes a nervous sip of coffee.

"You remember, about two years ago Congress introduced a bill on the floor to tax houses of worship. Well, we, of course, opposed this action with other churches. Christian tradition is clear about the separation of Church and State. Lot of good that does! But, I have a feeling it isn't over yet."

"...So, you think Congress will pass this bill and more important, is the IRS going to enforce this new law if it passes?"

"Father, we had no idea this action was passed in Congress. When we were first notified about it, Congressman Newell assured us that it already passed by a wide majority in both Houses. Well, it turns out that the President vetoed it and sent it back with a letter questioning the constitutionality and the abrogation of a long-held practice of separation between Church and State. And mainstream media didn't even cover this. They want to pass this quickly and keep it under the radar."

Stan reaches for his second croissant as he weighs in on this initiative from a government looking for more money. "I can see where the Church can lose a big portion of its revenue. Do you think Congress will amend the bill or override the President, Greg?"

Greg stands and carries his towering frame over to the window as he drinks from his large cup. He's trying to be delicate about this, but he can't stonewall and play with words any more.

"Yes, Father, Congress can override the veto and pass the bill into law. Or it can amend the bill to clarify a percentage of all revenue. When I called Newell's office, they were considering 2% of gross income. You see where I'm going with this?"

"You don't think they're going to do it, do you?" Stan asks with alarm.

"Yes, I think they eventually will. In a couple weeks, 60 Minutes is doing a feature on this bill and the news will finally get out. A spokesman for the church is planning a nationwide boycott of Congress. Media knows they can't keep this quiet and is actively calling for the church to give up its tax-exempt status! This can snowball into a system-wide taxation policy affecting not only us but all exempt houses of worship. Welcome to the New World Order, Father."

They sit silently, both in deep thought about the connecting outcome of civil law and how it can challenge the long-held practice of tax-exemption. Centuries old churches normally take hundreds of years to enact even the most subtle changes. And they're not about to submit to taxation because Congress says it's now okay to tax churches.

The pieces are falling in place for Stan now. He realizes that taxation under the law and management of non-taxable 501 (3) (C) institutions are two classifications headed toward a collision course. And the primary casualty will be the church. He now recalls the troubling comment Greg dropped on him at Christmas.

"More damaging will be once Washington taxes income, states will most surely decide to tax church properties," Greg continues. "Since most states are financially under water, they have been looking feverishly for other revenue sources as they simply cannot raise property taxes anymore now. But in the meantime, Congress continues to spend like drunken sailors!"

"I see the problem." Stan admits sheepishly, shaking his head. "It's enormous! What's the next step?"

"We have a conference call at the end of the month in Chicago. It will include, the hierarchy, both councils and our legal team. I want you in on this. It's crucial we adopt some form of action that protects the church, probably invoking Church-State separation statutes.

"Father, I know the Vatican has been discussing the impact this ruling may have on Catholics. I'm sure their legal department is looking for some loopholes as well as the constitution to protect the church, even if they have to establish a new classification of exemption. In any case, they will not stand for the tax. With all the properties they have— it would bankrupt the church. They even look upon it as sinful.

"Father, we are looking at a perfect storm here. Early American values have established the church as a social charity necessary for the spiritual health of its citizens...in harmony with the vision of the founding fathers. Meantime, our culture has evolved to diminish the importance of church and consider it as nothing more than another thriving business. This legitimizes the invasion of the tax man storming into the hallowed houses of worship, an incursion once considered unthinkable.

"Having succeeded in enlisting the support of the culture at large, now we shall hear loud banging on the church door from the tax collector. In other words, the long standing status of the church to safeguard the moral principles of human behavior are challenged by emerging social norms demanding harmony with the *New Normal*. So, we have the tail wagging the dog, so to speak. What ever happened to right and wrong?"

"Well, Greg, cultures don't usually move in harmony with established models of religious institutions. You have to understand, society does continue to change, oftentimes in a direction we don't approve. So, you must admit, somewhere down the road, a clash is certain to occur."

"This scourge is in the beginning phase," adds Greg. As conditions continue to change, it's clear the time has long last arrived where the tax man will finally be included in church board room meetings across the country."

"Church independence was carved in stone in the early days of the Republic when the church was looked upon as the spiritual support of the citizenry. Look, Greg, it's easy to cling to tradition and proclaim steadfastness to it. When it is threatened, the difficult thing to do would be to defend the legacy and resist not so much by prayer, but in practical ways that bring results.

"These realities have been shaping for a long time and we know we can't turn the clock back. It really comes down to this: do we want to be obedient and submit to an unlawful law and eventually risk extinction as a church, or should we struggle to find a way to preserve the church?"

"Extinction, Father? Isn't that extreme?"

"Greg, it's not about losing just tax exempt status! Society at large is systematically moving to render the church unnecessary and force it to share society's tax burden. Moreover, the American public feels the church operates as a business and shows little interest in the plight of the people. In short, they have become sympathetic to the proposition that it's finally time for churches to pay up!"

Chapter 17

PASSAGE TO NAZARETH

S tan looks forward to meeting with Famir and eager to find out
what's on his mind. He parks in the lot reserved for patrons of TJ's
Tavern and Grill and walks into the pub toward Famir who's waving
him over. Stan wears a holiday sweater under his parka while his friend
is more formally dressed with a jacket over an open collar and sporting
a manicured full beard. They shake hands and embrace.

"Happy New Year, Father!"

"The same to you, Famir."

They shift some chairs and sit around a high round table.

"Very quaint place," Famir says.

"Yes, it's small but they have great burgers. I don't know why it's
called a tavern."

"Maybe because they make more money on beer and spirits
than food!"

"You know, I think you're right. Thanks for coming out to Sycamore.
So, how was your Christmas?"

"Oh, it was wonderful. I met some new neighbors once I decorated
the house with lights and hung a big star on the front door for the first
time. Funny, I've lived in Elgin for three years and no one would wave
or greet me. I think they were frightened when they noticed a strange
name on my mail box and thought I was a Muslim. Once they saw
Christmas lights, everything changed. Father, the irony is I am an Arab!
But, not all Arabs are Muslims."

"That's right! Most people don't understand that. Well, you were born in Nazareth which is in modern Israel."

"Born and raised with the best formative education in the biggest Arab city in Israel! And that's what I want to talk to you about. I left almost six years ago, as you know, but I still communicate with my family and my wife's family. Father, Nazareth is home to St. Gabriel, the Orthodox counterpart of the Basilica of the Annunciation. It was built on the site where Angel Gabriel brought the good news to Mary over 2,000 years ago.

"When I left, there were a dozen churches in town. Now four are active while several are in disrepair. When condemned, these properties become ward of the municipal government. That's how church properties are lost throughout the years. Well, I'm told things are changing over there and incidents are more common."

"How do you mean?"

A waiter arrives to take their drink and food order. They place their order including a couple steins of draft.

"Look, Father, Nazareth has about 80,000 people and 75% are Muslim, 25% Christian. And the Christians are diminishing rapidly."

"Yes, I know, there's been a steady decline in the whole Middle East for the last hundred years..."

"That's my point, Father. Christianity is slowly being erased from the whole area. And Nazareth is the birthplace of Christianity. My replacement, as director of the Arab/Christian Cultural Center, disappeared last year. One day he didn't come home. He just vanished! No one knows what happened to him."

"What do you want to do, Famir?"

"My apologies, Father, I ramble...I need to go back and see for myself what is happening. My wife and two children and her family are there. I used to text freely and keep in touch, but in recent weeks, connection has been limited to certain hours. But I can't return on my own..."

"Famir, what can I do to help?" Stan can see Famir is very upset and he's trying to be helpful.

"I need a passport with diplomatic immunity to insure my safety. My visit will be far less than three months, so a visa won't be necessary. Father, I have a PhD. from Oxford and have taught in several universities, here and abroad. I can qualify for most any peace mission under the auspices of the U.S. or U.N., but I need the paperwork to support and protect me...I thought maybe you can talk to the bishop. He may know someone in the state department to help."

"Famir! You left that region years ago by the skin of your teeth. And your picture may be on every light post in the city, with a bounty. What makes you think that some document can protect you? You can't be sure if there's anyone left in government that you even know who would protect you. Do you have any friends there besides family? I mean in government. I don't think there's much security for you if you depend entirely on the reputation you left among Christians. You realize, everything may have changed."

Famir was hoping to hear more positive news from his trusted friend. He had convinced himself that a path would exist through the church or other philanthropic organizations to get him there with some immunity from growing local social cleansing.

Two big baskets of burgers arrive crowded with large crispy fries and pickle. They clink their steins to a New Year's toast. Stan orders another round of beers.

"I'm not familiar with these international protocols," Stan asserts between bites, "but I will find out what I can. I know the bishop plans a trip to the Holy Land next Easter. Surely he would know the mechanics of travel in that region. I will be talking with him at the end of this month about other issues and I will definitely get some answers for you."

"I sure appreciate it, Father. I trust you will do what you can. Thank you."

"For sure! Give me a couple weeks, I hope to have something for you. By the way, I don't know if you noticed, but Christianity is on the defensive here, as well."

"I know, Father, there are global forces that are taking advantage of Divine silence and are building a tower to worship a secular godhead, one that people can see, feel and relate to."

The waitress passes by and asks if they want anything else. Both waive the dessert and she places the check on the table near Stan slightly touching his hand. Famir reaches over and grabs the check. Stan smiles at the waitress, at the same time troubled by Famir's last comment.

"Don't be silly, it's my treat. Thank you for seeing me and taking interest in my problem. Let me know when you have something."

"Okay, I'll be talking to you soon."

Chapter 18

COURT RULING AT MADISON
Gustafson v. Continental Petroleum Co.

Regarding case #29906 (Gustafson v. Continental Petroleum Co.), Judge Clayton Lewis of the U. S. District Court of the Western District of Wisconsin, has reviewed evidence to determine if the case meets the requirements of a "Class Action" case. To date, 319 Wisconsin residents represented by plaintiff have filed complaints for injuries and/or deaths from environmental incidents along the Rockstone Pipeline route through the state.

In consideration of the evidence presented and in view of the number of people affected, Judge Lewis ruled that the case qualifies as a "Class Action" case. Attorneys were advised to prepare for discovery including documents and sworn testimony and/or depositions admitted as evidence and other compelling investigatory revelations.

So far, two offers to settle from the defendant have been rejected and attorneys for the plaintiff are preparing to go to trial before a jury. The judge announced a trial date of April 23 with jury selection beginning on April 10. Attorneys for the defense were advised that offers to settle can be filed at any time, subject to acceptance by the plaintiff and by the court.

"This is the updated information I'm recording from the court hearing on February 6, 2020. We will explain what happened in a special meeting of the board of Continental Petroleum at corporate headquarters in Milwaukee on February 10th." (Jim Winters)

* * * *

Jim plays it over several times with his team to make sure he covered everything that went on in the courtroom. He looks at Bob Haeger, a younger lawyer brought in to replace Jordan who couldn't take the heat and left the firm last month.

"Bob, you've been quiet, what do you think?" Jim asks.

"Things do look bad, Jim, but not totally lost. I'm trying to think through an idea. Give me a minute to check something out."

Bob sits in a nearby couch and starts tapping on his phone.

Inside the board room, J. R. Morrison is addressing the board prior to convening the official meeting with the legal team. Jim Winters watches Morrison through the glass waving his hands with authority as his voice carries loud and clear through the soundproof windows. Carol Stempke and two other girls in the reception area cast a troubling glance toward the board room and then at the four lawyers whispering among themselves.

"Jim, how do we position ourselves in there?" asks Pat Mackey.

"We just tell them the truth, that the plaintiff represents so many victims, the judge ruled the case a 'Class Action.' We made a motion to strike, but it was denied. There was nothing more we could do about it. At that point asking for a dismissal of the case on the grounds that others shared in the contamination would have been a moot point."

"The judge also denied a motion of 'Shared Liability' with the paper mills," asserts Roger.

"That's right guys, we were thrown in a corner with no place to go," says Jim.

"Any act that threatens the environment and human life with eco-logical damage in this state, you're pretty much guilty until you prove innocence beyond a doubt. And juries have little or no sympathy for the defense because it represents a large, greedy corporation interested only in profits. Roger, you go first and explain all the affidavits supporting the complaint and list the injuries and casualties.

"Pat, you pick up on shared liability case we tried to make since there is strong evidence that the paper mills are also complicit. Also, point out that the industry is a major source of tax revenue for the state. And they're not going to bite the hand that feeds them. So, we're the target for all of Wisconsin's eco-problems. I'll handle the questions that will follow and give them our plan of attack in the courtroom. We still have a job to do. But, between us, unless some miracle comes our way, I don't see a way out of this.

"And to make matters worse, attorneys for the plaintiff have filed an injunction against any attempt to shield the company from liability in case it decides to file for bankruptcy."

"Do we include that part?" asks Roger.

"You bet!" Jim continues, getting more upset. "Let it all hang out and let them worry about the next step. We're doing our job, but the deck is stacked against us. Continental should have been more careful and spent more on detection systems to isolate leaks and ruptures and repair them before causing damage. Also, two attempts to settle only aggravated the plaintiffs as the amounts offered were laughable."

Bob jumps up and waddles over to the others. Although his facial features are well-proportioned and trim, he's a bit round around the middle and sports a strange gait.

"Hey, Jim, I don't care what you want to say in here, but I'm thinking about the bigger picture: the trial we have to face. I believe we can pursue an argument in court that may be our only defense, an argument that's solid and difficult to deny."

"What are you talking about?" asks Jim, already anxious about the whole thing.

"I'm talking about exonerating the company of all wrong-doing. I did some preliminary research since Monday and I found a path to clearing us. There's a lot of work to be done before trial. We've been looking in the right place but we didn't go far enough to round up all the horses. We need to interview a lot of people, get depositions and we must have key people testify. And we only have a couple months to pull this off!"

"What the hell are you..." Roger interrupts and is instantly cut off.

"Look everyone!" Bob now in a loud whisper, "let's go in there and do what you said. Give them a Bad News/Good News scenario. Make them sweat first, but in the end, tell them the team is working on an iron-clad defense, a way to emerge unscathed. Trust me, when I get some more data together, Then I'll explain it all to you. We need to work like hell to get it done. Let me call the next meeting. People, our victory lies in the courtroom, not in the boardroom. And I need to know I have your support."

"You got it, Bob" Jim says with confidence as the others nod in agreement. "We have no idea what you're talking about, but we're excited by your positive attitude. I for one haven't felt anything positive around here for weeks."

Morrison now waves Carol and the legal team in. Carol grabs her tablet and approaches the group.

"Well, it's time! Let's go in and join the party," she says with hesitation. This is one meeting I don't care to record. I think everybody needs a stiff drink. Good luck in there, guys!"

Chapter 19

"RENDER UNTO CAESAR..."

On Friday, January 31, Stan parks in front of Greg's house and honks the horn. He is about to walk to the house, but the front door opens and Greg rushes out with binder under his arm. A gust of wind opens Stan's trench coat to reveal a clerical suit with collar as he slips inside the car.

"Hi, Greg, sure is cold this morning!"

"Good morning, Father," he shouts. "I didn't recognize you in that outfit!"

"Come on, you know I wear my black suit and collar when I have to."

"When is the last time you took that suit to the cleaners?"

"I can't remember," Stan says laughing. "You said on the phone that your company has an office downtown Chicago where the meeting and conference call will take place. I thought your office is in Hartford."

"Hartford is the corporate headquarters. We have six other offices around the country. Anyway, it's a great place for the meeting with a long table and a conference phone. On hand physically, will be Bishop Mark, the other council members—I think three of them are able to make it, you and I. On the conference call will be four members of the archdiocesan council, two attorneys from Washington and Archbishop Philip."

"I was thinking about this whole thing last night, Greg. You, know, this is a real government overreach into the affairs of the church. Historically, government kept out of church business even if complaints of wrong-doing reached the state attorney's office. The only time they got involved was when public monies were miss-handled. Beyond that, government stayed clear of church issues.

"But this...this is definitely government crossing over the constitutional Church-State separation."

"You're right, Father, bring it up in the meeting. I'm sure the lawyers will have something to say about that. There is a difference between secular taxation and a tax exempt church which renders a public service. The two have been separate for 250 years. There hasn't been a problem because during all these years, governments levied taxes on business, individual labor and equities.

"Plenty of revenue is generated to take care of the country's programs. The church was left alone and the two entities had respect and stayed out of each other's way. But fiscal irresponsibility and unimaginable government debt have brought the tax man to the church looking for money. Fact is, the system of taxation is still issued by Caesar; and matters of the soul are issued by God."

The almost 2-hour drive into downtown Chicago allowed for some silent moments for both to do a lot of thinking. Stan turns on the radio to catch the morning news. Following the weather report, a news bulletin crashes into their consciousness to temporarily get their mind off the church.

...and this just in: reports have come in regarding the virus that originated in Wuhan, China, last month. There is evidence the virus has spread to Japan, South Korea and Thailand according to the World Health Organization. The U.S. has suspended entry of flights from China. Meantime Chinese authorities have cancelled all transportation in the affected area. More details will follow on the six o'clock news...

Neither of them express much concern over the news, as they are deep into the crisis at hand, and besides, they feel this is a problem on the other side of the earth and doesn't affect them. Greg shows him the way down a ramp leading into a garage on Wacker Drive. They get out and take the elevator to the 18th floor. Greg checks his watch: 10:30.

"They should all be here," he says. "The bishop arrived last night and stayed at the Windham. I'm staying in the city tonight. I forgot to ask you, can you take the bishop back to the diocese when you leave?"

"Yes, of course," Stan pipes in. "I'll talk to him after the meeting."

The doors open and they walk passed the embossed sign on the wall: *Lab-Rinth Pharmaceuticals Inc.* toward the conference room. Greg walks ahead to connect with council members. He bows before the bishop and greets two other gentlemen and they begin walking slowly into the room. Stan hangs back to read an explanation of the company name on a plaque.

Lab: A medical research facility where miracles are created
Rinth: An uncharted mythical island in Norse folklore some-where in the North Sea, where, once found, offers healing and life-long immunity from physical and moral infections

Stan enters the conference room and a man in a suit with a dioc-esan pin on his lapel closes the door behind him. Stan's still intrigued by the phrase "Moral Infection."

"Hello everyone and thank you for coming this morning," Greg gets everyone's attention. "We've all been briefed about the new TAX burden facing the church. Today we will clarify the developments and discuss options we can exercise to mitigate the risks we face. In Chicago, besides Bishop Mark, we have two council members, Father Stan and myself; and on the call will be the Archbishop with three council mem-bers from New York and two lawyers representing the church from Washington.

"Your Eminence, are you there?"

"Yes, Greg, and thank you for getting this meeting together."

"Is everyone else connected?"

"Yes, Sam and Peter here from Washington."

"Yes, Perry, Chris and George in New York with his Eminence."

"Thank you all," Greg speaks into the conference phone. "I hope you all saw 60 Minutes a couple days ago and have a good idea of the impending demands upon our church as well as other houses of worship. Your Eminence we would like you to give us an overview response from the church about this unprecedented tax issue."

"Well, that program is social-based, driven by a determined effort to imperil our church order. As you know, we receive our mandate from Holy Tradition. The church has held steadfast to the unchanging truths of the Holy Gospel. Societies continue to evolve through time, but the eternal truths of good and evil, right and wrong prevail.

"Gentlemen, our own government is moving forward to impose a tax on the ministries of the church. Our best defense is found in scripture. In Luke 20:19 Jesus clearly defines government's role when he said: *Show me a denarius. Whose face and name does it have? Caesar's they replied. Then give back to Caesar the things that are Caesar's and to God the things that are God's.*

"Furthermore, In Luke 3:11 Jesus said to the tax collectors: *Collect no more than you are required.* However, as you also know, the federal government and states are strapped for money. Corruption and fraud aside, revenues will diminish more because of impending lockdowns. Now, the Church is fair game!

"I've read the arguments of those individuals who choose to interpret the law in a more relative manner to suit their agenda. They are spreading the notion that tax exemption for churches forces all Americans to support religion, even if they oppose their existence. They rationalize that a tax exemption is a form of subsidy and the constitution is against government support of religion.

"Simply put, our church looks upon the government tax as outrageous, even immoral. It's an invasion into the church coffers: outright stealing of the people's money that's already been taxed!"

The Android phone goes silent for a minute until some static introduces another speaker.

"Thank you Your Eminence, this is Bishop Mark. Gentlemen, it's a fact that there is no better way to destroy the church than to tax it! Even if the tax is the smallest percentage possible, the door is opened for increases down the road. Also, if any conditions are attached to our tax exempt status, it's the same as imposing a tax. When the genie is released from the bottle, you can never put him back. Also, an old Arabian proverb says: *Once the camel gets its nose inside the tent, his body will soon follow.*"

"Thank you, Your Grace, Sam and Peter, here. We want to call your attention to a subtle ambiguity in the law: the 1954 Johnson Amendment prohibits a pastor from talking from the pulpit about political elections or candidates. Depending on what the pastor says regarding political events, the tax code allows the government to tax a church.

"Clearly, there's no way to determine if the pastor crosses the line unless there happens to be an IRS agent in the congregation to record the homily. Any other testimony would be hearsay. The government will be forced to monitor church services and punish those whose pastor violates the law. In short, these vague tax codes represent a path to censorship of religion. Sadly, the free exercise of religion cannot survive under such conditions."

"Hello, everyone, Peter here. Sam is right. I think we are looking at is an attempt to re-fashion what used to be a sacred separation between government and the Church. It is understood that monies collected for charitable goals cannot be used for personal benefit to any individual. That's understandable, but how do you monitor these actions?

"Violations would have to be flagrant, like a pastor purchasing a Kandinsky painting or a pair of Christian Louboutin shoes for his wife. Even then it's difficult to investigate and prosecute."

Stan leans over the speaker. "This is Father Rybak. Thank you so much everyone for all this meaningful feedback. What I see happening here is an incursion into the inner workings of the church, a clear violation of the 1st Amendment that's been in force since the early days of the Republic. It begins once you start re-defining specific legislation to fit an evolving economic and social framework.

"In other words, you take advantage of opportunities to re-fashion by exploiting other possible options, which create a very slippery slope. Gentlemen, once we submit to rationalization, we discover options and wiggle room that did not exist before. For example, the revelation that church funds may not have been spent in the interests of the parish. That's when objective principles laid down by the founding fathers lose their relevance and taxing bodies now smell a new scent of money from a historically forbidden venue.

"Please pay attention to what's happening here. I see this tax issue, however benign it may seem now, as a prelude to a more sinister objective. It's a head-fake to take our eye off the ball while governments, federal and local, dig their hand into the church coffers. These people are not only smart, they're cunning. The mission here is to render the church socially unnecessary and irrelevant since it stands in opposition to secular social models. And the best way to achieve this goal is through taxation."

"What do you mean, Father?" asks Bishop Mark.

"I think, the economic crisis is an excuse to bankrupt the church. Look at what's happening! As government gets bigger and people depend more on it, our elected officials in Washington prefer us to pay homage to government instead of God."

Greg now leans in. "Listen, Sam, in your opinion at this time, what is our best defense if this decision gains traction into our religious institutions?"

"For now, I think we should begin to look at the First Amendment:

Congress shall make no law respecting an establishment of religion or prohibiting the free exercise thereof...

"We view this as a constitutional matter. If governments obligate the church to pay taxes, to accommodate social and economic needs, then we can allege with great constitutional support that we are being denied "the free exercise" of our faith. In addition, the Religious Freedom Restoration Act (RFRA) imposes a higher standard of review for government actions that burden a person's religious exercise. We see this to be the basis of our position so far. It's a matter of civil encroachment into the sovereignty of a religious entity. We'll research this approach for now. We'll see what happens."

Following two hours of fruitful discussions, Greg thanks everyone and says he will send a copy of the minutes and a notice for a follow-up meeting in next 60 days. He approaches Stan.

"Father, thanks for taking the bishop with you. As I said, I'm staying in town overnight; people from the FDA are coming tomorrow. The government selected us to develop a vaccine. We're one of three companies involved. I may have to go to Washington and to our research facility in Rochester. I'll be in touch. Don't forget to have lunch. I had sandwich sacks catered."

"Sure, Greg, I'll take care of the bishop—great news about the vaccine! Good luck. I will take a couple sacks of food with us. I'd like to get going and get back before dark. Thanks again. Stay in touch."

Stan takes two bags of food and walks over to the bishop to tell him he will take him back to Rockton. He checks his watch: 2:30.

"Your Grace, I'll get the car from the garage. Give me ten minutes and then come out the front door. I'll be in a Subaru."

In a few minutes they're on the expressway heading northwest.

"Your Grace, are you worried about what's going on?"

"Not worried, yet, Father. But I'm concerned about what's happening in this country. Things are changing too fast. I'm afraid the saying 'In God We Trust' is only found engraved in the money, not in people's hearts."

"I agree. What I see in this new assault on the church is a more sinister agenda."

"What do you mean?"

"It's really not about government's need for more money. They can get all the money they need from the Fed. I think it's an orchestrated plan to remove religion from our lives and consider the church as an obscure cult. Your Grace, you are right, Government and corporations are on course to create a new social-based Godhead to replace faith and rule over the New World Order.

"If the church cannot pay the tax, the government then has the power to shut it down. This trend can not only weaken the importance of church in our lives, but it can actually destroy it."

"That's right, Father. Who knows, maybe one day while the IRS audits our books on a Sunday (as all the days of the week will have equal value), Holy Communion may be replaced by 'Happy Hour!' How about confession? If they have their way, social workers may be brought in instead! Father, now I am worried!"

They drive a few miles in silence and Stan decides to change the subject for now.

"Your Grace, if I can ask for your help on another matter..."

"Of course, what do you need?"

"A member of my church of Arab descent is worried about conditions in his homeland, Nazareth. His name is Famir and he's trying to find a way to go back with some immunity for his safety. He is worried about his wife and children, her family and his own family. He wants to know if you're aware of a way since you visit the area regularly. I told him I would ask you."

"Why is he worried about his safety? Nazareth has been relatively safe."

"Well, about six years ago he was Director of the Arab-Christian Cultural Center in Haifa. The city was growing more Islamic, 75% Muslims, 25% Christians. Incidents began to occur weekly as cleansing reared its head in the area. Anyway, he got word that he may get picked up by Palestinian extremists for questioning about his peace initiatives in Nazareth. He fled to Europe to finish his studies and then settled in the States."

"Well, I think, he's a marked man. I don't know what I can do for him. Do you trust him?"

"Your Grace, he's more Christian than many Christians. He's like a brother!"

"Let me make a few calls. I'm already arranging for my trip to Jerusalem in April, talking to the consulate and embassy. I'll let you know what I find out."

"Thanks for your help."

Chapter 20

DOING THE RIGHT THING

S now has been falling in Sycamore for several days keeping the plows busy on the main streets. Stan even has to fire up the little Toro to keep the lanes to the church clean between plow appearances. He enters the office and begins taking off boots, parka, hat and gloves. He freshens up in the bathroom and looks over Stacey's shoulder as she's typing a letter to the church membership.

"We should send these out before I return to school," she says.

"Thanks for your help during the holiday break," he responds while sitting down at the computer to work on his essay entitled: *Doing the Right Thing*.

"Stacey, I feel the need to write about the illusive nature of doing what's right. I really believe mostly everyone has instincts to be on the right side of ethical behavior, but things get in the way to distort and alter the desired action. In the process, they're convinced that their questionable actions are not only necessary but justified.

"Lately, I'm focused on the process that empowers the intellect to consider other paths, that marginalize the direct route to doing the right thing. Also, I fear we may have lost the ability to recognize the right course of action."

"Honey, people out there are pressured to behave in a way that leads to success. So, they're going to do what's necessary to achieve their goals."

"I know. But my pamphlet is going to show a simple path, a path we have lost."

Stan began putting down his thoughts on the subject during the holidays and found himself adding more and more material; and now it has turned into a 20-page paper. Ethical principles of human behavior and why we need them is the primary theme.

"I believe I'm offering a constructive approach to re-discover the simple path, the path from which we normally stray. I plan to print and distribute it in the community and have regular workshop sessions to reinforce.

"A part of me does feels this approach is too simplistic and juvenile, much like Sunday school for adults; and people may not buy into it; doing the right thing for whom? And yet, that's the problem! I'm convinced that the path to the truth should be simple and direct. Reasoning, rationalizing, over-intellectualizing merely invites fog to settle in to obscure the path."

Stan's phone vibrates. It's Famir.

"Hello Father, how is 2020 starting out for you?"

"Very well, actually. It's an exciting time where projects are planned and dreams are imagined. I'm glad you called. I was going to call you tonight. I did talk to the bishop about your situation..."

"Oh, really! That's wonderful. Did you find out anything that may be helpful?"

"Well, yes and no. But we need to talk about this privately. When can I see you?"

"I can come to your office this afternoon, say 2:30?"

"No not here. I'll meet you at TJ's Tavern at 2:30."

"Okay, see you there."

Stan pulls the copies out of the printer and folds them into a 24-page script. He looks at it and he's getting excited about connecting with people in a different way. He is convinced that people are inherently good; it's just that Right and Wrong have gotten a lot closer together, almost running into each other. He decides to call Tony about printing copies.

After waiting on hold a few minutes, Tony picks up.

"Hey Tony, this is Stan."

"Hi, Father, Happy New Year! Did you get my e-mail?"

"Yes, I did. Glad things worked out. Listen, I want to ask you about printing some pamphlets for me. Do you have a price list for booklets?"

"Hold on a minute, I'll get a catalog from sales. I don't want to palm you off to them. I can take care what you need. Father, I owe you big time!"

"Okay, what size is it?"

"It's letter size folded in half."

"Okay," Tony finds the listing. Minimum booklet size is 32 pages and we have to run 10,000 copies."

"Wow! I have only 24 pages. And what am I going to do with that many?"

"That's the best buy, Father. I can get these for you for about .10 each and then take 20% off for non-profit discount. You see, this project has to be printed on our web press because it has a binding module at the delivery. Father, once on press, 10,000 booklets can be printed, folded and stapled in under 3 hours. And, Father, you can take the rest of the year to pay. I'll stand behind it. Now it's time for me to challenge you!"

"What do you mean?"

"Is this booklet part of the ministry, and you want to distribute them to church membership and maybe to other churches?"

"Yes...that's a great idea."

"Well, if you expand the mailing list, 10,000 isn't that many is it? By the way, do you have any illustration in there?"

"No, it's just text copy."

"How about if I take it to the art department and get some illustrations to support copy and make it more interesting to read? Creating a self-cover and adding photography and illustration, you can increase it to 32 pages easily. Look, Father, come and see me when it's ready and our people will show you ways of getting it done."

Tony feels good about helping Stan with his project. It makes up for some things he neglected to mention about his problem with Gus. He recalls talking about it with Rita.

"You didn't mention the separate account to Fr. Stan, did you?" she asked.

"No, of course not! Just the separate company account. I couldn't admit to him about having yet another personal account. You remember, it has already generated over $6,000 under the name of Tony Cassata Associates at Wells Fargo Bank."

"How did he help you then?"

"He showed me a way out with Gus that made sense."

Tony kept separate records locked in his office. He told himself this was a temporary thing and that he would make it up to Gus with a new client he was working on for additional business.

"Thanks so much for your help, Tony," Stan interrupts Tony's brief daydream. "I'm sure I can come up with a few more pages. I'll see you soon."

"Great! And thank you, again."

Stan is grateful for the reciprocal advice. And he's right about dissemination. If the message is good enough to put into print for a few, then it should go out to as many people as possible, not just to a few in his church. "Does it merit mass distribution?" he asks himself. And this is the second question he places in the back burner for future consideration along with Thoreau's question about fishing: *Is it the fish we're really after?*

In any event, he feels a sense of excitement at the thought of creating awareness and enlightenment in people. He's not sure if it's vanity or genuine happiness at the thought of helping others. He adds to the text and reads it through again and again second-guessing himself on the value of his writing. He examines a sentence and feels a tornado of mixed-up words whirl around in his head as he's trying to balance a plethora of pressing issues.

Stan can visualize some illustration to enhance understanding. He also begins thinking about sending copies to the church's national publication *The American Observer*. He checks his watch and rushes to his car. A few minutes later, he's pulling up at TJ's. He walks in and sits at a table in the far corner of the restaurant. As he's a little early, he orders a couple beers and he spots Famir coming in.

"Just in time!" he announces. "I ordered us a beer."

"Hello, Father, thanks for seeing me again."

"You're welcome, Famir." He leans closer to him. "Listen, I told the bishop that you and I are close friends, like brothers and asked for whatever help I can access for you. The bishop checked with the embassy on your behalf. He said you can't get diplomatic immunity because you have no official diplomatic function.

"The bishop already has clearance and local authorities recognize him and know of his humanitarian programs that help all people, Christians, Jews, and Palestinians alike. So, here's the good news! He said you can join his group which leaves April 8 for Tel Aviv and returns April 22. It's a two-week stay."

"That is wonderful, Father. I don't know what to say..."

"But, listen, you have to do two things. First, you need to get a passport with a Christian name—and I know this is not right, In fact it's fraudulent and illegal. But the group's mission cannot be jeopardized. Also, have a clean-shaven face with short hair and wear glasses, but not sun glasses..."

A bar maid arrives.

"Another round, guys?"

Stan shakes his head and hands her a ten spot. He eyes her gait as she hustles away.

"This is to avoid any suspicion that anyone in the group has other motives for being there. In addition, you have to attend meetings and a workshop at the diocese on your assigned tasks while over there. And when you contact your people in Nazareth, do it on your own time without drawing attention to yourself. Do you agree to all this?"

"Oh, my God! Yes! This is great. I don't know how…"

"Look, Famir! The passport thing is your responsibility. We can't help you with that and how you do it is your business and it can't be traced back to the diocese or to me, understand? You have to do this before April.

"One final warning. If you are picked up while over there, the bishop will disavow any knowledge of your true identity. He said your presence is already placing the group at great risk."

"I understand perfectly. Thank you so much, Father."

"Okay, keep me posted on your progress. Call me and we'll get together before you leave. We'll review everything you're supposed to do and I will give you something to take with you."

"Okay. There is one more thing you can do for me."

"What's that?"

"My house in Elgin. Can you find a needy family to live there until I return? I'd like to stay at least two months. I paid utilities in advance as well as taxes. And if there is no danger for me there any more, I may stay longer. Also, if things do not go well and I can't come back right away…I just don't want the house to be empty. If we can help some family, I feel better about it."

"That's very thoughtful of you. I'll try to find someone."

Chapter 21

A Plague Upon the land

Well into February, the world's attention and resources shift to deal with an international pandemic that's spreading over the earth. An invisible enemy marches across the land with great prejudice toward all colors and faiths, all cultures and beliefs; it claims hundreds of thousands at the outset and sickens countless more. It soon becomes clear the virus afflicts the frail and old and those who scoff at its power with reckless abandon.

The death toll rises quickly and hospitals are stretched to the limit. Within just several months, people think and talk about nothing else. The unseen infectious foe separates people more and starves them of human warmth, as contact is stripped away. Leaders decree more distance around us as bond with friends and even family is torn away. The All Saints Loons had to shorten the basketball season, finishing with a 3-7 record.

Stan wonders if perhaps this is a lesson; that we cluster among our own too long ignoring strangers and others in need. So, further apart we're forced to drift in fear.

"Maybe this pestilence is penance for the gated life we live. It could be a lesson to separate us even more until such time we amend our ways and consider a stranger as our friend; until our heart for mankind swells; until we decide to do the right thing," he says softly. He bows his head as this new reality weighs on him heavily.

These thoughts take center stage as Stan adopts a wait and see position, hoping this scourge will go away as quickly as it arrived. In spite of travel ban and precautions taken, the United States announces its first death on February 29 while tens of thousands more are infected. By the middle of March it reaches across oceans to cover every country on earth.

On March 30th Bishop Mark sends out an encyclical to churches in his diocese calling for a 30% maximum attendance with face masks and appropriate distancing in compliance with national and local ordinances. *That's just great,* Stan fumes. *Easter services are around the corner and instead of the usual 200 faithful, I have to restrict it to around 60.*

He quickly asks Michelle, a temporary volunteer for Easter services, to prepare a letter to the church membership about the new regulation.

"Make sure you mention that they have to call the church office to reserve space before every service as we can only allow 60 people at a time. Board members will have to check off those coming in and monitor their distant seating—how do we turn people away who haven't reserved and refuse to comply?"

"I don't know, Father, I never experienced this before."

"Neither have I! You know, the bishop didn't specify the start date. Good Friday is in three days! How do we alert everybody that quickly?"

"We can't, Father. By the time this letter reaches them it will be after Palm Sunday. And that's a big attendance day!"

"It sure is. We do not have enough notice. Prepare the letter and make it effective after Easter, beginning April 19. Don't send it out during the services. I want people to focus on Easter, not on a lockdown. We'll mail it out on Good Friday so they have it the following week."

While Michelle starts on the letter, Stan opens an email from Greg:

Conference call meeting for April 16 cancelled. Will advise when re-scheduled. Pandemic crisis taking center stage. Church tax issue put on back burner. Except for Nazareth project in April, I will be in Rochester for most of the year working on vaccine.— Happy Easter. Stay safe.

Stan looks out his office window and watches Famir's car park by the side door. In minutes, a man walks into the office Stan does not recognize. Besides a face mask, he has a butch haircut and wears round glasses. Without saying a word, he takes off his coat, then his mask... then his glasses.

"Famir! I didn't recognize you."

"How do you like my disguise? Look, no beard, short hair and these fashionable glasses!"

"Perfect!"

Famir produces his passport to show a clean-faced man with the name of Miles Jackobi. Also, he takes out his driver's license to show the same photo and name in case he's asked for another I.D.

"They look pretty genuine to me."

"It wasn't easy to do this, Father..."

"I don't want to know about that. What will you be doing while abroad?"

"The bishop has me in charge of distribution of donated items at the *Pilgrim's Center of Care* in Nazareth. I know of the facility in the open market district. It's a medical center, but they also distribute food and other items to the needy. In demand this year are shoes, hats, sun glasses, T-shirts, water and of course, food."

"Well, Famir, it looks like all is working out fine. You get passage to the area and in return, you help out in distributing good will. It's a win, win. I'd like to ask you if you have room in your luggage to take some pamphlets to give away. I had these printed with the bishop's approval."

Stan hands him a package of 200 copies.

"This is not much. Give me another package. I'll make sure the people get copies with other items they're given. I see it's in English. What is this about, anyway?"

"Thanks, Famir. I appreciate it. It's about doing the right thing. Why don't you read it while traveling; it's not that long. Have a good trip and stay close to the group. Wear your mask, I hear the region is also infected with the virus."

"I know, I will be careful. You know Father, at the cultural center in Nazareth, there are educated people versed in many languages. Even though some residents understand English, it would be more beneficial if your message was translated in Hebrew and Arabic. I know people who can do this."

"Really? I never thought of doing that."

"Well, you can reach more people this way."

"Let me know what you find out and text me, okay?"

"Of course, I will. Thank you for everything. By the way, here are the keys to the house and the address. Happy Easter to you and Stacey. I will be in touch."

* * * *

Two days later, Father Stan appears in the altar to celebrate Saturday night Resurrection service to a standing room only congregation. Prayers are read and psalms are chanted as the service progresses toward midnight climax.

A Sycamore police car patrolling the area stops at curbside. Two officers notice a full parking lot and cars parked along the street for blocks. They also notice the size of the church. They get out and approach the church entrance. One of them opens the door and sees wall to wall people shoulder to shoulder. A trustee of the parish informs the officer that there is no seating available but he can stand by the wall.

"Sir, excuse the intrusion, but this group is illegally gathered. I don't see masks and people are sandwiched together. They should be six feet apart. Didn't you get a notice?"

"Yes, we did, but that was only two days ago. This is Holy Week! There was no time to alert the people. A letter is in the mail, but nobody got it yet."

"I'm sorry, sir, I have my orders. You must get word to stop the service and get the people out of here, like right now!"

The president of the parish walks to the front of the altar and stops the chanting. He then goes in the altar. Stan rushes to him.

"What's going on? Do we have a fire?"

"No, Father, police are disbursing the crowd because the virus is getting worse."

Commotion in the sanctuary builds as people start filing out thinking there's some kind of emergency. In minutes the church is empty leaving a trail of unlit candles on the pews and floor.

Chapter 22

TRIAL AND TRIBULATION

For the past three months Jim Winters, Bob Haeger, Pat Mackey and staff have been busy with interviews and depositions from plaintiffs in the class action suit. Some victims would not volunteer any information at first, but once they heard that it could be proven that Continental may not be the guilty party, but rather, two paper mills in the area, they became alarmed and more cooperative.

Bob was careful to convince them that if they proved Continental was not responsible for the damage done to land and people, much time would be saved. So, exonerating Continental would put the focus where it belongs: paper mills. And people would be on the way to receiving compensation from the companies that are truly responsible.

"Look, you know and many others know, that the real polluter here is the paper mills," Bob explained to a man wearing an oxygen mask. "Someone has to force them to become compliant to safety regulations. Time is wasted trying to make us the bad guy since we just came on the scene a couple years ago."

The jury selected last week was composed mainly of residents from Madison and Portage. None of them are in the vicinity of polluted areas or associated with those who are. Witnesses, one after the other testified about their illness and about the loss of loved ones in such a convincing and passionate manner as to win over the most indifferent jury.

Face masks were provided by the court for the elderly and those who felt vulnerable to infection and wanted extra protection. Several jury members wore them and a few elderly in the courtroom including a gentleman in a wheelchair.

The pandemic, although spreading widely, had not yet reached alarming levels in the States. Also, it seems the rules of engagement vary in different areas. Some states are stricter with masks and distance while others, not so much.

The fatal blow for the plaintiff's legal team occurred when on cross-examination, each witness was able to verify a timeline of illness that began long before Continental's pipeline was even installed. To be sure, many became terminally ill during the pipeline's service in Wisconsin, but the initial damage from methane gas had already claimed hundreds who underwent treatments long before the pipeline went into service.

The defense team questioned witnesses from the chemical industry all of whom revealed the perils of methane gas emitted from paper-making waste in the mills surrounding Lake Winnebago. In addition, several witnesses took the stand to verify that relatives had passed away from this affliction as far back as 30 years. Whatever complaints were filed at the time were subsequently dismissed for lack of evidence.

Following lengthy testimony from credible witnesses for eight days, the defense motioned that in view of mounting evidence produced, the case against Continental Petroleum be dismissed. And the judge agreed. The plaintiff's attorneys realized that the last several days laid out an iron-clad prosecution case against the real guilty parties that had escaped accountability for decades.

Although relieved by the favorable outcome, Jim still has lingering issues with his company's safety record. The courtroom victory did little to alleviate a growing personal condemnation associated with an immoral company. Evidence still shows that Continental did then and continues to have accidents and explosions. It did turn its back on spills and pipe breaches and did drag its feet on repairs and restitution.

Jim thinks of Stan's advice, still trying to make sense of it. Mixed feelings, mainly negative, continue to occupy his mind. Stan's advice to leave the company after he exonerates it, does not hold the company morally liable for what it did and for what it will continue to do.

Why did he suggest I try my best to defend the company? he thought. *Does doing the right thing have to yield to conditions and other options? Why didn't he urge me to resign and have no part in a company involved with fraud and cover-up?*

Jim feels this verdict will simply embolden the company to continue such practices and rely on the creative genius of his legal team to defend and justify wrong-doing, legally. He is troubled by two witnesses who recently became terminally ill from his company's reckless actions. He can't shake the painful image of their drawn faces on the witness stand after they took off their masks. Unfortunately, their complaint was lost in the pool of a collective case aimed in the wrong direction.

All smiles, Morrison walks over to congratulate his team.

"Jim, brilliant work! I have to admit I had my doubts, especially with those 300 plus people signed on the complaint." He squeezes Jim's shoulders shakes everyone's hand and invites them to his office Monday morning. Jim forces himself to congratulate Pat, Bob and Roger on a great job, especially Bob's research and legwork.

Pat goes to the plaintiff's legal table and shakes hands with their lead attorney.

"Good working with you," Pat says. "We hope you guys don't drop this case. You have evidence to present a great case and go after the real culprits. It would be a damn shame if all the people you represent are left out in the cold because the state's attorney is gun-shy to go after the paper mills. You know they're going to continue polluting the area with great impunity."

The attorney stares at Pat, walks away, then turns.

"So will you guys! Have a nice day, counselor," he says with sardonic grin.

Chapter 23

RESEARCH AT ROCHESTER

G reg Elliot swipes his card and enters a lab. He wears a long white coat with name badge hanging on a lapel. Following protocols, he is preparing a preliminary rationale for a vaccine based on how the infectious organism causes the disease. Since they were selected to develop a vaccine couple months ago, the company has focused its energies to expedite this program.

In addition, the government called for an accelerated vaccine development from early stages of disease definition, extensive research, through clinical trials to licensing. So, Greg tackles the first hurdle: research and discovery phase.

"Greg, we've done the initial lab tests on animals," says a research chemist holding data sheets, "and I believe we have found a practical application to develop a vaccine candidate."

"Excellent, Wayne. Continue with the research and testing in animals to determine its safety. We have to generate a report on detectable side effects in animals. You realize, to move forward to the pre-clinical stage, we have to first establish its safe application to humans."

"Yes, I understand, we have several approaches in the works until we reach a consensus for the best research direction."

"Very good, Wayne. Also, keep the manufacturing facility clean and operational in case the FDA does a spot visit."

"You got it! Enjoy your break."

Greg walks into his office down the hall. The last two months have been fraught with research obstacles with some dead-end outcomes.

The lab has been on a 2-shift schedule and finally, they are on the threshold of isolating a vaccine candidate. This will enable them to continue to complete the pre-clinical phase.

The FDA will then examine the data and research results as well as the manufacturing facility and hopefully, move the process forward to submitting an Investigational New Drug Application (IND). This will hopefully open the door to Phase I clinical trials by summer.

"When do you think we'll have a vaccine to market?" asks Wayne.

"I don't see it happening in less than two years—unless we get some federal money to add another shift. I know there will be pressure from Washington to get it out much earlier."

The researchers and technical people have their work ahead of them until the next series of data is available. This can take another six weeks minimum. Greg is looking forward to taking a break; and the Easter trip to the Holy Lands coming up shortly will be perfect and fit right in the schedule. He'll come back in May, if not earlier, to help move the project along to Phase I even before summer. But he can't understand why they're not using a drug they've already produced against this type of virus: Pneumochlorin. Data shows it's most effective, especially in severe cases. He's surprised no one has even mentioned it.

Greg sees his phone blinking and picks up.

"Greg, it's Maggie Preston. What do you want to see me about?"

"Got a minute now?"

"Sure, come on up."

Margaret Preston, Vice-President, Head of Vaccine Research, sounded serious. Greg hopes there's no problem with him taking time off right now. More important, he needs to know about the silence over Pneumochlorin. He takes the elevator up to the 8th floor and makes his way to a glass door with her name and title in gold letters. He goes in the carpeted area and faces a receptionist.

"Go right in, Mr. Elliot."

He enters her office while she's on the phone, facing a window. She gestures for him to take a seat on an adjacent leather couch. She stands tall in a navy pants suit with a red paisley scarf around her neck.

Greg enjoys coming up here. It must be the carpeting and high ceiling, giving an open-air effect, quite different from the tiled floors of a congested lab environment. She puts down the phone and comes to sit on a similar couch across from him.

"Sorry I couldn't see you last week. What's up?"

"Maggie, what's the deal with Pnemochlorin? It's our product! Why aren't we producing more of it to meet this crisis? It's already a proven..."

"Greg! That was Philip on the phone. He has been in close negotiations with the White House for a few weeks now. Well, we got the extra money: $2 Billion. That's why we can't talk about Pnemochlorin. In fact, marketing has already released data that it may not be effective against this type of strain."

"But, Maggie, we already know..."

"Greg, forget Pneumochlorin! We have to be on the same page here! We've been selected to develop a new vaccine and got a chunk of money to run with it. Here's the catch. We have to get final FDA approval and produce 100 million doses and distribute them by February of next year! What do you think?"

"Wow! That's like a year away including distribution!"

He walks over to the window, rubs his face and tries to calm the rumbling in his gut. He turns to her and stays on topic.

"All I can say is I'm glad we started on this two months ago as though we only had a year. And it turns out that's all we have. Yes, we can do this—we got the jump on it and are ahead in pre-trial prep."

"Are you still taking some time off?"

"Yeah, I scheduled about ten days in mid-April. I can cut it short if I have to. My team has to finish animal testing, side effects and create reports for pre-phase. They will need at least a month to complete this segment. I have Wayne in charge of it. He can reach me any time if something comes up. Meantime I'll be in touch with him regularly."

"What's the next step when you get back?"

"We'll be ready for FDA approval for pre-clinical data. That's when we get the green light to proceed testing with humans. At that point we'll go on a 24/7 schedule."

"Okay, Greg, keep me posted on your progress...and remember..."

"I know! Vaccine!"

Chapter 24

EASTER IN ISRAEL

At noon on April 10, the American Airlines jet taxis slowly toward the terminal in Tel Aviv's Ben Gurion airport. It finally reaches the gate and all engines are turned off. As expected, everyone stands and scrambles for their bags; then they wait for the longest time to get off. Finally, Bishop Mark and his group connect visually and inch their way off to meet at the Avis car rental booth. Greg, in charge of this year's mission, makes sure everyone stays together.

Going through customs was easy for everybody, except Famir. The agent looked at his passport, then looked at him. He then asked if he had other identification. Famir produced a photo driver's license with the name Miles Jackobi. The agent re-checks his papers and lets him pass but continues looking at him as he walks away.

More waiting greets them at the Avis counter. The extended van they arranged for is not available because it had not been returned yet. So, they have to settle for a smaller van with a luggage rack on top. Fortunately, two young men in the group, Louis and Steven, negotiate all the bags and secure them with straps. Louis gets behind the wheel and begins the 50-mile trip to Haifa.

"Does the driver know the way?" Famir asks Greg.

"Oh, yes. Louis usually takes us. He follows the shoreline road far away from the West Bank. He knows the country well."

Famir feels the need to ask the bishop about Nazareth and if he can reach family so they know he is here; but he thinks it's best to wait and talk to him privately. He does not want to call family with everyone listening. Just passed the town of Hadera, the van must stop at a checkpoint.

"I'm not aware of a checkpoint at this location," Louis says.

An Israeli soldier comes to the driver's window. They all have to produce passports. Satisfied that everyone's from America, he hands them back.

"Where you go?"

"We're going to the Pilgrim's Christian Foundation in Haifa to distribute humanitarian aid and to Easter services in Nazareth," the bishop leans over to say. "We come every year for two weeks to help the needy with food and clothing."

"Okay, go! Happy Easter to you, Christians!"

The bishop turns to face everyone.

"Listen, everyone. We'll be in Haifa in about half hour. We check in the hotel, freshen up, get something to eat and set up our distribution booth for tomorrow. Everything has been delivered. We'll have time to drive to Nazareth for services tonight at Church of the Annunciation. It's only about 20 minutes away."

He looks at Famir and sees him nod in agreement.

Late afternoon temperature reaches a comfortable 65 degrees. The bishop is dressed in black with a grey vest and a gold chain looping into a vest pocket while the others wear shirt and casual jacket. Within a few minutes, Famir points to the Church of the Annunciation in the distance with its towering cupola.

"Look, everybody, when it was built in 1969, the 2-story basilica was the largest Christian Church in the Middle East. At first Nazareth was a Jewish city, then Christian; today the city is mainly Muslim with a 25% Christian minority."

Greg cautions Louis to drive around to the west side so they can enter into the lower level, the sunken grotto that has the original home of the Virgin Mary.

"Listen, everyone," says the bishop, "this is the site where the angel Gabriel came to Mary to give her the good news—and upon this cave this massive basilica was built."

As they enter the darkened area, they walk into church history where Christianity was born. In the silence they can hear haunts of the past rush through the clay walls that whisper of a new paradigm on how to live. They notice a Latin inscription on a wall:

"Here the Word was made flesh and dwelt among us."

Moving toward the sanctuary, a statue of a young Mary welcomes all who visit her home. All around are preserved remnants of Byzantine and crusader churches. They proceed to a small altar with seating around it. Bishop Mark begins the Friday vespers as he's done the last few years here.

Steven, a young man in the group, chants the responses to the petitions and starts reading from Matthew a series of events that led to the capture, sentencing and torture of Jesus. The bishop turns and faces the people. He notices other pilgrims are drawn to the service and join his group to fill the small sanctuary. The cantor steps forward to recite the 1st epistle of Paul.

At this point Famir steps away quietly from the congregants and moves into a private area of the grotto while tapping at his phone. He tries several times, but there is no signal. He continues to retrace the path up the stone steps and closer to the entrance. He calls again and hears the ring sequence. Someone picks up.

"Hello? Amira? Hello?"

"Famir, is that you? My God! Where are you?"

"I'm here, in Nazareth. Look, I can't talk much now."

"Why? Come home. I call family, everyone misses you and wants to see you."

"I can't now, I'm with a Christian group here on a mission. We have to go to Haifa. Tell everyone I'm okay."

"Why you go to Haifa?"

"I'm helping the group distribute food and clothing at the Pilgrim's Christian Center. I had no choice; it was a way to come back home. I call you again when I get free time."

On his return to the service, he hears the end of the Gospel reading. More prophesies are read followed by chants and prayers. By now more visitors and pilgrims have come to join the faithful. Twenty minutes later when the readings end, the bishop turns to the people for the dismissal.

All file out quietly, not realizing they have just participated in a service on the sacred ground of the Virgin Mary, a revelation that will settle in their conscience in the days and weeks ahead.

Chapter 25

Troubling Developments

The Pilgrim's Christian Center lies in the heart of the Market District in Haifa. On Saturday morning, Louis parks the van at the outskirts of the district so they would have to walk about 3-4 blocks to their pavilion. And a sensual walk it turns out to be. They are immediately overcome with aromas of coffee, frankincense, turmeric and cinnamon.

Greg alerts everyone that this city is the spice capital of the Middle East. Soon, they notice the scent of pomegranates, fresh honey, cumin and chili powder, all fresh and exposed to the open air. As expected, Steven begins to sneeze and Louis joins him with a couple of his own.

Boxes of an assortment of food items are placed on the counter. Behind are racks of clothing, shoes and other household items; and each box gets a couple of Stan's pamphlets. Those who receive a box sign a tally sheet to record disbursements. Bishop Mark confers with Famir on inventories while people begin lining up for whatever they can get.

"Miles!" the bishop asks, "Do you know if we still have a Christian mayor in Nazareth?"

"No, Your Grace. Geraisi's 40-year rule ended a couple months ago. The new mayor is Ali Samal, a Sunni Muslim and to confuse his Christian critics, his first act as mayor was to declare a holiday for Annunciation Day on March 25. Also, he's considering a proposal to rename the neighborhood 'The Virgin Mary Quarter.' I don't know, if this is a head fake, we have to wait to see what happens."

As they're discussing local politics, an Israeli police van arrives at the pavilion with multi-colored lights flashing. Two young officers approach the group and post themselves in front of them. They bow slightly to the bishop and ask Famir for his identification. He reaches in his inside pocket and produces a passport and a driver's license.

"Miles Jackobi?" the officer asks.

"Yes, that's me."

The other officer shows two large photos of him, one taken at the customs office and another picture from police files that's quite different with the name "Famir Karim Masoud."

"These photos are of the same person," he announces as he shows them to everyone. The officer settles his probing eyes on the bishop who gestures he knows nothing about this.

"You need to come with us to the station for questioning," he fires at Famir. "We believe the captain will want to know who you really are, why the disguise and why you are here."

"Listen...the reason I..."

"Please! Save it for the captain."

As expected, the bishop displays shock at the allegation but he knows he must stay out of this. He denies knowing anything about Miles' other identity and Famir realizes that he is on his own.

"Bishop Mark," the officer continues, "your presence here is appreciated—an important humanitarian task for our people. We need to know how you came to include him in your group."

"He came highly recommended by one of my priests—a hardworking member in his community. I, personally do not know him. I just needed another member to complete my team. Nobody suspected him of being someone else."

Without realizing it, the bishop has just denied knowing Famir three times.

The officer then looks at the rest of the crew and asks them to also come and make a statement and answer a few questions. The pavilion is shut down and everyone except the bishop files into the police van. It drives away leaving in its wake a line of people waiting for food.

Bishop Mark is left alone in the market square. He checks the time, walks to an outdoor café and sits at a table under a yellow umbrella. He reaches in his pocket for a folded note he carried. He opens it, reads it again and then tears it in small pieces.

Moments later, a casually dressed man wearing plaid trousers and a fisherman's hat, approaches looking at the bishop. He sits across from him and takes his hat off revealing only a horseshoe of hair.

"Bishop Mark, thanks for meeting me here. How is your stay in Israel so far?"

"Well, not so good. My team was just taken to police headquarters for questioning. One of my people is suspected of dual identity. I'm sure they'll clear it up."

The gentleman produces a card. "Let me know if there are any complications."

"Thank you." The bishop looks at his card: Benjamin Morris, Deputy Director of Special Operations. "So, how can I be of service Mr. Morris?"

"A very dangerous man," he begins in a low voice, "will be attending the Symposium on World Religions in New York City in September, next year. Assuming they have the pandemic under control by then, we expect you to register for this event."

"Why is he dangerous?"

"Ibrahim El-Awad is a Palestinian terrorist responsible for the bombing that killed 85 men, women and children in settlements in the West Bank two years ago. We believe he will attend this event as cover for a meeting with others involved in a plan to bomb a site in New York."

"How can a bishop help in any of this? You expect me to kill him?"

Both enjoy the humor for a moment, then Ben hands him a B & W photo of El-Awad.

"We've been unable to corner him as he has two acting doubles that conceal his whereabouts. He has an Islamic crest tattoo on his right arm but so do the other two. However, there is a noticeable burn mark on the inside of his left wrist, a childhood accident. It is the identifying mark."

"Ben, I'm not CIA. Why are you telling me all this?"

"Because no one would ever suspect you. We know there will be diverse seating arrangements. The committee wants religious leaders to mix with other faiths in the spirit of brotherhood. When the seating charts are finalized, we will have you next to him. We just need to make sure that he is the one. A sniper will be positioned at a deadly distance. Once you give the signal, he will be taken out. You will be sitting on his right for a better view of his burn mark.

"We will monitor the organization of this event in the coming months. We know things will change continuously. But you can be sure you will know the latest up to the final moment."

"Mr. Morris, you are using me! And what do you mean things will change?"

"Once the seating chart is complete, his security team will change it shortly before the evening. We will know when that happens, that's why we don't have you next to him on the first round. I will contact you on developments in the customary manner.

"Yes I know, Bishop Mark, I use you, because I need you. That's what people do in life, use one another. If you help us pull this off, I can guarantee that Nazareth's mayor Ali Samal will be most cooperative to uphold human rights and insure freedom for the Christian minority. And I can get it in the municipal record as a matter of policy, no matter who is in office.

"Bishop Mark, I will be contacting you regularly with developing updates. Please know, your cooperation is much valued and appreciated."

Rising Tensions

Meantime, the police van arrives and parks in front of police headquarters, a modern towering glass building. Police escort the four inside, walk through security scanners and wind up in a waiting room. No one is cuffed, but an armed guard stands by the doorway. A plainclothesman approaches the group and asks for Greg, Louis and Steven to accompany him into a side room. Another officer escorts Famir into an elevator.

"Do any of you know this so-called Miles Jackobi to be a Palestinian under the name Famir Karim Masoud?" asks the detective as he loosens his tie. Everyone shakes their head. He examines their faces for a moment and appears satisfied.

"I understand. You are all free to go. Someone will take you back to the pavilion. Please continue your valuable service."

"Excuse me, sir," Greg asks. "Where have you taken Miles?"

"There's no such person. You mean Famir! He's being transferred to our intelligence unit in Nazareth. We have to detain him for further questioning." He will have an opportunity to call you soon."

They enter the van and the officer drives them back to the marketplace. They find Bishop Mark in front of the closed pavilion.

"What happened over there? Where's Famir?"

"They suspect he's a spy!" says Greg. "Who recommended him to the group?"

"Father Stan knows him well. He vouched for him and I suggested he join our team as we needed another person anyway—Listen, Greg! I just got a text from Miriam. We have problems growing with this pandemic. Churches were closed last Easter Sunday by local government. And they will remain closed until further notice. How can they just decide to shut us down? Stewardship pledges have fallen and now parishes won't be able to pay their bills."

"I know, Your Grace, I received similar messages about thousands of casualties and hospitals are filling up."

"Greg, we should head home. See if you can get us on an earlier flight. We can't stay here another week. Where are Steven and Louis?"

"They went back to the hotel. What about Famir?" he inquires already suspecting the worst.

The bishop raises his shoulders and eyebrows. "What can we do?"

Greg's phone vibrates in his vest pocket. He picks up.

"Hello? Hello? This is Amira, Famir's wife. The Pilgrim's Center gave to me this number. Famir supposed to come home to see us today. And nobody answers his phone. Sorry for bother. You know where is he?"

"Hello Amira, my name is Greg, leader of our group. Police came to the pavilion and took him to station in Nazareth for questioning..."

"Why police? Question for what...?"

"Listen, we don't know. You should go to the station and find out for yourself. We don't know anything else. I'm sorry. Tell us what you find out because we have to leave for the States earlier than planned."

Later, Greg exchanges the group return tickets to Wednesday the 15th, five days earlier. They just have to change to a different flight in New Jersey. He hasn't heard from Amira or Famir; and police have not returned his call. Louis agrees to go to the police station the following morning on the 14th to find out about Famir's release.

They close the pavilion early while Steven tells the manager about their early departure and to arrange for another team to replace them. Greg sends a text to Stan for the new pick up date and time from Rockford. They have to get a flight to JFK in Newark, N.J. and from there, a flight on American Eagle to Rockford.

"What's going on? Why the hassle—coming back so early? Everything Okay?" Stan fires back.

"Things not good Father—explain when we C U."

Chapter 26

MISSING IN ACTION

The next morning Famir is brought into an interrogation room which has a large two-way window and two cameras in the opposite corners. He sits and waits while observers watch him through the window. Within minutes a man in a military uniform comes in and sits opposite Famir.

"Why was I kept here," Famir can't wait to ask. "Why am I being held, I didn't do anything!"

"You are Famir Karim Masoud?"

"Yes I am, why am I detained? And why am I before a military person?"

"My name is Captain Nathan Barocas of Israeli Security. You are here because you come to our country with mixed identity and you are held under administrative detention until we find out your real purpose. So, talk. Why are you here?"

"I come from the United States to see my family in Nazareth."

"But, why would you come disguised as someone else with a different name? This is a puzzle, yes?"

"I was afraid of the Palestinian extremists picking me up."

"Why you afraid of Palestinians? You are one!"

"No! Check the record. Six years ago, I was here as director of The Arab-Christian Cultural Center. I am an Arab Christian. I had to leave the area...they were after me because I was promoting peace in the region..."

"Have you been to the West Bank since you came?"

"No, the group I'm with took the shoreline route to Haifa from the airport. I have no business in the West Bank. Check with the Pilgrim's Christian Foundation in Haifa. I'm not a Palestinian connected with violent extremism. I am a Christian! I came with the group on a humanitarian mission."

The captain lights a cigarette and offers one to Famir. He declines. Barocas stands and walks by the window making a gesture to the glass. Two guards enter the room and grab Famir. They wrap a chain around his waist and cuff his hands.

"What are you doing? Am I not free to go now?" he pleads.

"We have to check your story. You will hear from us soon."

The guards pick him up and leave the room.

"Wait, don't you have to charge me with something? You can't just keep me here. Can I get a lawyer? Don't I get a phone call?"

The captain begins thinking about the Emir Odeh case. Emir and his wife went on a hunger strike in military prison to protest unlawful killing of Palestinians including children during a peaceful demonstration in the West Bank in April. She starved herself to death while Emir is still detained.

Captain Barocas is aware of many imprisoned for no apparent crime and can't help feeling a level of injustice, that maybe the state policy need not confiscate all human rights. He no longer supports that Israel is still in a state of emergency after 67 years. But, he has an official duty to enforce existing policy. He laments he cannot do the right thing and wonders if other officers feel the same.

"Listen!" Barocas responds with stern voice as if reading a script. "You are held on administrative detention because you are considered a suspect, a threat to Israeli security. You are in military custody. The due process or as you call it, 'Habeas Corpus,' does not apply to your case. We can hold you indefinitely until we are satisfied with your story. And if we are not, a trial date will be set. Then you can have your lawyer. As I said, you will hear from us soon."

"A trial? For what crime?"

The guards take him away and the door behind them slams with a loud thud, drowning out his continuous cries about his criminal treatment and the absence of basic human rights. The captain goes back to the office where a call is waiting for him. He is told that a woman named Amira has been waiting to talk to him. She claims to be Famir's wife.

"Hello, this is Captain Barocas. What can I do for you?"

"Hello, sir, my name is Amira. I understand you are holding my husband Famir. Did he commit a crime? What can you tell me?"

"Amira, your husband came to Israel disguised as someone else with a fake passport and identification. So, we are holding him on suspicion under our administrative detention program until we can check his story. Do you know why he came disguised as someone else?"

"I'm sorry, I don't know. But he is a man of peace. He left five years ago because radical Palestinians were looking for him. Maybe he came with other name so they won't pick him up."

"Well, we will check on all that. Thank you for the information."

"When can I know what happens, Mr. Barocas?"

"We should have full report in about a week. Call back then and talk to Sergeant Adelman. He is handling this and will know about the next step."

Unhappy Return

The flight from Newark to Rockford was just over two hours. The bishop, Greg and Louis sit in a waiting area while Steven goes to a Starbucks to get coffee. Louis goes with him and Greg attempts to call Amira's number hoping to get a connection. Surprisingly, she picks up.

"Hello? Is this Amira?"

"Yes, is this police station…?"

"No, Amira, Greg Elliot from the Pilgrim's group. Did you go to the station to check on Famir?"

"Oh, yes, Mr. Greg. I have to wait, because police check Famir's story. They can't say anything else. They say I call back in a week to find out. I don't like this, very worried what they will do. Bad things happen to Palestinians especially West Bank and Gaza."

"But Amira! You know Famir is an Arab Christian—he's not a Palestinian activist!"

"Yes, you and me know this, but I don't think they believe!" She begins crying. "I worry our children and me, we not see him again. Too many people die just because of suspicion."

"Listen, Amira. I'll check from here to see what can be done. Please be patient and don't lose hope. We sent Louis to the station too, but he could not find out anything either. I will call again when I know more."

Amira thanks him for understanding and trying to help, but deep in her heart she knows what happens there. She's aware that people disappear on a regular basis, peaceful people who are well meaning but get caught up in the crosshairs of an overzealous security policy.

They sit quietly and wait for Stan to arrive. They reflect on their shortened stay in a country in a continuous search for peace and security, where Christians, Muslims and Jews confront the dynamic of peaceful coexistence on a daily basis. Greg's phone lights up.

"Hi, Greg, I'm just coming up the arrival ramp now. I'm driving Tony's Chevy van."

"Okay, I see you. We'll be out right away."

They come out with a baggage cart and start loading up. Bishop Mark gets in the front and everyone else follows. Famir is nowhere to be seen.

"Where's Famir?" Stan shouts, at the same time processing the reality that he may have been picked up.

"Father Stan," the bishop begins in a low, empathetic voice, "we have bad news."

"What do you mean, Your Grace, is he alright?"

"He's fine, but he's detained by Israeli police. We're worried his disguise got him into terrible trouble..."

"I'm afraid that's my fault," Stan utters quietly. "I urged him to change his identity so those fanatics won't recognize him."

"Father," Greg says reaching in his pocket. "Here is his wife, Amira's phone number. She is in touch with the police almost every day. Call her for the latest news."

"Well," Louis pipes in, "we didn't realize that Israeli security is running a police state over there. Apparently they think Famir is a Palestinian disguised as a westerner. For them, it's a security risk to let him go. His wife even tried to explain why he had a different name, so, an investigation began into his story. We won't know his fate for another week—maybe."

The ride to Rockton is a journey in silence. The only sound is the engine's hum and the flutter of the wind when someone opens a window. Stan thinks of the often repeated phrase: *The road to hell is paved with good intentions.* He also fears that his friend may be imprisoned indefinitely just because they suspect him. Above all, he holds himself responsible for Famir's fate and he's honor-bound to do whatever it takes to secure his release.

Chapter 27

FALLEN ANGEL FALLS

At breakfast, Stacey tries to help Stan snap out of his depression. Holding a mug of coffee, he picks up a fork, stares at his eggs and for a moment they turn into Famir's large forlorn eyes.

"I just can't eat anything now...I'm sorry."

"Listen, honey, you can't beat yourself up about Famir. You tried to help him and it didn't work out. It's not your fault. Didn't you tell the bishop about the advice you gave him?"

"Yes, the bishop didn't want additional risks to jeopardize his relationship with the local police. I told him about the I.D. change and passport and he felt okay about it."

"So, he agreed to it. It's not like you engineered the whole thing on your own! Besides, even though the disguise didn't work, the bishop still walks away clean!"

"I know. Look, I have to go to the diocese and talk to him about it. Maybe there's something that can be done. Where do we have that painting of the hands?"

"What painting? You mean Sophia Konton's canvas? I think it's in the basement. We had no wall space for it. What about it?" she asks curiously.

"I want to give it to the bishop, for his name's day. St. Mark's Day is in a couple days. You remember, Sophia gave it to me in return for helping her petition to be registered as an authorized iconographer in the archdiocese. Anyway, I think he would love it. And I can remain in his good graces."

"Okay, I hope it helps."

Temperatures in the mid-40s have finally washed away the salt and lingering mounds of snow that's been on the ground for weeks. As the gate opens, the familiar squeak has now progressed to an irritating squeal. Stan's car meanders along the winding driveway of the diocese compound and leans into the call box.

"Bishop Mark's residence, do you have an appointment?"

"Hello, Miriam, this is Stan Rybak."

"Hello, Father, I'll ring you in. Is he expecting you?"

"No, but he's going to love what I have for him."

The gate opens and Stan drives up and parks at his usual spot. He walks up the path carrying a 3' x 2' wrapped canvas toward the huge doorway which opens as he's approaching.

"Hello, Deacon John. I haven't seen you in a while," he says through his mask.

"Hello, Father Stan." He lowers his mask. "By the way, it's Father John. I was ordained last month."

"Well, congratulations! Welcome to the 'Golden Rule Club,' where no good deed goes unpunished!—don't mind me, Father, not having a good year so far. Will you remain in the diocese?"

"Not sure; actually I'm waiting for a parish assignment shortly."

"That's wonderful. Maybe in South Bend?"

"That would be perfect, but I don't know yet."

Bishop Mark walks into the reception area to see what all the commotion is about.

"Father Stan! What a surprise. What do you have there?"

"Your Grace, in honor of your name's day coming up, I bring you a real painting created by Sophia Konton. You remember, she was the only woman iconographer in the country. This is an adaptation of Michelangelo's *Creation of Adam* in the Sistine Chapel. You notice the hands do not touch..."

153

"Yes, Father, I know the painting. Man has fallen short of God's image, but is forever trying, forever reaching to touch the hand of God. Where did you find this?"

"Actually, she gave it to me as an act of gratitude when I helped her make her way into the man's world of iconography. Sadly, as you know, she passed away a few years ago. But her work is visible in many churches and museums. May I suggest, Your Grace, that this work replace the Fallen Angel for two reasons.

"Firstly, this diocese and this building ought not be defined by a 'Fallen Angel,' but rather, by a painting to show man forever reaching for the Hand of God, even though no mortal can ever touch God. And secondly, on display, this painting will honor the work of a devoted Christian woman who spent her short life painting images from the mystical to the Divine."

"Very well put, Father, thank you." The bishop looks at Father John. "See to it."

Father John takes down the Fallen Angel print and places Stan's gift. The size is slightly smaller, but fits perfectly. The bishop and Stan walk into his office and close the door. The bishop walks around his desk and sits in his high-back chair as Stan pulls his chair closer.

"Your Grace, I must tell you, I'm extremely upset about Famir's situation. I feel responsible after advising him to change his identity. Who knew that they would take photos at customs and then do a computer profile search on him?"

"Not your fault, Father. Apparently they had him flagged as a person of interest and when they got a photo match—that did it."

"But he's innocent, he didn't do anything wrong. His disguise did not have a sinister motive, he was just concerned about his safety. You must know some people over there. What can we do to help him?"

The bishop shakes his head. "Nothing." But, Ben comes to mind!

"Wait! I did talk to a Benjamin Morris, when we were in Haifa. He's Deputy Director of Special Operations."

"Who is that?"

"Father, he is 2nd in command at Shin Bet—you know who they are! Israeli Internal Security Agency. I have his card."

"Can you call him? Does he know you well enough?"

"Believe me, he knows who I am. I can call him at midnight—they're eight hours ahead—and ask him to intercede in this. He owes me!"

Chapter 28

Operation "Save Famir"

Stan's Subaru grinds uphill to park near the ICU unit of Mercy Health Hospital in Rockton. He's visiting Harry Paulus, a member of All Saints who's been on a ventilator for two days. Approaching the waiting room, he finds his family sitting quietly, awaiting word on Dad's condition. Estelle, his wife, notified Stan of the Covid-19 infection last week.

"Father," a nurse draws closer with mask on, "Mr. Paulus is not able to breathe on his own since Monday. You may go in for several minutes and then allow the family to visit...it doesn't look good."

Stan walks into the room, a most unpleasant task he often has to do in his ministry. He looks at a man on life support with eyes closed and hands folded in repose. With hands outstretched, Stan looks up and whispers a short prayer. He pauses for a minute as he listens to the machine breathe. He walks back to the waiting room and consoles the family. A bereaved wife thanks him for his prayers as they begin their painful pace toward the room.

He hurries back to his car to see an alert text from the bishop.

"Checked with contact person regarding Famir. Come in to discuss."

"How timely," he thought. "I'm right here!"

He calls Miriam at the diocese, says he's coming to see Bishop Mark and to open the gate and door for him. He parks and approaches the doorway to watch it open as he draws near.

"Good morning, Father. Please go right in. He's waiting for you."

"Thank you, Miriam."

Stan enters the bishop's office as if he's a regular fixture in the diocese.

"Good to see you again, Your Grace." He sits near the desk almost rubbing against the corner angel head. "What did you find out?"

"First of all, Father, please observe the new rules for congregating in church. There is nothing I can do about that for now. Your parish has already been shut down once. The next time there will be a fine."

"I understand."

"Regarding Famir, here's what's happening—and this is very confidential! This fellow Benjamin—he talked with the prosecutor's office and found out that Famir is scheduled for trial on June 8. He is charged with espionage. In such trials where the defendant is from another country, they typically appoint a sort of 'public defender' to represent him."

"Is the defender like our own here?"

"No. He is just window dressing. They just have to show that they provide a defense for the accused. But once you're accused, it's pretty much a guilty rubber stamp."

"So, Your Grace, there's nothing we can do?"

"Oh, yes there is. Benjamin was able to clear a path for an outside attorney to represent Famir. Whoever it is, he's supposed to submit his credentials and get authorization as a defense counselor. So, Father, find him a lawyer and get him over there. That's his only prayer."

"I wonder what the likelihood is of getting him off."

"I asked him that. He said in certain cases, an outside lawyer can often affect a dismissal. They have to do this sometimes to show they have a fair justice system."

Stan thanks the bishop for intervening on Famir's behalf.

"By the way, Your Grace, were you given any contact information for an attorney to communicate with the justice department over there?"

The bishop nods and gives him a piece of paper on who to contact.

"One more thing, Father. Benjamin told me if the attorney does a decent job to defend Famir, that the judge will dismiss the case. Have the attorney present this to the presiding judge before trial."

He shows Stan an envelope.

"What is that?"

"Father, please! Tell him NOT TO OPEN THIS ENVELOPE! It's very important. Just make sure he gives it to the judge, as is, sealed, Okay?"

"Well, hold on to it...I think we'll come here before the attorney goes abroad. You can give it to him then with final instructions."

"Who is it to be?"

"I don't know, Your Grace, I'll be working on it."

"Also, on another matter," the bishop asserts. "There is a Symposium on World's Religions in New York next year in September. The date is not set yet, but I need you to attend, especially the dinner. It's important, you have to be there with me! More information will be released in June."

"What's going on, Your Grace?"

"Not sure, but something big is planned on that night. I'll keep you informed."

As Stan is driving back to his office, he's thinking about the bishop's cryptic comments. He's never heard him talk like that before. He shakes the thought away and Jim Winters comes to mind. He realizes that whoever this Benjamin is, he's a powerful person. He pretty much paved the way for Famir's acquittal. The lawyer must just present a decent defense.

At the office, he searches through his desk and finally finds Amira's phone number that Greg gave him at the airport. He punches the international code and the number and waits. He hears a phone ring and ring and then it stops without a signal for leaving a message. He leaves one anyway.

"Hello, Amira, this is Father Stan Rybak, Greg Elliot's friend. He gave me your number to discuss Famir's situation. When you get this, please call me. I finally have some information for you. Call me on the 800 number I just used."

The events of the last couple months have taken a toll on Stan and he is thinking about Saul's Resort. He remembers that the ice goes out around this time. He knows he needs to reset and regenerate. And Stacey is too busy with on-line teaching to go with him.

Maybe Tony can go; it would do him a lot of good, he thinks, but he knows he's too busy at the plant. Stan is still hoping that maybe, Jim would be available to join him at the resort for a couple days. He understands that he has been through a lot with the trial in Madison and perhaps needs a break, too; also, a perfect opportunity to bring up Famir's need for a lawyer.

Stan locates Saul Haddad's number and punches it. A woman answers.

"Hello this is Stan Rybak."

"Hello, Father, how are you? This is Meg."

"It's been a strange year so far. Listen, I want to come up for a few days. What's the situation at the resort now?"

"Well, we're still getting the cabins ready for the season, but you can stay upstairs in the main lodge. How many of you are coming?"

"Me for sure and maybe one more. I'm thinking on the 20th for 3 days?"

"That's fine, I'll put you down. Check in with Saul at the bait shop when you come. By the way, the dining room is big enough to spread people around. Only about 25 are registered for that time slot so far. Don't forget winter clothing. It's still cold up here."

"Thanks so much! Say, are the loons back yet?"

"Yeah, they are—made a racket when they flew in a couple weeks ago. I think they were looking for you."

"Ha! Thanks, Meg, see you in a few days."

Stan is getting ready to call Jim. He hasn't talked to him since the Continental trial. As he's ready to punch his number, his phone begins to play "We gather together..."

"Hello, Father Stan? This is Amira, can you hear me?"

"Hello, Amira, I can hear you fine. I want you to know I feel very bad about Famir's arrest. He has been like a brother to me. It's unfortunate what happened...but listen to some good news. I asked my bishop to help and he was able to talk to someone important in the justice department."

"Oh, really? What you find out?"

"This man told my bishop that we need to get a lawyer from America to go over there and defend Famir. His trial is set for June 8. The defense lawyers they provide do not work for the interest of the accused. I can't reveal details but I have a close attorney friend I will talk to. He works for an oil company, but he's between cases right now."

"Oh, my God, you think possible to free Famir?"

"I have to ask him if he can take the case. But we have to raise some money to pay for expenses of..."

"Listen Father! Don't worry about money. I can get money to free Famir. Tell me how much you need."

"I don't know, Amira. Let me find out more when I talk to him. I have to call you back, Okay?"

"That is wonderful. Thank you so much for your helping."

The next few days proved very productive as Stan was able to settle a few nagging issues. When he called Jim he found out he no longer works at Continental. He took a severance package and has enjoyed a less stressful schedule. Stan also learned Jim's wife just filed for divorce and he is finishing a liability case in the next two days at Eau Claire, Wisconsin.

Just when Stan thought his idea won't work, everything falls in place. He relates Famir's tragic saga to Jim and asks about his availability in June to defend him in Israel. He assures him he will be paid. They can discuss the details at Saul's for three days on the 20th—his treat!

"That sounds great," Jim responds enthusiastically. "Perfect timing! I can drive up from Eau Claire and be there around mid-afternoon. A case of wrongful arrest, a chance to brush up on International Law and get out of the country for a while? Why not? Above all, this is an opportunity to do the right thing for someone."

Following a lengthy conversation with Jim, Stan calls Amira with the news.

"...Listen, Amira," he says clearly on the phone, "Jim Winters said he would do it. He needs you to testify that Famir is a Christian. He will secure sworn affidavits from the bishop, Greg, Steven and Louis, all the people in the group, to explain and justify his disguise."

"Thank you, tell Jim I'm so grateful! What about money?"

"He said he just wants enough to cover expenses. His legal services are pro bono. He said $5,000 should be enough for travel and expenses."

"Wonderful! Send me bank information, Father and I wire the money."

Chapter 29

REGENERATION AT SAUL'S

S tan brings Jim up to date on his conversation with Amira. They agree to meet at the main lodge tomorrow afternoon. The only thing on his mind right now is escape—flight to the natural refuge where therapy is not a word, but a treatment for the body, mind and soul.

Approaching the resort in early spring is much different from summer and fall. Stan listens to the familiar crunching of gravel as he drives up to the main lodge. Unlike the regular season, he sees ample parking just next to the raised terrace. The cottages are being cleaned, with attendants coming and going, doors opening and closing, cleaning supplies and garbage bags moving back and forth.

Stan checks in at the bait shop.

"There he is!" yells Saul Haddad, behind the counter. "Glad you could make it, Father. Anybody joining you? Say, where's your mask?"

"The same place where yours is. Yeah, my friend Jim Winters, the lawyer is coming later today. What's biting out there these days?"

"Well, the cold morning air, for one…You know the drill, Father. Fish bite twice a day: before you come…and after you leave! Seriously, if you go out before ten o'clock, (which is the best time) better wear gloves and head cover. Even though it may be in the early 40s, that wind has a way of making it feel like 20s."

"How warm has it been lately?"

"Oh, yesterday it got up to 'bout 55 around three o'clock. The ice was a couple feet thick this winter. Most of it is gone on the east side, but you may find some ice still floating on the west shoreline. In fact, if you listen, you can hear it melting. Father, I have you two at room 112 upstairs, main lodge, okay? Some of the workers stay up there. You need any bait today?"

"No, not today, Saul. I never fish the first day. Thanks."

He hauls his fishing gear and duffle bag up the stairs and into room 112. Jim asked him to bring an extra winter jacket and head cover for him since he was coming up dressed more lawyerly. He unpacks, puts clothes away and drops a pair of jeans, a coat, a couple hats and a pair of boots on the other bed. Stan now makes his way down to Long Lake for his usual ritual.

A brisk 45-degree noontime breeze forces him to zipper up as he walks slowly onto the pier. The planks are still wet as well as the familiar bench. It must have rained before he arrived. A wake on the water surface causes his buoy to rock back and forth. The sun shines through heavy cloud cover and then hides behind a grey cumulus. He sits on the bench, stretches out his legs, shuts his eyes and savors the hooting of the loons and the clinking ice crystals in the distance.

I wonder if they know I'm here, he thinks. *Maybe it's the Adviser.*

Stan is wishfully thinking. He knows that May and June is mating season where all the studs are showing off to snag a mate. He realizes there will be a lot of loon calls, but they won't be calling him at this time. He also hears loud clinking of glass, like someone knocking bottles together. He recalls that's what Saul meant when he said you can hear the ice melt.

He stands and reaches up as the sun floods across his face for the longest time. He smiles and enjoys the warm freedom, freedom from the chaos in the world...freedom from regulations and freedom from face masks. He watches a small boat slowly inching its way toward the pier. One man is sitting in it hunched over holding a rod and wearing rain gear, reminiscent of Winslow Homer's "The Herring Net" painting. As he approaches the pier, Stan grabs his line and ties it to the pier ring.

"Catch anything?"

"No," says an older man, as he shakes off his hat. "But I sure made the acquaintance of many fish. They just weren't in the mood today, I guess."

"Too bad." says Stan.

"Why too bad?" the old man inquires. "I accomplished everything else—except catch them! It's all about the pursuit, you know! I also met a couple beavers around Monet's bay."

Stan reaches out his hand and helps him onto the pier. He feels good grabbing the hand of another human and standing next to him. He looks at his watch: 12.30. They hear the bell ringing from the porch of the dining hall.

"You're back just in time for lunch, old timer!" Stan says affectionately.

"Not a coincidence, sonny, planned it that way. Name's Matthew."

"Mine's Stan. Good to meet you."

Stan helps carry a couple rods while they walk uphill toward the dining hall. He looks up and sees Jim walking down to meet him.

"Hello Father, when did you get here?" he shouts through his mask.

"Oh, about an hour ago—meet Matt. Matt this is Jim Winters."

Matthew stares at Stan as though he's a famous celebrity he didn't recognize.

"Father," the old man says, "name's Matthew, not Matt. In your church service would you announce the Gospel reading according to Matt? Good to meet you Jim—by the way, that mask won't help you out here."

Jim is taken aback from unsolicited advice coming from someone he just met. *What a thing to say,* he thinks looking at the old man wince with his red cheeks and whiskers. Stan is also jolted by the sudden irreverent correction that digs deep into his ministry.

"Forgive me, I'm too old to mince words or beat around the bush. What I'm saying is, out here, we're drawn to water, to its cement-like aroma, to the scent of iris and lilies that you'll find at Monet's bay and to the smell of pine." Now looking at Jim, "how will you ever experience any of this with that muffler covering your face?"

"I'm sorry, I ramble, but there's no infection to fear out here. The only infection you'll catch is regeneration. Now, that's contagious! You see boys, nature calls us all to water. It's the best therapy in the world! By the way," looking at Stan, "the excitement isn't in catching fish. The excitement is in fishing! Nice to meet you both. I think we'll be separated in the dining room. Have a great stay, boys!"

After that little sermon, Matthew hikes slowly up the hill without looking back, leaving a high-power lawyer and an ecumenical priest speechless. Jim takes the mask off and throws it in his car. When he returns to that perilous uncivilized world, he knows he's going to need it. They walk into the dining room and Jim spots the old man at a nearby table. He waves and points to his naked face. They all share a big grin.

Stan sees Meg as a server today behind the buffet counter. As there are only 20 some guests scattered throughout the large dining room, Jim and Stan stand in line with some distance and get their food in minutes. At the counter, Stan greets Meg with a question.

"Say Meg, who is that old guy named Matthew, you see him over there?"

"Oh, yeah, that's Matt Larson, the only poet in the county."

"A poet? Pretty smart guy," says Jim.

"I don't know that much about him, he's kind of quiet, keeps to himself. I do know he's a retired college professor from Madison and has a mailing list of people in his area he e-mails poems to. I think he said he sends a poem every month to about 150 friends."

They sit down at their assigned table with deli sandwich, potato salad, fruit and drink. Both enjoy the food and look forward to sharing many events of the last few months. Stan moves the Rybak I.D. tag out of the way.

"So, Jim, tell me about Continental. I heard on the news that the case against the oil company was dropped. What happened at the trial, and why did you quit?"

"Father, you won't believe it. Two of my best lawyers, Pat Mackey and Bob Haeger, they tore the prosecution's case to pieces. I got to hand it to them. Initially, Bob saw a big hole in their case: all the defendants were suffering from toxic methane gas produced not by the oil company, but by the paper mills in the area. This happened long before any pipeline was laid."

"Wow, your boss must have been impressed!"

"Yeah, everyone got a huge bonus—I received $10,000, can you believe that?"

"Why did you leave the company if it wasn't your fault?"

"Oh, but it was, Father. Last couple years, we were polluting the area even worse than the mills. We took advantage of a time frame technicality and proved that Continental was wrongfully cited and the state's case was misdirected. Father, it was only a legal victory. Morally, it was a travesty. That's why I had to leave and change my life—I think I need another sandwich, great potato salad—be right back."

Someone from another table comes to greet Stan.

"Good to see you, Father, just get in?"

"Yeah, a couple hours ago—say, I don't see Charlie. He usually comes up in spring..."

"Father, Charlie passed away in March—he got the virus, just ate him up in a couple weeks. Nice guy! What a rotten shame! Anyway, good to see you, enjoy your stay and keep warm."

Jim returns with another plate of food. Both are eager to talk more and catch up. Jim takes a bite of his sandwich and looks at Stan.

"Father, I understand you're having some issues with the church."

"I'm afraid this has not been a good year so far with the pandemic, tax man pounding on the church door, Famir arrested in Israel and the government is about to close the church. Other than that, things are manageable."

Stan unloads these concerns on a trusted friend and also listens to Jim's divorce.

"Once I left the company, she allowed a personal financial restructuring to erode our relationship and couldn't handle the adjustment. In other words, when the big bucks stopped coming, she couldn't deal with it. Fortunately, the break was clean as we hadn't started a family."

They continue sharing events and experiences as they make their way to the great family room next to the dining area. The fireplace is raging and all the mounted heads and trophy muskies on the wall take notice of their entry. Jim doesn't mention fishing as neither of them is inclined to go out today. They walk around the room and view old photographs on the walls from the early days; like taking a tour down memory lane beginning with the 1890s.

They stare at old gritty black & white pictures with horse-drawn wagons on dirt roads, old cabins long gone and re-built; and people, with baggy shirts and long denims. But a wide picture of Long Lake looks the same today as it did then, except for a longer pier. Stan is impressed that water never changes with time.

It's one of the many eternal elements around us we don't notice or have any control over—like air and fire, he muses.

Stan opens a small bottle of brandy and pours some into two glass tumblers. They sit in huge comfortable couch chairs and watch the fire in silence for a few minutes. Dancing flames also reflect off their drinks, mixing fire with the silky liquid. Jim gets up and moves a burnt log to make room for a new one. Sparks fly and crackle throughout the room.

Both settle back and give in to the brandy and the comforting surroundings. Although much of the day is still ahead, they feel this relaxation is part of the resort therapy as they enjoy fellowship and uncommon tranquility, After all, the purpose of being here is to unwind and feel at peace, whether on the water or in the comfortable confines of a fireside. There they are, two adults in mid-afternoon, closing their eyes in peace like children lying on the warm palms of the creator.

Chapter 30

BOTTLES, LOONS AND LURES

The next morning, a quilt of fog lies over Long Lake, barely above the water line. It's as though someone covered the water to keep it warm through the night. Stan has already brought fishing gear to the pier, loaded the boat with cushions, rods and tackle boxes. He watches a couple loons make their way toward the pier. They glide along as though sliding on a cloud. One of them looks Stan over. He waves to it assuming it's the Adviser. He checks the gas and makes sure the oars are on board.

Following a sumptuous breakfast, Stan and Jim are ready to go out. Pulling away from the pier at slow speed, they pass the buoy and venture out. Shafts of light sneak through the clouds to burn off some of the mist. Alabaster birches stand guard along the shoreline while two eagles glide among the pines.

"Let's check this shore, Stan...I mean Father."

"Out here, Jim there is no class structure. Nature looks upon us as the same. So, Stan is fine. Try casting about ten feet from shore, there's a drop-off."

"What are you using?"

"I'll try a Mepps Bucktail," Stan fires back. "You?"

"I've got the winner right here: a double cowgirl!"

They cast and retrieve for a while as more sun starts coming through.

"I talked to Amira, yesterday," Stan says. "You have no idea how excited she became when I told her you'd be defending Famir. As soon as the money arrives, I'll send it to you. What's your schedule with this case?"

"I haven't planned anything yet, but I've been thinking about it. First thing I need to do is check the legal protocols and the military justice system in Israel. I know of a colleague who practiced there. I'll be talking to him soon."

"What about the affidavits from the Nazareth group?—Whoa! I think I got something!"

Stan reels in a huge weed from the roots. He cleans his lure and casts out again.

"Well, I know their system doesn't honor Public Notaries. They don't tell you that part. So, they can throw out all depositions and suddenly you have no case. We'll have to take everybody to a judge to notarize the documents under oath. I know someone in Rockford that we can go to."

A wind shift now carries a loud clinking noise from the west shore which blends in with occasional loon calls, making it a noisy morning. After casting for ten minutes, they decide to check the western shore where all the noise is coming from. As the boat approaches the ice edge, a few columns of crystals crash against the boat and shatter.

Jim picks up a chunk to see that the ice melts vertically in little columns that separate and bounce into each other like bottles; truly a natural symphony that echoes loudly through the channel. He casts into a separation in the ice a few yards away and gets an instant hit.

"This is not a piece of ice," Jim yells. "It keeps pulling, see the pole jerk?"

"I think you caught a nice one," shouts Stan.

Jim sets the hook and now the fish is pulling line. He loosens the drag a little to allow it to run, but he's worried that his 10-pound line is stretching over a jagged chunk of ice. He starts reeling in slowly without resistance.

"I don't know, Stan, it feels like a lake trout, just sluggish, almost dead weight."

"Maybe it is. Bring it in slowly. Does this mean you don't want to talk about the trial now?" They both laugh loudly. Jim continues reeling most of his line until it just stops. Only about 20 feet of line out there, he tightens the drag, pulls gently but nothing happens. He lets out a little slack and waits. Suddenly, a big walleye jumps out of the water onto a floating slab of ice.

Stan grabs his cell and takes a video of a 30-inch walleye bouncing on the ice. It's easy to reel in now. Jim leans closer to the ice, pulls it and the fish slides and bounces onto the boat without a net.

"Wow! I never caught a fish like this before!"

Stan holds it next to the ruler: just over 31 inches. They both look at the beautiful fish lying just under the gunnels with gills opening and closing quickly. They gaze at the 15-pound beauty for a minute, then Jim pries his lure out of the lower jaw. Both pick it up and gently place it in the water. The fins begin to fan the water and soon the tail awakens. In seconds, it swims away revived and renewed, wondering what happened.

"This fish has just experienced an awakening, a re-birth," says Stan in a tone reminiscent of a mystical epiphany. "I hope we, too, can experience the same renewal while we're here." Jim looks at him and realizes that was a prayer.

"You really look at this place as sacred, don't you?" Jim queries.

"It is, Jim, look around you. Imagine if you have never been in a setting like this and somebody brought you here blindfolded. You sit a moment and listen to the sounds around you. Then the blindfold is taken off..."

"I suppose I'd be amazed."

"You bet! But later, when you come again and again, it's never like the first time, is it?" Stan probes.

"I suppose not..." Jim hesitates not knowing where this is headed.

"That's my point! The excitement wears away until the once breath-taking scenery becomes wallpaper and is taken for granted."

"I understand, but you can't be in a state of awe all the time."

"I get that, but we allow ourselves to flat-line and see everything in the same plane. Look, there are very nice people that come here often, but when they leave, the level of renewal they feel usually depends on the fish they caught, not so much on the experience."

The morning wind picks up and the boat is drifting back toward the pier all by itself.

"I don't know, I think when you catch fish like I just did, the adventure lies in bringing it in; and the time before you see what you caught is where the excitement is."

"Jim, look! I remember Matthew's reply when I said 'too bad' he didn't catch anything. He said he accomplished everything else, except to catch fish. And he was pretty content. What do you suppose he meant by that?"

There is no need to start the motor, the wind has guided the boat close to the pier. Jim uses an oar to bring it in.

"Come on, let's go to the bait shop and show the video of your catch. Looks like your name's going up on the board, buddy. Ha! It's like you went ice fishing without drilling a hole!"

"Okay Stan, leave the stuff in the boat. We'll go out later so you can hook onto something."

"Hey, Saul," Stan shouts as he pulls out the screen door. "Take a look at this. How often have you seen a fish caught like this?"

Others gather round to see what Stan is talking about. He turns on the video.

"Look, first Jim gets the hit. You know the drill, the fish runs, gets tired and then gives up. He pulls it in...watch this! A 15-pound walleye jumps onto the ice, then bounces across the slab and pretty much jumps on the boat by itself!"

"Now I've seen everything," says someone holding a minnow bucket. "This is sure one for the books, Saul."

They head on to the family room until the lunch bell. Jim goes up to the room while Stan stretches out on one of the lounge chairs, his phone resting on a side table. He shuts his eyes to rest and reflect. The phone lights up with two texts. One is from Bank of America, that $5,000 was deposited in his account while the other from Father John at the diocese states "Thanx for new painting—love it!"

A loud lunch bell shakes Stan awake as he and Jim come down the stairs to get in line for lunch. Today the main fare is grilled cheese with salad and chips.

"Jim I just got a text that your money has come in. When we sit down, I'll cut you a check for the $5,000 and you'll be all set. With churches limiting our ministry, I wish I could go with you—I know I can get Father John to fill in for me."

"Can you, really?"

"No, the bishop forbids it. What Famir needs now is not an old friend, but a good lawyer."

With trays in hand, they sit at their table. Jim picks up on Stan's church problem.

"So, you were saying about the churches. Are they closing because of the virus?"

"Not really closing, but they may as well close. I'm getting less than 20 people that the usher has to spread out. It is crushing my ministry. I can't have gatherings, meetings, Bible study or choir practice. We can't even get a quorum for council meetings because some of them are afraid to get out and come.

"And then, we have the tax problem where the government wants to tax donations, revenue-producing events and bequests."

"Wow!" says Jim. "How is that working out?"

"Well, we don't know yet. Since the President vetoed the bill and the pandemic hit, it's been tabled for now."

Stan takes out his checkbook and writes a check for Jim and thanks him. Jim finally calls him "Father" when leaving the resort.

Chapter 31

MULTI-LINGUAL MINISTRY

Unless by appointment, All Saints Church is closed during the week. So, Stan does most of his work at home—except on Saturdays, when he opens the church and the office. This is usually the day when he prepares his sermon for Sunday and other bulletins as well as setting up the on-line church service. He came back from Saul's Friday evening and didn't connect much with Stacey because he went straight to bed. The next morning at breakfast Stacey announces she's coming with him to church.

"You have time?"

"Of course. We haven't talked since you came back. I know you were tired. I'll come along, we'll catch up and I'll help you with the mail."

"Sounds great, honey, thanks! How is the on-line teaching going?"

"It sucks! Stan, this is not teaching, it's just class management. Everything's in the software, so a teacher isn't required. Anybody can run the class because I'm not really teaching, you know? And I don't think the kids are learning much. Besides, there's no way of knowing if you have their attention."

The ten-minute drive to church on this Saturday takes almost half hour because of a water main break that re-routed traffic. Just as well, because Stacey introduced a topic while riding that required some time for Stan to process.

"Stan, I think we should discuss something important."

"Of course, honey, what's up?"

"You know we're both in our mid-30s and we did agree when we married eight years ago, that we both want a child."

"Yeah, time really got away from us. I know what you mean. I was just holding off for the right time—can't believe it's been eight years!"

"Well, you still want a child don't you?"

"Of course, I do."

"The time is at hand, Stan!"

A big smile stretches across his face as he finally pulls up to the church. He unlocks the office and pushes in a pile of mail that's gathered the last four days. Stacey tends to all the envelopes on the floor with gloves and spreads them on a table while Stan goes in the office. A few minutes later Stacey comes in with the mail.

"Here are some utility bills, mail about recycling and solar panels, four donations, a letter from the diocese, a pound of junk mail, a letter without a return address and a large envelope from Nazareth. You know a Dr. David Brunner from the University of Haifa?"

"No, let me see that—by the way, save the solar panel literature. We should take a close look at that option." He quickly opens the large catalog envelope to find slick, camera-ready proofs in Arabic and Hebrew. He then unfolds a letter and reads it aloud:

10 May 2020

Dear Father Rybak,

My name is David Brunner from University of Haifa, Language Arts Division. A mutual friend, Famir Masoud, asked me to translate your paper on "Doing the Right Thing" in Hebrew and Arabic. As a trusted friend and colleague from the university, I was happy to grant his request as he's done many favors for me. Enclosed please find a complete translation of your paper in both languages printed on high resolution paper for reproduction.

175

Some sentences had to be rephrased but the meaning remains unchanged. Good luck with your project.
Yours Truly, —Dr. David Brunner

"Wow, isn't that nice! I had forgotten that Famir suggested I start publishing in different languages for broader coverage. What a guy! When did he get the chance to do this for me? I think he got arrested the second day in Haifa."

"He's truly a friend, Stan. I'm glad Jim agreed to represent him. When you called me from the resort with the news, I was really happy. Famir is all alone over there!"

"What's in the other envelope?"

Stan opens it and a money order falls out. He looks at it: $1,000 made out to All Saints Church. He reads a short note:

Father, you don't know me, but I read your pamphlet and I think everybody should read it and take steps to follow your guidelines. Enclosed is money I know you need to spread the word. Keep up the great work! —Anonymous

"How do you like that?" Stacey shouts with excitement. "A nameless benefactor, who believes in what you're doing, sends you money to continue and expand your message. What an endorsement!"

Just as they're both congratulating themselves, the office door chimes go on. Stacey goes to the door to see a man waiting.

"There's someone here for you, Stan."

"Oh, yeah, it must be Tom, the youth adviser. He said he would stop by today. Let him in."

"Hey, Tom, let's go out, I need your input on something."

They both go outside and walk to the side of the church.

"You see this side here and the other side has grass," Stan points. "The front of the building has grass. The rear is reserved for the departed from the community. I need you to get the kids involved this summer to dig out the grass on both sides and grade the soil so we can develop organic gardens. The grass in front is okay. But what else can you do with grass but look at it? Let's grow something of value! We can use the fertilizer money and lawn mower gas for seed and natural soil nutrients."

"Yeah, it's a great project for them. They can plant now and harvest in the fall. Crops can end up in food pantries and food baskets for the needy. Father, it's a feel-good project!"

"Great. But, they have to wear masks and observe safety...don't see a problem, do you?"

"None at all. We will need more garden tools. Maybe we can rent them from Home Depot. I'll do a virtual meeting and get the kids together and check with you next week."

After Tom leaves, Stan mentions the church garden program to Stacey.

"That's a great idea, Stan," she says. "I can oversee the project if you want. You know I believe in the power of youth!"

Stan is now thinking about his pamphlet.

"So, who would want my pamphlets in Hebrew and Arabic?"

Stan's query became a rhetorical question for Stacey. She begins searching for organizations that can distribute the pamphlets to various locations that speak the respective language. While Stan is working on his sermon for tomorrow, Stacey announces some sources for his pamphlet.

"Listen to this, Stan. *The Arab-American Institute, The Center for Arabic Culture* and *The Arab-American Family Support Center* are organizations based here in the states that deal with immigration and cultural issues. These are great outlets for you.

"Also, *The Jewish Voice for Peace* and *The Israeli-American Council* are similar organizations that promote cooperation and harmony. Why don't I prepare a form letter and attach a copy of the respective language pamphlet and sent out to these places and see what happens?"

"That's a great idea, Stacey, except for one problem."

"What's that?"

"We don't have any of these foreign language pamphlets. We just got the art work now!"

"Well, get on the phone and call Tony! Now you have a budget, so get them printed."

Stan is excited at the prospect of a bi-lingual dissemination program. Since Temple has a minimum of 10,000, Tony can do a split run of 5,000 each to get started. And he now has the money for it.

Chapter 32

PRELUDE TO A TRIAL

The day finally arrives when Jim has to travel to Tel Aviv. His flight leaves from Rockford to Newark at 12:15 P.M. He already has the affidavits, notarized under oath before a judge, with photographs attached. He has to appear at the President-of-Court Chamber in the District Court in Haifa on the first of June, a week before trial, for registration and pre-trial motions. He had already sent in his credentials and was approved as an auxiliary defense counsel.

He is aware that there is no jury system in the Israeli justice department, so cases are conducted before a judge (or judges). In cases involving national security or espionage, trials are held in the form of hearings before the bench and usually without observers or press. Famir's will be such a case. Jim is comfortable with that procedure where his case will be directed to the bench as judges are more interactive with case arguments.

One thing he hasn't gotten to yet is finding a court-approved interpreter. All court proceedings in Israel are conducted in Hebrew. He's already going to need more money as the rate is around $600 per day. There is an agency that hires out interpreters in Haifa. So, once he arrives three days early, he plans to connect with Amira, review her testimony and secure more funds. Then he will reserve an interpreter for the half-day pre-trial and the trial a week later, hopefully for a day.

Following coffee and donuts, Jim and Stan arrive with masks in place at the diocese at 9:30 for a final discussion before Jim leaves. Stan has offered to take him to the airport. Miriam shows them in, Jim in a summer suit with briefcase and Stan in his priestly outfit.

"Have a seat gentlemen, how's your time?"

"We're fine," Jim glances at his watch.

Bishop Mark marches into the reception room, all smiles with envelope in hand.

"Well, I guess this is the day."

"Good morning, Your Grace," says Stan. "Thank you so much for all your efforts. I'll be taking Jim to the airport."

"Listen, Jim, I don't know if Father told you about this envelope. You are not to open it, it has the Shin Bet security seal. You are to hand it over to the presiding judge before the preliminary hearing."

"I understand, Your Grace."

"Also, you have Benjamin's private number. Don't call him unless it is absolutely necessary and only after four o'clock."

"I got it."

"Excellent! God be with you. I would like a moment with Father. Will you excuse us?"

Stan and the bishop go to his office.

"Father, I need to tell you, the pandemic is getting worse, as you know. Any infections in your church?"

"Yes, we have three that I know of. Thankfully, they are recovering."

"Can you confine the ministry to online?—for safety, mind you."

"Yes, I can. Attendance has diminished; only a handful attend. What about money, Your Grace? I can't send you anything this month. I'm hoping for some revenue from the pamphlet. There's no price tag, but organizations have been generous with donations. Will you be okay for now?"

"I'm fine, thanks for asking. Stay with it Father, we'll get through this. On the bright side, now that you mentioned it, I hear your pamphlet is well received. Excellent work. Since we can't congregate, you provide the message in another way."

"Well, Your Grace, it's not intended to replace church services."

"Father, isn't the church ministry all about Right and Wrong, Good and Evil?"

Stan stands to pay his respects, checks his watch and rushes out of the office and shouts a goodbye to Miriam. Jim is waiting for him in the car. He quickly gets on the road toward the airport while Jim is reviewing paperwork. The ride is quiet at first.

"You know, Father, I really had a good time at Saul's last month. The few days there were not only relaxing, but also therapeutic. I was able to think better and deeper. And I was no longer worried about the trial in Israel. I know things will fall in place."

Stan pulls up to the departure entrance and helps Jim with his bags. He takes out an envelope and asks Jim to give it to Famir. They walk to the counter and Jim checks in. They lock arms. "Remember," Stan issues a friendly warning, "if you hear the distant call of a loon, it means you tamed the adversary and have the case by the tail!"

"Okay, I'll be listening."

Flying into the Future

The taxi driver tells Jim the ride to Haifa from the airport is over an hour. A bit disoriented with the night-time flying, time changes and Israel being eight hours ahead, he needs to set his bearings.

"What day and time is it?" he asks.

"It is 9:15 a.m., Monday, June 1, 2020. Get in."

The driver adjusts his rear view mirror and fixes on it as though he's looking for something. He waits a few moments, checks his mirror again and finally moves into the stream of airport traffic. Jim is busy looking over his notes but notices the visual drama between his driver and a yellow VW following behind.

Hardly a scenic route, Jim finds the ride to Haifa a bit less than exciting—really not much to see along the way. Highway 2 Coastal

Road is beautiful and fast moving. The view includes open fields with some scattered small buildings. Clearly, a boring ride—except for the VW, still following some distance behind. Thankfully, mid-day traffic is light and 45 minutes later some palm trees decorate the road to Haifa.

"Tel Aviv is for Jews and Haifa is for Arabs, yes?" the driver decides to speak.

"Oh, that's interesting. I didn't know that!" says Jim, amazed by the sudden burst of information.

Minutes later the taxi arrives at the Colony Hotel. The driver asks for $34.60 U.S. Jim hands him $40 and is surprised to actually receive change in shekels.

"Oh, no," Jim insists. You keep the rest. Thank you!"

The driver feels obligated to carry his bag and briefcase to the desk at the hotel in downtown Haifa. His tail watches him from a safe distance, but not safe enough to evade Jim's keen eye. Because he lost a day in the zone changes and half a day flying, he was concerned about being on time for the hearing.

Fortunately, it's early and he has time to meet with Amira later this morning. The courthouse is less than a mile away, a leisurely stroll later this afternoon. The problem now is the tail. He must talk to Benjamin about this.

Jim checks into his room and unpacks his clothing and paperwork. He checks his phone for messages and emails. He places a call to a client, but it doesn't go through. The traveling tired him a little, so he collapses onto his bed for a few minutes. When he opens his eyes, he realizes 40 minutes have passed.

He decides to go for a walk before calling Amira. He steps outside wearing only a short-sleeved shirt and begins his stroll downhill toward the business section. He scans the street and sure enough, there's the VW following. He quickly steps into a café, orders coffee.

Moments later, the door opens and in walks his tail no longer sporting a Panama hat; this time, a flat cap, hoping to confuse his target.

He sits in a booth at the other end by himself, his back to Jim. Now Jim is beginning to worry about his safety. He pulls out his phone and punches Benjamin's number. Fortunately, someone answers it.

"Mr. Morris? This is Jim Winters. I'm here for the Famir case."

"Hello, Jim! How is everything going so far?"

"Well, I have to appear at a hearing later today. The judge will determine if the case goes to trial and I know what to do—but I have a problem. Sorry for calling you."

"It's okay. What is the problem?"

"I'm being followed ever since the airport. He's even watching me now. Can you check on it and get rid of the tail?"

"Yes I can. Don't worry about it. Go about your business and good luck in court."

Jim quickly punches Amira's number.

"Hello, Amira? This is Jim Winters. I just arrived in Haifa."

"Oh, my God, you here!" she shouts.

"Can we meet today? I can take a taxi to your house to discuss Famir's defense."

"Oh, No! No, not here. I drive to Haifa, what hotel you stay?"

"Colony Hotel."

"Yes, Colony. Nice place! I can be there in one hour time."

At this time he notices the man wearing a flat cap talking on his phone. Soon, he jumps out of the booth, leaves some shekels on the table and rushes out of the café. On his way out, Jim smiles as their eyes meet.

"Amira, there is one thing that came up. I realized that courts here are conducted in Hebrew and I need to hire an interpreter for one and a half days at a cost of $900."

"Okay, I bring $1,000 more money."

"Good, you can park inside the hotel and come to the restaurant. We can have lunch. I'll be wearing a red tie."

Jim returns to the hotel, freshens up, secures a mask and heads downstairs to the restaurant. He totes his briefcase to review Amira's important testimony while waiting. He is taken to a table and orders coffee. Moments later, a different man arrives several tables away with a direct view of him. He is tall and thin wearing a light grey blazer over an open collar. He peers over a newspaper eyeing Jim's every move.

Not another one! Jim is thinking. He quickly inspects his notes about the agenda for today and next week and that Amira needs to testify on the 8th on Famir's behalf. A waiter arrives to take his order.

"Just coffee for now, thank you—waiting for someone."

He's wondering about the mysterious envelope. He takes it out of his case, examines it; feels like several sheets of paper.

He suspects that maybe it's a directive to ultimately acquit Famir after going through the process to defend him. That's why he was told to present a strong case for innocence. He also wonders what kind of a deal the bishop made to have this kind of intervention. In any case, Jim feels he has an advantage over just coming in cold as a hot shot lawyer from the United States to defend someone accused of espionage. He quickly hides the envelope in his case. He now notices a woman walk in looking around.

Amira spots his tie and walks toward his table. She is short, kind of plump wearing a long black leather coat and thick heels. An off-white scarf covers most of her light brown hair.

"You are Mr. Winter?"

"Yes, Jim is fine. Nice to meet you Amira..."

"Jim, I'm so happy you decide to help Famir. He is all alone in jail all this time. I could not get him out on bail."

"Have you been in to see him?" Jim asks.

"Yes, I am allowed only 10 minute time. Jim, they beat him. Why they hurt him?"

"I don't know, they must believe he is a Palestinian operative, so they try to get information from him."

"But he don't know nothing about Palestinian business," she announces "and when they move him to detention center in Haifa, is difficult to see him."

A waiter returns, takes their order. He wants another demitasse of coffee, she orders tea. The tall man in grey gets up and walks out, a newspaper under his arm.

"Amira, listen carefully. This afternoon, I'm going to court for a hearing on the case. Famir and I will hear the charges in a 'Reading' given by the judge. We respond to them and declare that we understand the charges.

"Then, a Preliminary Hearing follows where Famir admits or denies the charges. If he denies the charges, the prosecution argues the merits of the state's case. Then the judge decides to either dismiss the case or go to trial. Our case may go to trial next Monday morning at ten o'clock."

"Do I have to come and talk today?"

"No, this is just a hearing today to see if there will be a trial."

He hands her some papers that explain what she needs to say as a witness—that Famir has always been a Christian and that he is an educator and a family man. She needs to explain clearly the reason for his disguise when coming back to Israel.

"I will introduce you as a witness to explain all this; and I will ask you specific questions so we don't leave out any important information. Be careful, the prosecution will cross-examine you and try to make you unsure of what you say. Just be confident in your testimony and maintain your composure. There is nothing to fear. Their case has no basis. So, read over the material and call me if you need help."

The waiter returns. He orders breakfast. She doesn't want food now.

"Will they question Famir?" she asks.

"Of course. I will see him later today before the hearing and review what he needs to say. Unless I hear from you sooner, I will meet you at the President–of-Court Chamber next Monday at 9:30. Tell them you are a witness in the Famir Masoud trial."

"Okay, I will be there. Thank you so much." she hands him an envelope and waves goodbye. He looks inside and finds ten crisp $100 notes. Next stop: Hall of Justice, to see Famir. But he realized he didn't eat anything yet and it's too early for the detention center. Jim noticed Amira was in a hurry and they never got to order food. He watches her walk away briskly, talking into her phone with urgency while gesturing with the other hand.

The waiter brings a bowl of fresh yogurt and an assortment of cheeses and two eggs with diced tomatoes and shallots along with hot bread rolls. He leafs through the *Hamodia,* a daily paper and finds the English section.

The lead article decries the lack of due process and human rights toward Palestinians in Israeli prisons. And no distinction is made between PLO or Hamas Palestinians and peaceful Palestinians. His attention turns to the enticing breakfast with periodic glances at the story. He nods his approval to the waiter.

"Inside military courts the only defendants are Palestinians who comprise a 100% conviction rate." He reads on to learn that many suspects are detained in "Administrative Detention without being charged, some indefinitely."

"In national security cases, they are interrogated, often beaten to extract information. When the evidence against them is conclusive, they are tried, convicted and sentenced to a minimum of 10 years—all this while the government claims to adhere to the presumption of innocence."

As suspected in most countries, Jim understands the difference between the democratic principles of human rights they champion and the reality of treatment they deliver. In any case, he knows he has to be careful how to proceed and not to be cavalier in his defense approach.

He leaves the hotel and begins a brisk walk toward The Hall of Justice, about 15 minutes away. He can't shake the image of Famir being abused and beaten while incarcerated for over seven weeks without bail.

Finally, he will be charged today. And Jim understands that judges take an active role in the proceedings.

As Jim approaches the justice building, he is impressed with the modern look. An attractive curved frontage showcases the entrance and a height of four to five floors. He notices the narrow windows of the upper floors and suspects this area is for detainees. He walks in through an impressive doorway, places his case on the conveyer and passes through the scanner towards the information window.

"My name is Jim Winters, an American attorney. I represent Famir Masoud who is being held here. Here are my papers and a certificate of approval to legally represent the defendant. I requested a meeting with my client last week by email. We have to appear at a hearing today."

"Please, to wait," she says while calling someone over to her station. A man talks with her in Hebrew, she hands off the paperwork and then withdraws.

"My apology, Mr. Winters, the attendant did not understand all that you said. Can I help?"

Jim has to repeat everything, whereupon the attendant nods and asks him to be patient.

"I will check on all this, alert the detention center that you are here to visit Famir Masoud. Please wait and you will be called."

After thirty minutes, a young page comes before Jim.

"You are Jim Winters?"

"Yes, I am."

The young man pins an I.D. tag on his lapel and hands him a clearance pass to the detention center and courtroom for the day. He reads the English instructions from a printed sheet and points to a bank of elevators.

"This pass is for today. Use lift there. Go to level 4. Turn right for visiting room."

Jim follows directions and lets himself in the visiting room. He sees a long table divided by clear glass reaching the ceiling. On the other side is a mirror image of a table with chairs. He sits and waits, a phone nearby. In a few minutes, a guard escorts a man in waist chains and ankle cuffs into the room. It's a man with disheveled hair and scraggly beard wearing a camouflaged jumpsuit. He sits across from Jim and picks up the phone.

"So good to see you, Jim. Been a long time," he says from the side of his mouth.

Jim can't respond right away because he's outraged at Famir's condition. His lip is cut, he can't open his mouth, has a swollen left eye and a bruise on his forehead.

"I'm so sorry to see you like this," Jim grimaces. "Do you get any medical care?"

"No, only if you are bleeding. Interrogations happen at any time. Sometimes I'm dragged out of bed at two in the morning; other times in orderly fashion during the day. They ask why I come back to Israel, they ask who is my Palestinian contact, they ask if I was involved with the West Bank bombing two years ago. When they don't like my answers they hit me…"

"Listen, Famir, in about 1½ hours you will sit with me in court and we will put a stop to this treatment. There will be a hearing where the judge reads the charges against you. You are to say that you understand the charges. Then you will be asked how you plead. I want you to deny these charges and say you are innocent. The prosecutor will then reinforce his case by stating the risks you pose to national security. The judge then decides if there will be a trial next week. By next week it will all be over. Trust me and hold on, okay?"

"Okay, Jim. Thank you. See you later in court."

Chapter 33

PRESUMPTION OF INNOCENCE

Jim walks into the district courtroom chamber, a narrow room with high ceiling and blank walls, unlike the larger courtrooms in America with a jury section and a gallery for guests. On a riser, a wide massive solid bench stretches to near 12 feet to accommodate up to three judges. Below, facing the bench, are two long tables with chairs—one for the defense and the other for the state prosecutor. There is no jury box as arguments are directed to the presiding judge.

He lays his briefcase on the defense table and sits to arrange his paperwork for the hearing. Soon, two men with cases walk in accompanied by a woman holding files. They sit at the prosecutor's table next to Jim. They greet one another with a polite nod. One of the men passes out ear phones and does a sound check. As expected, Jim's interpreter arrives with a roll-on case. He sets up his audio and drops several ear phones on the table.

"Hello, you must be Jim. My name is Michael. I set up communication audio. When you speak, direct your comments to the proper parties and do not look at me. Whatever you say will be interpreted and transmitted to both the judge and the prosecutor. And whatever they say to you, will reach you in English in my voice. Any questions?"

"No, I've done this before."

"Do you have payment please?"

"Here is $300 for today. I will pay you the balance next week at the trial."

For the next few minutes, shuffling of papers, loud whispering in Hebrew and a continuous low grade buzz are the only sounds. The interpreters take a seat behind the tables with mics fastened to their coats. They make some adjustments to the equipment.

Abruptly, a door opens at the rear and an armed guard escorts Famir to his table. Famir is in cuffs attached to a chain around his waist. Jim notices he's cleaned up and groomed, even a trace of make-up to conceal bruises. They review the procedure while a guard stands behind Famir.

Jim checks the time: 4:10. Just then a door opens behind the bench and a black-robed judge walks toward his seat holding a file. His robe is loosely fastened in front revealing a white shirt with black tie. All stand during his entry. They put on head phones and Jim asks the bailiff to hand the special envelope to the judge.

"Please be seated," the judge says and opens a folder. He takes the envelope and lays it down. "Will the accused please stand."

Famir stands. At this point so does Jim. "Your honor, the defense requests that the restraints be removed from my client during the proceedings."

"Request denied. To all interested parties, I shall read the 3-count indictment against the accused." He looks at the accused.

"You are Famir Karim Masoud?"

"Yes, I am, your honor."

"Famir Karim Masoud, you are charged with conspiring to conceal your identity by presenting fake passport and identification to enter Israel; you are charged with spying for the Palestinian Authority; you are charged with conspiring to compromise the state's national security. Do you understand these charges against you?"

"Yes, I do."

"May it please the court, your honor," asserts Jim, "my client denies these charges; he's been wrongfully accused. I shall enter into the record affidavits of five individuals including a U.S. Christian bishop who attest to his Christian identity. These sworn depositions were given and recorded in front of a state district judge."

"But, your honor," the prosecutor jumps in, "if this man is a Christian and has no connection with the P.L.O., then why did he go to all this trouble to conceal his appearance and produce fake I.D. and fake passport? Police report noted he looked suspicious."

"Counselor?" the judge peers at Jim over his glasses.

"Your honor, perhaps Famir can best explain in his own words."

The judge agrees to hear his testimony as he adjusts his headphones. The guard escorts Famir toward the bench. Famir clasps his hands and assumes a pleading tone.

"Your honor, I am an Arab Christian, have been all my life. I was born and grew up in Nazareth and have been an advocate of peace all my life. Six years ago I was Director of the Arab-Christian Cultural Center. Because of my peace initiatives, Palestinian militants were after me. I narrowly escaped to the United States. I needed to come back to see my wife and two children, but I had to be careful, they would not find out I was here...

At this point the judge opens the envelope given him.

"Your honor, this is the reason for the disguise and fake passport," he continues. "I am not a spy and I mean no harm to the state. I was concerned for mine and my family's safety."

The judge asks the defense to produce the affidavits. The bailiff takes them to the bench. There is silence for a few minutes. Then the judge addresses the prosecution.

"Counselor, do you have a redirect to the testimony?"

"Your honor, we do not accept the defendant's story. He came to Israel with false identity to connect with Palestinian insurgents. We suspect he has ties to terrorist activity in the West Bank and is a threat to national security."

"Your honor," Jim jumps up, "there is no evidence presented that my client is a Palestinian operative. That is only an accusation. Suspicion alone, because of his name, is not evidence; and...even looking suspicious is not a capital crime, your honor."

"I agree, counselor. This case is dismissed for lack of *prima facie* evidence to support the charges. The defendant is free to go and the scheduled trial date is hereby cancelled."

The prosecution attorney is stunned at the verdict. He has witnessed less serious cases go to trial that ended with convictions. Meantime, Famir can't believe it's all over. Jim, too, is surprised at the sudden acquittal. The guard unshackles him and instructs him to go to claims and retrieve his belongings. At this time, Jim hands Famir an envelope.

"Father Stan asked me to give this to you."

He removes the headphones and opens it to find a letter from Stan:

Dear Famir,

I pray every day that your case will be dropped. I'm confident Jim is going to do the best he can so that justice prevails. He knows how to do the right thing. I also want to thank you for getting the translations for me, they came a few days ago. The professor spoke highly of you. I'm in the process of getting new pamphlets printed in Arabic and Hebrew. Thank you. You are truly a good friend. Also, I took the liberty of placing in your house a family with two children. Last month, he lost his job when a factory closed. They have no other income. I told them you are out of the country and when you return, they would have to find other housing. Let me know if it's okay. – Stan

"So, now you can go where you wanted to go all along: home."

"Yes, Jim. I don't know how to thank you. Now that it is finished, you have some time. Come to our home today so my family can thank you. Can I use your phone?"

"Of course."

He punches Amira's number. "Hello Amira? I'm free! The judge threw the case out. They had no basis to even go to trial..."

"What? I can't believe it! No trial next week?"

"No, I tell you, it's all over. Jim did a great job! I'm bringing him home with me to meet the kids. You have anything ready?"

"Oh, yes, yes. I cooked food I planned to bring you today. So, now you two come home."

Jim hands over the extra $700 to Famir and explains Amira gave the money for the interpreter and he won't need him anymore. While Famir goes to get his belongings and check out, Jim calls to reschedule his return flight. After being on hold for the longest time, he's able to get a seat on a red-eye at midnight.

He's reflecting on what happened a few minutes ago and is stunned, himself. He never imagined it would be this easy. The prosecution's case was circumstantial, at best. He's amazed how a judge can make all the difference in a case.

No wonder Palestinians are treated with great prejudice, he thinks. But what he'll probably never know is to what degree the secret, mysterious envelope played a role in Famir's acquittal.

Part 3

Chapter 34

REUNION WITH DISTANCE

T he warm summer months have taken some sting away from the virus as people begin to relax social restrictions. The infection and death rates have stabilized, more so in certain locations. Under rules of face covering and distancing, some activity is allowed again. Even houses of worship are calling back their people to "Reunite with Distance," a new phrase that has caught on. Restaurants and places where people gather carefully resume their activity observing strict guidelines to curtail the spread of the virus.

With the bishop's permission All Saints Church is also back in service, somewhat. August attendance has improved but travel is still at a trickle. Following Sunday morning services, Stan steps up to the pulpit to face some 60 faithful, conveniently spread to fill the sanctuary.

"Today I want to share some thoughts on *Justifiable Wrong-Doing versus Evil.* When someone lies, do you think he lies deliberately, without reason or motive? Of course not. One can lie to appear acceptable, to cover a wrong or to achieve a certain outcome. And usually, that person is convinced the act is justified.

"Why do we manipulate situations and people? Perhaps to achieve control over others, to become successful; or maybe, because we're frightened, so we need to be in charge. And why do we hurt others? It may well be fear, fear of insecurity, fear of not being able to advance our cause. Again, we feel comfortable with our actions.

"A young man came to me last month after he stole a car. I asked him why he stole. He said he was trying to save enough money to purchase one but he lost his job, and now, he needs a car to look for other work and be able to get around. He said he worked hard and he deserves a car more than the elderly couple who owned it. He watched them and they rarely ever used it. He said he felt it was the right thing to do. When he finished his argument, he looked at me. I shrugged and said, 'so, why are you here, telling me all this?'

"With regeneration and renewal, we are able to face our flaws and see them for what they are, not what we want them to be—and then, tame them. It can be done with prayer, meditation and resolve. But there is one reality that only prayer can help, and that is Evil. My friends, evil is wrong-doing without reason, motive, justification or rationalization. Evil is deliberate!

"Evil offers no benefit to any person, society or culture. Evil is malice for its own sake. Man is capable of doing immoral acts and can explain them, atone for them. But the power of evil as a force inflicts pain and suffering for no reason, no justification, no explanation. Can you tame evil? The answer is NO! When you see it or feel it, when you sense it's near you, you must run in the opposite direction and seek God's help. Alone, you don't stand a chance."

Stan did not mean to deliver a fire and brimstone sermon, but he found it necessary to clarify the difference between wrong-doing and pure evil. He recalls what a visiting monk said once at the seminary when asked why he prays all the time. "I continuously fill my mind and soul with the things of God, the Jesus prayer, other prayers over and over again," he said, "but if I get distracted by the world and stop even for a moment, evil can enter uninvited and corrupt me."

He walks near the church entrance and notices only one of his pamphlets is left on the counter. One of the ushers told him last week that people take extras to mail to friends. He brings more copies and makes a mental note to call Tony about the French & German pamphlet delivery. He thought he saw him at the service. But he must have left.

Stan had secured a mailing list for Europe and the mailing house is supposed to run the copies through the machine and ship them out. Fortunately, more donations have come in to pay for all expenses.

He's also been thinking about Famir. He hasn't heard from him since his release from prison six weeks ago. He understands that he needs quality family time to get re-acquainted with his wife and children after more than six years, but it isn't like him not to send a quick message or a text to stay in touch. He is also concerned about renting out his house. Why would he do that unless he planned not coming back for a while, or perhaps, at all? Although it's just as well, a needy family found a temporary home since Famir was captive for almost two months.

Stan did speak to Jim a couple weeks ago who learned that everything went better than expected and there was no need for a trial. Stan plans to call him tomorrow as well. The bishop, Greg, Steven and Louis also have inquired about Famir. Since everyone put in a lot of effort on his behalf, they're anxious to find out how it all went in Haifa even though they know the final outcome.

Regarding the pamphlet, the next and probably the last translation Stan needs, is in Spanish. For this one, he has a Spanish-speaking parishioner to call on. He teaches Romance Languages at NIU. Stan realizes the Spanish market is the biggest next to English, so he figures maybe 20,000 copies should be a good start.

The unexpected donations from the pamphlet so far has paid for all expenses related to it and there's $4,700 balance in the account. Stan is expecting more donations to come and is visualizing a steady revenue stream once the distribution expands into Europe and the Hispanic regions.

He feels this extra money is God-sent, as it makes up for the shortfall in pledges and also helps sustain the diocese until this scourge is gone. Stan took Tony's advice and added donation information at the bottom of the last page. It is discreetly printed as an optional act of generosity and is not intended as a solicitation.

Chapter 35

RENDEZVOUS AT WEST BANK

Getting around in East Jerusalem in the West Bank is no walk in the park. There are physical obstructions forcing detours, barricades and numerous armed checkpoints. Many of the barricades are moveable, some are permanent. It all depends on what orders come down from military command. The Israeli government which claims control over all of Israel, has also built underground tunnels in this area. They facilitate movement for Jewish residents in the scattered settlements. Once they know the tunnel system, they can avoid many of the checkpoints and obstructions.

However, Palestinian inter-village travel is almost impossible because of road closures and the infamous "Forbidden Roads" policy. This policy forces them to use longer routes to navigate from one town to another. Only those with special permits are allowed to travel on all roads.

A 90s Mercedes coup travels southbound on Route 60 towards Jerusalem. After many twists and turns, valleys and hills, the driver approaches a checkpoint in Jenen where certain vehicles bearing yellow plates cannot continue. But the driver produces a permit with top military clearance and an accompanying photograph: Famir Karim Masoud. He is greeted and allowed to proceed.

An hour later he reaches Jerusalem, passes Gilo where the road joins Hebron Road. Without hesitation, he turns this way and that way on several streets as he's most familiar with the area. He passes the

Western Wall, turns again, passed the Damascus Gate and finally spills onto Sallah Eddin Street and parks in front of the Rivoli Hotel.

Famir walks briskly through the main door and into an elevator. He exits on the 3rd floor and approaches meeting room 309. He opens the door to see six people sitting around a table talking with face masks. Upon his entry, they stand and applaud vigorously.

"Glad to have you back..."

"We didn't think we'd ever see you again..."

"How did you manage to..."

These and other boisterous shouts in Arabic fill the room. Famir sits at the table and lays down his binder. They take their seats too.

"I had lots of help, gentlemen. Thanks to generous funding from you, a lawyer from America came here to defend me and I was acquitted. He was able to prove I am a Christian and I had a disguise to protect myself from all of you."

Everyone laughs for the longest time. Famir notices two men dressed the same with similar features. He had heard of Ibrahim but never met him; maybe it's one of them.

"If it wasn't for my friend Jim, I'd be rotting in chains for the next 20 years...and I had no major role with the bombing in the West Bank two years ago."

"Well, you weren't involved in the inner workings of that event," says Mohammad Najjar, "but we count on your help with the next one. Welcome back!"

"Next one?"

"Yes, and more to come," asserts Ibrahim El-Awad. "Until we have a country to call our own. Gentlemen, let's remember, before 1948 Israel used to be Palestine and Jews living among us were less than 10%. Now, everything is reversed... Famir, please meet Sadiq one of my doubles. He and Ahmed, who is not here, help confuse our enemies who have been after me for years. I rely on these two who have great courage. They accompany me everywhere I go. Without them I could not survive!"

"You all know, we have a few settlements in Gaza," interjects an elder, steering the group back on subject, "and some area in the West Bank this side of the Jordan River—and even then, we have to live under siege. We were supposedly given Gaza and West Bank, but they were never ours to call home. For the past 70 years, Israel kept expanding their presence with settlements in both regions..."

"...and even, here in East Jerusalem," another man in a robe pipes in, "Jewish neighborhoods are cropping up all over. The sad fact is, we still do not have a home. And the two areas where we have roughly five million people, it is a partial presence and they are 70 km apart."

Ibrahim quickly takes the floor to redirect their attention. Barely over five feet, he stands tall and proud like a little Napoleon with pitch black hair. He appears more focused on the here and now, whereas some of his compatriots love to reminisce and feel sorry for themselves.

He grew up in Gaza and went to school with Mohammad Najjar. The latter considered him a man of peace until it became clear that they were destined to have no more than scattered settlements. He pulls his mask off and reveals a thick black beard.

"Gentlemen, we all know the history," El-Awad continues speaking with authority. "The big powers have decided our fate long ago. The celebrated UN partition plan never materialized. Forty percent of the West Bank and a portion of Gaza Strip does not make a country! When Israel annexed the West Bank in 1980, the world community condemned the act. A lot of good that did! Also, Israel will never give up Jerusalem as they consider it their capitol. But for us, East Jerusalem shall be the capitol of the future Palestinian state!

"Now, let's get to the business of the next event. We need to let the world know of the injustice forced upon the Palestinian people. It's the global power establishment that needs to be tamed. The big powers need to acknowledge us and pay attention to our cause.

"Look, we don't have an army or air force to achieve our goals like the Israelis. All we can do is raise awareness that things have never been right since the establishment of the Israeli state. Allah knows it is the right thing to do! We have justice on our side that will celebrate our actions. One day righteousness will prevail! And here is where you come in Famir."

"What can I do?"

"You will return to America and connect with our affiliates in New York. They know of the plan and are busy with various strategies. You should stay in New York; don't go back home. They are of no use to us now. Your contacts will review all the details with you and stay in touch. There is a lot of work to be done."

"When is this event?" Famir asks with anticipation.

"September 11, 2021, 20-year anniversary of the towers. Also it is Patriot's Day in the American calendar. But on that day we will be the patriots. What better time to get attention and let them know things need to change!"

Ibrahim hands him a list of New York contacts written in Arabic as well as his own private number. Famir takes it and slips it in his binder while noticing a large scar on the pulse side of his left wrist. Ibrahim has a final thought.

"Famir, since the event is a year away, perhaps we can get you in touch with our people at New York University for a teaching position. I'll let you know."

"Thank you. That would be a good thing." They all embrace and cup their hands with slight bow.

Chapter 36

STANDING UP FOR RIGHT

A strong morning sun filters through a foggy mist as Stan sees himself in front of All Saints Church. He watches a figure in white walking toward him slowly, bathed in light like an apparition. He is dressed in an Islamic robe and wearing a pillbox hat.

"Famir! Is that you? My God, you're back! Why haven't you contacted us? Everyone is worried about you. I talked with Jim and he said everything turned out better than expected—why are you dressed like that?"

"Father, even though I have Christian roots as my foundation, I'm still an Arab by race. And as such, I am connected to the Arab struggle for nationhood in the Middle East. Westerners find it hard to understand this. I am tired of hiding my identity."

"But who are you, really?"

"I am a devout Christian, I am also an Arab in search of a home. Why can't people grasp that? This allows me to have a Christian support system and an Arab identity at the same time.

"For example, Father...take the Greeks. They are Christian, but those who left their country as adults still identify with their ancestral home. My problem is, my ancestral home ceased to exist in 1948 when Israel took our land. And 70 years later, all I can point to is a few isolated pockets in the West Bank and Gaza Strip. And life there is almost under siege for us because in reality, Israel wants it all."

"Famir, I understand, you are not a bad person. You have good reason to feel the way you do. I know you to be a sensitive man who responds to human emotion, pain and suffering. You are a good man swept up in *a righteous struggle to make things right. But Famir, two wrongs don't make a right!"*

"I don't know what that means, Father. That's a cliché. Is it wrong to want a home, especially if we once had one and it was taken away? Isn't this what you always said, to always try to do the right thing? Why does everybody accept the injustice that was done just because the global powers said so?

"We were even prepared to accept and be content with the West Bank and Gaza. But Israeli encroachment in those areas never stopped. To this day, they keep developing settlements on land they decreed to be ours! And the UN that created the partitions in the first place, does nothing about it! Stan stands spellbound with bated breath, but the image of Famir gets hazy and gradually begins to fade away. He watches him disappear while still talking until the voice fades as well."

Stan is startled to consciousness by the hymn 'We gather together...' and jumps up to answer the phone, but he can't find it. By the time it plays the whole hymn, he hears a message signal. He can't believe it's Famir. He punches the numbers.

"Hello, Father, I feel I haven't talked to you in months. I miss everyone."

"Hi, Famir. Jim brought us up to date on your detention and hearing, but we got worried when you didn't contact us. We tried several times to call, but our calls did not go through."

"My apologies, Father, when I was released I suddenly got my life back. Amira has been so understanding and helpful. She never gave up hope. And my children—wow! They have grown so much. You, understand, I needed some quiet time to refresh and regenerate, as you would say."

"Of course! By the way, thank you for the translations. I received them from Prof. Brunner. You won't believe the response I'm enjoying.

Everyone loves it. So, aren't you at risk staying there? When are you coming back? We miss you."

"Oh, Father, since I'm no longer involved with the Cultural Center, I was told the pursuit for my capture was cancelled. But I have to stay clear of any peace initiatives and I can't run for any local office. So, there is no reason for me to leave my home here in Nazareth. Thank you for all you did for me. Without your efforts, I would still be in prison without any hope. You all did a wonderful thing and I will never forget it. I owe you my life, Father."

"Famir, we saw you needed help and we felt badly about your arrest. I was the one who suggested a different identity and disguise. And that cost you almost two months of your life. Anyway, we put our resources together and did the right thing for you. I will tell everyone that you are very happy now and staying home with your family. We will miss you."

"You are all welcome to visit," he quickly adds with excitement. "By the way, I was kept in detention for exactly 50 days. I counted every one of them. I look forward to seeing you. There are so many historical things I can show you here. I will call you periodically so we keep in touch. Stay well and good luck on the pamphlet."

When the call ended, Stan begins thinking about the uncanny coincidence of his dream of Famir and then a real phone call from him immediately after. It's as though Stan is made aware of a side of Famir he never knew. Just then, Stacey walks into the bedroom.

"Hey, sleepy head, were you on the phone? I came in a few minutes ago and you were out cold."

"Something weird just happened. I had a dream that Famir and I were talking in front of the church. He was wearing Islamic robe and hat and talking to me about the injustice in the Palestinian community in Israel. Then the sound of my phone woke me up and guess who was on the phone? Famir! Weird, no?"

"No, it's scary! What did he say to you in the dream?"

"He said he's forced to have a dual identity. First, he's a Christian, but then he's also Arab and still looking for a home that was taken away...and he's honor bound to make things right..."

"What do you think that means?"

"I don't know," Stan says, "except that he feels a duty to support Palestinian right to exist. Funny, how all we hear from that region is the right of Israel to exist."

"What about on the phone? Did he say the same things?"

"No, on the phone he was nonchalant about his liberation. I mean he was grateful and all that, but casually said he's not coming back, because they're no longer looking for him since he's not involved in peace missions. He said his place is at home with his family now."

"Stan, I can understand about the family thing, but the other stuff? I don't know. Yeah, in a way I feel like we were all used for a different purpose, maybe for a higher cause. We were kind and caring toward one person; and that allowed him to succeed in a greater cause. Maybe, overall, that's a good thing."

"Look, honey, we did whatever we could to help him with his problem, and I'm glad things turned out well for him. And we feel good about it. Let's not keep score. It's a win, win and leave it at that."

"I know, Stan," she continues as though on the cusp of something important, "but don't you see, all of our efforts helped liberate Famir from a prison on the other side of the earth. We look on it as a kindness that restored freedom to a good person to achieve good things that eventually help others. But what if Famir's reason for going back was not just to reunite with family?"

"Wow! Your mind is working overtime! Come to think of it, in my dream he did not accept the axiom that two wrongs do not make a right."

Chapter 37

SOIL AND THE SOUL

S tan and the youth director, Tom, are outside the church inspecting the organic farm. The young adults in the parish undertook to till the soil in spring, seed and fertilize according to organic guidelines.

"It's been a team effort, Father. Since spring we have been learning all about organic farming from Sunshine Farms here in Sycamore. Mr. Jordan was most helpful in teaching us all the secrets of soil care and use of proper natural fertilizers and biological pest controls. He even came here to show us how to control insects, weeds and pests naturally."

"That's great, Tom, you all have done a great job. You must now know that man's relationship with the earth is a sacred one. It's a matter of giving back to the earth what we take from it. So you learn to take care of the soil that gives you food. Few people realize there's such a thing as Ethics in farming."

"Thanks, Father, you're right. Well, anyway, the fertilizers we use are mainly bone meal which is high in phosphorous and feather meal with the highest level of nitrogen. We also used compost and organic fertilizers from animal and human waste. That part the girls weren't crazy about handling. So, what do you think?"

"Fantastic, Tom. Show me what we have!"

"Okay, on the north side of the church, you can see several rows of zucchini, then rows of tomatoes, cucumbers and beans. On the south side, we have beans, beets, potatoes and of course, corn. All plants enjoy east-west exposure to the sun. So, they get sunlight all day long. We had to protect the perimeter with chicken wire, so the rabbits don't eat everything. Mr. Jordan gave us more than enough. The girls felt sorry for the rabbits so they actually made a small patch for them in the back with grass, carrots and cucumbers."

"That is interesting! Tom that's the ethic of care exhibited by women. Not that we wouldn't do things like that—we just don't think of it! Anyway, when is harvest time?"

"I would say in a couple weeks, although we may start gathering tomatoes next week so they don't get overripe. Smell the tomatoes, Father? Now that's organic-natural food!"

"We received about a hundred small baskets—they're in the family room. You know what you need to do, right?"

"Not sure Father. Do you want an assortment or keep the veggies in separate baskets?"

"Well, see what your inventory looks like, but maybe start out with assortment baskets first. Be sure to include a couple non-perishable items that we've been collecting all year long, like dry goods and can goods to fill the basket.

"Let me know when you've finished and I'll post the news online and on our outdoor signage. We have many in our own village in need of food. Thanks so much for your hard work. I really appreciate it, Tom. We are doing a lot of good for people in need."

Tom has to leave and Stan heads back to the office. On his desk is a Fed Ex package. He tears into it to see samples of his pamphlet in Hebrew and Arabic. There is a note:

Enclosed are samples of your first foreign language pamphlet. As you can see, it turned out really well. The copy blends in with the same illustrations. We delivered 10,000 to the distribution com-pany. I believe they have your mailing list to send them out. Also, enclosed is the invoice. Usual terms, Father. Good luck. —Tony

Stan's phone plays the hymn. He picks up. It's Edith, his mother.

"Stan, Dad is in the hospital! He ran a high fever last night, shaking all over and he had trouble breathing. An ambulance took him to NCH hospital here in Naples. I'm here now. They say it's the virus. I can't even be with him, he's quarantined."

"I'm so sorry mom, how is he doing?"

"They put him on a ventilator, it doesn't look good, son. But he's on a treatment that has worked with other patients."

"What is it, mom?"

"I don't know."

"Mom, ask if it's Pnemochlo...something. That's the miracle drug that has worked."

"Okay, Stan, I'll check. I have to go now. We'll talk later."

Suddenly, the church farm output is pushed to the back of his mind and Stan is now preoccupied with a personal problem calling for his undivided attention: his dad. In his ministry, he has witnessed three elderly people from the parish who were infected and recovered with this drug. It's already been tested and used for years. It's available and cheap. But he knows the big pharma community does not recommend it because they're looking for lucrative government contracts for new vaccine development.

Why does everything have to be about money? Why does the big picture get distorted and people just can't bring themselves to serve the simple task: to do the right thing without conditions or attachments? Stan can't help fielding these troubling thoughts.

He's convinced that over-thinking, deceiving, scheming, complicating, manipulating and over-intellectualizing has driven mankind to the brink of dehumanizing itself toward ultimate self-destruction. He feels a chill go through his body at the thought that maybe it's already too late; that people can no longer recognize the right thing. They may see it for others, but are blind to it for themselves. He thinks of his conversation with Tom this morning and the relationship we have with the earth.

211

If we take care of the soil and provide moisture and nutrients, it will deliver a cornucopia of nutritious food. Similarly, if we contribute and take care of people in need around us, our higher self shall be enriched with the moral nutrients from good works; and our alms-giving will renew the people we touch. Above all, our soul shall rejoice.

Stan's triumphant train of thought is interrupted once more with the Valerius hymn. He picks up.

"Hello, Father? This is Greg. I just got off the phone with the bishop. He invited Jim to discuss the Nazareth event and asked me and you to join them. Do you have time this afternoon? I can pick you up at two o'clock. Can you go?"

"Yes, sure! I'm eager to find out how it went in court."

"You know, when we came back after Easter, none of us knew what happened nor could we find out any information except that Famir was being held under 'administrative detention.' That's a fancy phrase meaning 'locked up in a cage with surprise interrogations and beatings at any time, day or night.'

"Even his own wife barely got to see him two or three times. She noticed scars and bruises every time—listen, I'll see you later."

For Stan, the ride to Rockton is filled with additional troubling allegations and suspicions of Famir from Jim's experience with him and his wife Amira.

"Well, you know Greg, Jim's a lawyer and lawyers always probe into all the angles and sometimes come up empty."

"Father, he's a lawyer, not a detective. Jim would not reach any conclusions unless there was probable cause for suspicion."

"Like what?" Stan asks defensively.

"Well, Amira, for example. He said she acted strange when they first met at his hotel. He wanted to go to her house to discuss Famir's defense. But he remembers she objected strongly to his visit and instead, drove to meet him at his hotel. When they finished, Jim said she left the hotel in a hurry, and began talking loudly in her phone with hand gestures.

"Also, she showed no hesitation to pay $5,000 for Jim's expenses and then, another $1,000 for the interpreter. It was as though she already had plenty of cash on hand, especially for his defense."

"So, what does all that prove, Greg? Just because she has money? Maybe she didn't want him to come to her house because it wasn't prepared for guests. You know how women are."

"I don't know, Father, I'm just telling you Jim's suspicions. Maybe he can shed more light on what he knows today."

Chapter 38

FUNERAL IN FLORIDA

William Rybak lies peacefully at Annunciation Church in Naples. Family, friends and co-workers shuffle quietly to get a glimpse of the waxen face, an empty vessel that once was home to a man called Bill Rybak. Stacey, Stan and his mother stare at him imagining his wide grin and positive disposition.

They keep coming, young and old parade past, daring to cast a solemn glance. Everyone finds a seat and soon, the church is full of the living, with only one at peace: the one without a mask. Whispering breaks out in different areas, everyone sharing feelings and thoughts. Crippled words are offered to Edith's family in front as they pass by.

Soon, the priest comes from the altar to face the casket. Holding a cross, he begins the service with several prayers followed by additional petitions from the priest leading up to "Again we pray for the salvation of the soul of God's beloved servant William. Forgive him of every voluntary and involuntary transgression."

More praise and glory hymns are spoken and chanted as everyone stands and files passed the casket for a final look before the pall bearers carry William's remains to the hearse. The family attends a final graveside service, then everyone is invited to a luncheon at a nearby restaurant. Stan and Stacey help his mother into the car and proceed to drive to the reception. The ride there is very quiet until Edith breaks the silence.

"Stan, why didn't you assist in the service for your own father? I expected to see you participate and eulogize him..."

"Mom! I'm a member of the family and my place is with you. When it's personal, it's much different..."

"Yes, but it's your father, dear. You would be more involved in the service on his behalf..."

"You mean, I can use my position to influence St. Peter to open wide the gate for him? Look, mom, if you were a heart surgeon, would you perform open heart surgery on me? No, you'd be in the waiting lounge like any family member, hoping that the doctor in charge does as good a job as you would have."

Following another quiet spell, Stan changes the subject.

"Mom will you be alright here on your own now?"

"I'll be fine, Stan, we had a wonderful life together and as you've always said..."

"I know, mom, 'We don't select when we debut...and we don't select when we exit.' I don't know how often I can come and see you with the ministry and this virus."

"I know son, look we've made many friends down here. Did you see all those people at church? They are all from here. So, don't worry about me. But I do want to see my first grandchild. When is the big day?"

"Sometime in April, mom, maybe the second week."

"That's great, I'll be sure to visit when that day arrives."

The restaurant manager escorts the 25 plus guests into a private room. The priest acknowledges Stan to say Grace, but Stan defers back to him. Sitting across from Stan are a man, his wife and a little girl.

"We're very sorry about your dad's passing, Father."

"Thank you very much, and your name?"

"Yervent Alexanian, my wife Maria and daughter, Esther."

"Where is your home, Father?" asks the young man with bushy hair and glasses, trying to be sociable.

"I live in Northern Illinois, about 50 miles west of Chicago. My parish is in town, much smaller than Annunciation. How about you, what do you do?"

"I teach Ethics and Philosophy at Hodges University here."

"You are Armenian, right?" Stan probes gently.

"Yes, that's correct. My parents were from there. They escaped in the mid-1980s when it was part of the Soviet Union and came to America. But I was born here. If they stayed another two years, they would have seen a free Armenia."

Stacey looks at Maria and is impressed with her olive complexion, her poise and well behaved child.

"Maria, is your family Armenian also?"

"Oh, no. My father is Greek and my mother is Turkish."

"Very interesting," Stan pipes in. "How did they meet?"

"My father ran a ferry service among the northern Greek Islands in the Aegean. He would navigate through the various islands and end up in Mytilene near the Turkish coast. Then he'd make the journey back to Piraeus. On one trip she boarded at Mytilene on her way to Athens and it was love at first sight!"

As Stan listens to this adventurous romance on the Aegean, he's thinking about Armenia and how it was possible for the Soviet Union to relinquish control and yield to its independence. Then he thinks about the British who conquered Palestine from the Ottoman Empire in 1917 and who ultimately engineered the creation of the state of Israel on Palestinian land some 30 years later.

"Have you ever been to Armenia?" Stan asks Yervent.

"No, I haven't," is his reply leaving Stan to understand with his tone that he has no plans to ever visit that country.

"Well, One day you may wish you did visit the country of your parents. Don't get me wrong, there are people whose ancestral home no longer exists and they would give their left arm to get it back; and here you already have one and it's not on your radar..."

Stacey steps on Stan's foot to let him know he's out of line, but fortunately no damage is done. Meantime, some of Edith's friends come over to commiserate and keep her company while these deep conversations go on.

"You know, Father, you're right. Since the country was occupied by the Soviet Union, my parents lived under siege. And then the risk, the fear and expense of finally escaping to America, all I could think about was that I would never go there. And that impression has stayed with me even though it's been an independent country for 30 years now. Funny, how some feelings live inside you long after they should have been reviewed and altered. Thanks for resetting my compass, Father!"

"That's what I do for a living! Tell me, Yervent, in what context do you teach Ethics? I mean, do you invoke any absolutes about human behavior, or has everything become relative today?"

"Interesting question. Without getting too academic, let's just say that cultures around the world differ. What one celebrates, another may condemn..."

"I understand that. I meant in the United States primarily."

"Okay. That does not mean we have a homogenous culture. We have people here from all over the world who bring their culture with them. We are currently obsessed with diversity. That means we condone and are sensitive to values of individuals and groups even though they may conflict with one another.

"For example, if in an Arab family a daughter loses her virginity prior to marriage, this creates dishonor to the family. It may be morally acceptable to kill her to restore the family honor, whereas here, we condemn the practice. So, honor killings are justified in an Arab culture in America, even though they're tantamount to murder.

"So, with respect to Ethics, we no longer operate with principles, but with rules. Yes, you may say that principles and values have yielded to Relativism. Why? For one—and you know this better than me—the decline of the authority of religion in Western culture. When it comes to moral evaluation, we choose the path of least resistance..."

"Say, you two, cut out this academic talk," Maria rejoins her husband. "Are we ready to go? A pleasure meeting you, Father. Again, sincere condolences."

Chapter 39

SAUL'S REVISITED

All through the busy summer months, Jim kept asking Stan to go to Saul's Resort. He not only left text messages, sent emails, even periodic phone calls, he even pleaded and nagged Stan like a child begging for a new bike:

"Father, let's go this fall."

"How about one last time this year!"

"It must be beautiful up there now!"

"Surely you can get away for a couple days!"

Well, October has arrived again and Stan is able to secure a cabin for Tuesday, Wednesday and leave Thursday morning. Saul had to shuffle a couple people to make it happen. Stan informs Jim of the reservation but neglects to say that he's probably more excited to go than he is.

Stan finished breakfast with Stacey and caught up on things to be done. Now, he heads out to Hampshire to pick up Jim and then take route 90 to begin the northern journey. As he pulls up to his house, Jim is outside waiting for him. No surprise there. He loads up his bag, tackle box, rods and a bottle of bourbon and they are North woods bound.

Entering Wisconsin, both notice trees and shrubs slowly transforming from green to beige and ivory, especially the sugar maples. Around Madison, the maples acquire a rust color and burgundy on some of the Japanese maples.

"I suspect you've given this trip a lot of thought," Stan says.

"Oh? What makes you think so?"

"You've only been talking about it for months."

They both laugh and are thinking of ways to slow down the clock when they leave.

"Seriously, Jim, what are you looking forward to the most?"

"I don't know, it's hard to say. I guess just being there. I remember the time when I was ten, my parents took me to Disney World. There we were at the porpoise pavilion while my dad was explaining how smart these mammals are and all the tricks they could do. But I remember my mind was focused on the rollercoaster rides and I couldn't think about anything else..."

"So, what happened?"

"Well, when I finally got on the rollercoaster for several rides, it was over quickly and in the end it did not deserve all the anticipation and mental hype. Meantime, I missed out on learning about and enjoying the porpoises. The same thing about this place. You need to know where to look for lasting enlightenment."

"Jim, I think you're getting the picture."

North of Eau Claire, the October colors begin to resemble Van Gogh's palette. The honey locusts turn bright yellow blending with scarlet black gum trees while the dogwoods add another hue of orange. Then they notice the famous river birches that release their bark in sections much like the partial peeling of a banana where the peels curl and hang down. Unlike other forms of life, Stan knows these trees can be counted on to behave consistently year after year.

For the next hour, they listen to the motor and the waffling sounds of the wind inviting itself in from a partially opened window. Since last October, Stan can't believe all that's happened. The drama with Famir and the outcome of his release shrouded in mystery; the pandemic which included his dad on a long list of casualties; the church garden which helped over 30 needy families in the area; the impending tax levy knocking on the church door and the local trial with the oil company.

Several hours later the Subaru reaches Route 70 and proceeds to turn west toward 9-Mile Bar. It would be an unforgivable oversight if they just drive passed without checking in with Herb and Sally.

"Hey, Fatha, good to see you!

"Hi, Herb, you remember Jim from last spring."

"Yeah, how you doin? I remember you, looking really dapper like in GQ magazine. Where's the silk scarf?"

"Well, Herb, I learned to tone it down and simplify."

Herb leans on the counter as though to release a coveted secret. He looks left and right and lowers his voice.

"You know you guys come at the right time. Over at Saul's they were catching fish like crazy last couple days."

"Oh, we're not here to catch fish, Herb," Stan corrects him.

"Oh? Is it the beer and fresh air?"

"No! We're here to go fishing."

Herb lets out a peel of laughter only he can deliver. The commotion draws the attention of Sally and others hunched over the bar.

"You see, Herb," Stan now leans forward and lowers his voice. "There's a lot more to fishing than catching fish...catching fish is just an added bonus!"

Herb continues laughing and Stan realizes he just doesn't get it.

"What are you cackling about?" Sally yells at Herb. "Say Father Stan, you know the building next door, that we hoped you would buy?"

"What about it? Somebody buy it?"

"Yeah, you know, Dick's Sporting Goods gave Jack an offer they thought he couldn't refuse, a lot higher than what he was asking."

"Don't tell me that Dick's bought it!"

"No, Fatha," Herb breaks in, "Jack told Dick's to take a hike. He sold it to two local guys from Flambeau. They gonna sell fishing and hunting gear. Gave 'em good terms too, so they can get on their feet."

"That's good to hear," says Stan. "Hey Sally, how about a couple bottles of Leinenkugel so we can get in the right frame of mind here."

"You got it—on the house, Father," Herb pipes in. "Glad you didn't say *Get in the right Spirit!* All enjoy a hearty laugh, looking at Stan to make sure he didn't take offence. Sometimes Herb gets carried away and forgets who he's talking to.

"I didn't say that," Stan stares into Herb's eyes, "because you might think I mean a shot of whiskey with the beer!"

More laughter breaks out, everyone pointing at Herb. Jim looks at his watch: 5:30. They thank them for the drinks and start heading toward that long gravel road to the main lodge. They take in the colorful foliage along the road and notice Saul's farewell shingle pointing the other way. Soon the familiar dinner bell will sound at Saul's and they will know they are really here.

Chapter 40

Magical Loon Landing

The only available cabin fronts Little Bass Lake, which is just fine. This lake is a bit wider and deeper than Long Lake and you can see all the shoreline. It really doesn't matter to Stan as the Adviser will find them easy enough. They drop the fishing gear on the porch and take their bags inside the two-bedroom cabin.

Ordinarily, check-in usually occurs at the desk in any hotel or resort. But here, real check-in for Stan happens at the pier. They walk down a steep staircase and sit at a bench facing the wide lake. Jim doesn't say much this time. He knows his courtroom articulation skills have no audience here.

They wear lined jackets as the temperature slides into the 40s. Like two kids at summer camp, they close their eyes and breathe in the pine-scented air. Straight ahead the weakening sun is preparing to retire and paints an orange hue across the horizon.

While deep in thought, they detect a faint dinner bell sound at the outskirts of hearing range. "Duly noted," Jim whispers.

"Stan, we know trees drop their leaves every fall, face winter naked and then they're reborn in the spring with a new set of clothes. But what do evergreens do? Don't they have a shot at re-birth?"

"Well, we don't notice it," Stan responds, "but evergreens do shed their needles every two to five years. But it's a gradual replacement. Unlike deciduous trees, evergreens are not that dramatic about their regeneration. They do it gradually while showing off their green coat all year long. Say, let's get something to eat to help with our regeneration. We have half an hour before they stop serving."

"Good idea, Stan."

They sit at the Rybak table and begin eating a Caesar salad with hot bread rolls. Soon a server brings a platter of pasta and one of meat balls with a side dish of parmesan cheese. And for dessert, there's a soft serve machine about five yards away. A man with a teenager approaches the table.

"Are you Father Rybak?"

"Yes, and you are?"

"My name is Arthur, this is my son Robert. I wonder if I can talk to you for a minute after dinner..."

"Just the two of you?"

"Yes...we just came a few minutes ago. We're from Milwaukee."

"Why don't you join us, just the two of us here, and all this food. Please meet Jim Winters."

They sit and begin serving themselves and Stan feels the energy level rise from the two guests looking for a release. So, Stan breaks the ice.

"So, what's on your mind Arthur?" He looks at Jim. "My friend Jim is like a brother to me. You are getting the attention of a priest and a lawyer at no charge!"

"It's these video games, Father. They're not only violent where massive loss of life is a given...but I'm concerned about the lack of justice, you know, when the good guys win? Nothin' like that and practically anything goes! It encourages players to accept violence and feel okay about it..."

"How old are you, Robert?" Stan asks.

"Fourteen."

"Do you get to kill anyone in the game?"

"Yeah, that's what it's about, killing and winning."

"Does the game allow you to talk to those people so that the killing doesn't get to happen?"

"No, Father, that's not in the software, only chasing and killing them."

"What games do you enjoy playing?" asks Jim.

"Last year I was playing Fortnight—it was great! Then I got Hades and Cyberpunk and I really like them."

Stan looks at Arthur and asks the cost of these games.

"About $60 Father, but he earns the money by doing chores..."

"So, what's the problem?"

"I don't think such games are good for him, he's neglecting his studies and ignoring family..."

"Arthur, do you want my advice?"

"Why, yes, of course!"

Stan now moves all his attention to Robert. He tells him that his dad has cause to worry about the content of the games and that Robert needs to listen to what he has to say.

"Robert, you may not know it but if you keep this up, you could be destroying your future. Your dad may not know how to tell you this, but I do! You are to either throw these videos away or return them to the store. While you're there, ask if you can trade them all for *Airship Genesis/Pathway to Renewal*. It's a video game, but it doesn't rob you of a sense of right and wrong. The only violence is against evil.

"As for earning money for work around the house, since when is your father an employer? He brought you into this world. You live in his house, he feeds you, buys you clothes, pays for your school, medical and dental care. In short, Robert, you owe this man your life! And you want to be paid for taking out the garbage?"

Arthur and son look at Stan and Jim in shock from what they just heard. But Arthur knows Robert is overdue for a reality check.

"We rest our case," declares Jim.

"Anybody for ice cream?" asks Stan.

The next morning is a day on the water. Fortunately, it is sunny but the temperature is just barely 47 degrees destined to reach 65. Stan goes into the bait shop for a dozen large minnows for musky bait. They load the gear on the boat and Stan takes the back seat to man the motor. Jim sits in the middle facing the front. He checks his reel and runs the line through his rod. Stan navigates out of the pier at slow speed while looking for a lure to attach.

The morning sun is coming up behind them, shimmering through the golden brown hickories near the shore. Surprisingly, there is no wind and all the trees appear to be at rest. At about 30 feet deep, Jim sends a jig to the bottom hoping to lure a lake trout. Stan does the same thing, with an ideal rig under the calm waters. It allows for silence and contemplation where both lines gently bounce their lures on the bottom.

"So, the bishop was pretty upset about Famir," Jim recalls the meeting.

"Yeah, we all took a chance adding him in the group while he pretended to be someone else. Of course, that was my idea. It's a good thing everyone else is well known in Nazareth and they were released."

"What are the chances we'll ever see him again?"

"Pretty slim, I think, but you never know!"

"Say, have you heard from Greg recently? Does he still live near you?"

Stan's bobber sinks and line is being pulled quickly. He tightens the drag and reels in a little only to come to a dead stop. He reasons the boat was not moving, so the line must have been pulled from below.

"This is typical of lake trout," Stan says. "They will pull and run and then sit tight for the longest time and makes it feel like your line is snagged under a rock. If it could send a message, it would say: 'I can hang out here a lot longer than you can up there holding a rod.' Jim, why don't you try a minnow as bait and go down deep for a trout, walleye or musky."

"I'm doing just that. I still remember that walleye earlier this spring."

"I got news for you. You'll never forget it!"

While Stan is babysitting his lake trout and Jim is combing the deep for the big one, a large bird flutters overhead forcing Stan to duck really low almost losing control of his rod. At first he thought it might be an eagle which can scratch your face apart.

"Look, Jim, a loon almost hit me, ducked just in time."

"Look at him, he's still flying around us," Jim shouted.

They never saw anything like this before. A loon with an attitude. Stan recognizes the Adviser with the unusual markings. He waves both arms in the air, takes his phone to capture this special visit. The loon makes another pass and descends toward the bow. With cupped wings that break the fall, he lands gently on the wedge seat in front. Wings folded, he sits quietly to watch his friend. Stan crosses himself while Jim sits stunned—a lawyer at a loss for words!

Stan admires the heart-shaped crown with zebra collar and checkerboard wings and those tiny glassy eyes that see everything. He moves the minnow bucket gently closer to the loon with his foot. As expected, the surprise visitor investigates the contents. It bends down and grabs a big minnow, a favorite snack.

The bird then unpacks its wings, spreads them wide and fans the air repeatedly, pushes with its web feet and lifts off. He flies overhead silently, turns toward the middle of the lake and lands on the water, the minnow still wiggling in its beak.

A clear blue sky is backdrop to a low-lying white cloud and a dark charcoal grey one, side by side. Stan notices the white tufty cloud gradually but decisively, eclipse the dark one, a most unusual sight; though Jim's attention is drawn to a small fluffy feather left behind. Both grown men remain speechless through this incident. Stan holds up the quill.

"Jim, this is a gift of peace he left for us. Today, the excitement occurred not in the water but in the air. This creature crossed the line, from his habitat to ours, from his world, to ours...do you understand what just happened, Jim? Think about it! It conquered the fear that characterizes the species as a creature in the wild and he dared to defy nature's boundaries of safety."

THE TAMING OF THE LOON

"Exactly!" Jim exclaims, finally snapping out of it. "Stan, imagine a hunter tracking a lion. He follows the beast into its lair. He leaves his weapon outside and crawls in with a slain rabbit in hand and sits gently in plain view. There they are, two of God's creatures who would never draw this close in peace, sitting near each other. Then the hunter stands, places the rabbit down and slowly crawls out without looking back.

"Stan! That's exactly what the loon just did with us. The hunter is the loon and the rabbit is the feather. Do you know anyone with the courage to do something like that?"

Stan takes a nail clipper from his tackle box and cuts his line. The thought of struggling with a sluggish lake trout seems anti-climactic now. They both expect that one day the trout will loosen the hook's hold and spit out his $20 lure. In the meantime, a loon had been tamed and they witnessed an unnatural event they would talk about the rest of their lives.

Stan wonders how his ministry can develop such trust and courage in people where they summon the will and daring to cross over into uncharted areas of human understanding, where honesty and trust can conquer fear. His studies and his faith clearly demonstrate that Jesus boldly crossed over into man's lair many times to deliver his message of peace and love among all people. He encouraged those he touched to cross over without fear and extend their boundaries of kindness and caring.

Chapter 41

COMPROMISED TRIALS

B ecause of the ever-threatening pandemic, Lab-Rinth has been
given special consideration for a fast-track development of the
vaccine. The process is given a green light to be expedited with federal
government support. Since Greg returned, round-the-clock testing has
resumed with unprecedented haste and pressure. He is in his office with
Cecil Lynch, an FDA inspector.

Cecil has been assigned to monitor the pre-clinical data and help
move along the process assuring that tests are conducted according to
Good Lab Practices. Cecil is on hand almost every day looking over
everyone's shoulder. He must decide and approve that testing is safe
for humans prior to beginning Phase I.

"Cecil, what do you think, are we ready for the Clinical Development
Stage?" Greg asks.

"Yes, I believe we are. Remember, Greg, the main emphasis
throughout is safety. Once I check the reports, I'll give you clearance
to secure, say, 25 to 50 volunteers—Minimum 25, if you can't get more.
You understand they have to be healthy with no exposure to the virus…"

"Jesus, Cecil! I know that! We will look for adverse reactions with
varying doses. We will also find out how well the vaccine works to
induce an immune response which addresses the efficacy of the drug.
I will make sure you get reports on this part of the process as quickly
as possible."

"Look, Greg, I know we're all under a lot of pressure, but you have
to understand, I have a job to do. We let this vaccine out without

exhaustive testing just to satisfy the politicians, many will die and heads will roll in Washington."

"I appreciate your concerns. I, also, have a job to do and I'm not going to cut corners and deliver a product with inherent risks that could have been mitigated. My name is also on that vaccine."

"I understand perfectly, Greg. Let's work together and get this done right. We can work quickly, but we have to cover all our bases and not be guided by the calendar—or Washington."

"I agree. Thanks for your help."

"I won't be here tomorrow or Friday. So, we'll catch up on Monday, okay?"

Greg heads over to his office to catch up on paperwork and messages. He reads a report on animal side effects and discovers that a rat given a mild dose of the vaccine died. This development adds to an already sick feeling he's been stifling regarding the scuttling of Pneumochlorin.

He calls the lab to speak to Wayne.

"Wayne's phone, this is Spero."

"This is Greg, Spero. I'm checking if you received the toxicology report on the rat we lost."

"Not yet, Greg. Wayne expects it sometime today."

"Okay, thanks. We're going to need a side effects report from animal testing by next week; including several levels of dosage. Make sure the report breaks out the dose amounts."

"Will do. We should finish that segment next week, no problem. And I'll get that rat report on your desk when it comes in."

He opens his personal laptop to see what's going on with the church. There's an email from the bishop.

"Greg, please call me...it's important."

Greg checks the time: 1:00 p.m. He punches the diocese number.

"Hello, Miriam, it's Greg. The bishop is expecting my call."

"I'll put you through right away."

"Hello, Greg. We have a real problem! It's about money, of course. We have 65 churches in this diocese and we're not getting a nickel from any of them."

"What about corporate pledges, Your Grace?"

"Those have dried up too. Look, we can function as a diocese for the rest of the year by drawing from our money market fund. But I'm worried about the old people's home. We usually support it. But there simply isn't any money to keep the doors open. I hate to lose it to the state. You know what happens to programs they run!"

"Look, your Grace, let me check with our company. Maybe I can get some money for us. Give me a couple days."

"Thank you, Greg. Banks are no help now. I don't know where else to turn."

Greg thinks about the Federal money Lab-Rinth received. Surely they can spare a couple bucks to support a local charity. He punches Maggie's number and relates the financial problem of his church. He tells her that the nursing home under the auspices of the diocese is sinking in default and the company can sure use a deductible donation now that they received a big chunk of money.

"I don't know," she pauses, "I think Philip was looking to donate to the Malaria Foundation for African relief."

"Maggie, can't you request a local donation instead? People are suffering here as well! I guess you need to ask, which is the greater good?"

"Greg, let me see what I can do. I have a phone meeting with him tonight"

"Thanks for your help. All we can do is try. Let me know what you find out."

Greg's become aware of the domino effect this pandemic has on every facet of business and personal life. Everything and everyone is connected to the main hub of human interaction. If something serious happens to any part of the chain, everyone suffers. He calls the diocese again and finds out the bishop is in a meeting.

"Father John, tell the bishop, I should know one way or another later tonight or in the morning. He'll know what I mean."

"Sure thing, Greg. Will do."

The next morning, he checks his phone and sees a text from Maggie.

"Talked 2 Phil. He doesn't care one way or another. He said if he can help your church, why not! How 'bout that? Tell your bishop there's $1 million for his nursing home. I'll give you some papers that have to be filled out for the state and federal."

Greg can't believe it! He'll be the hero of the year with the diocese. *I'm not chairman for my good looks,* he thinks. He texts the diocese that all is well and he'll make a follow-up call later. He savors this positive feeling which mitigates the moral concessions building at the lab.

At the company the pressure for the vaccine is all over the building. Everywhere he looks he sees imaginary signs.

"Greg! Get that vaccine going!"

"Greg! The vaccine! You don't have much time!"

"Greg! How is the vaccine coming along?"

These alerts are bouncing around in his head as he makes his way to the testing lab. He feels the pressure to move the testing to humans hoping there are no snags in the immune responses in animals.

He checks his phone to see a text from the vice president's office.

"MP wants update on the trials ASAP. Advised Cecil Lynch to help move process quickly."

Great, he thinks. *Now I have the VP on my back. I wonder when I will hear from the Man himself!*

Just then Spero rushes in with a sealed report and hands it to Greg.

"Thanks, Spero. Is this the rat report?"

"Yes, it is."

"Anything on the animal side effects yet?"

"So far, Wayne shows a 2% reaction effecting the kidneys, and this is with minor doses. As of today, the percentage for regular dose (to be an effective vaccine), is approaching 4%."

"I need that report ASAP."

"You got it!"

He thanks him and waits for him to leave. He cracks through the seal and takes out the report. He follows through the diagnostics to the cause of death: Acute hepatitis. Greg knows this is not good. This will delay the approval process and many from Washington will come for his head, even the Man himself. He decides to change the cause of death to cirrhosis of the liver.

This finding suggests the rat already had the disease before taking the vaccine. Cirrhosis can't possibly happen that quickly from a vaccine. Therefore, as far as he's concerned, the report is inconclusive and has no effect on the accumulated data. He states these comments on his report filing. He signs the report and includes it in the research data. The only report he's waiting for is the animal side effects. If that checks out they will be ready for human trials which will put the program on the scheduled fast track.

The next morning, the animal side effects report is delivered in a sealed folder. Greg breaks the seal. He reads through the preliminary jargon and comes to the finding: There is a 4% side effect on kidneys when the normal dose is administered on 400 animal trials.

He knows this is an unacceptable ratio: 16 recipients out of 400 stand a strong chance of contracting kidney damage. In other words, for every thousand people who take the vaccine, expect 160 to experience kidney damage or failure. Reducing the dosage would lower the risk but will also lose effectiveness.

This is, indeed, a conundrum for Greg along with the guilt that's building with the rat and his involvement with the Pnemochlorin suppression. But there is no way he will spend another 12 weeks for further testing and be able to deliver a viable vaccine by February 2021. It's becoming clear, a moral hazard is forming in his mind. He can't believe he's prepared to alter the 4% to 1% and put lives at risk. How could he live with himself when the casualty numbers start rolling in by spring and summer?

"When they come to my lab for explanations," he writes in a personal ledger, "I must be ready to report that the virus must have mutated or the particular recipient group is showing unusually high adverse effects to the vaccine and that we have to start over with testing. It won't be the first time that the medical community had to return to the lab to improve the percentage of side effect risk."

Deep in his heart he knows all this is justification for wrong-doing and no amount of rationalization could ever make it right. Doing the right thing would be to disclose the unaltered truth about the finding and continue testing until the data clearly shows the product is as safe as can be. But this option has now become unthinkable.

He now wishes he should have walked away as the Pnemochlorin was shelved for political and monetary reasons when it could have saved lives. But then, he would not have gotten the money for his church. He realizes alongside the dark shadow of lies, fraud and deception, a good deed often emerges in the clearing.

Chapter 42

Escape to Classroom

A snowfall greeted Famir when he arrived in New York a few days ago. He secured a studio apartment on the 11th floor for $2200 a month on 7th Street, barely a couple blocks from NYU campus. Classes for the spring quarter already began this week, so he completed his academic paperwork online.

Because of his Sociology Doctorate from abroad, he was assigned *Socio 5501,* (Analysis of Cultural Organization) to teach on a Tues/Thurs afternoon schedule. With additional campuses in Abu Dhabi and Shanghai, Famir learned the university is famous for global education and enjoys a continuing formidable foreign student population.

Surprisingly, his class is small enough to meet at the university. Famir does not value on-line teaching either. He feels preparing yourself for class is a necessary act of learning rather than sitting in front of a laptop in your pajamas. Twelve students are able to maintain a comfortable distance in a classroom that accommodates thirty. The course focuses on the dynamics of cultural development in urban areas with special emphasis on minority groups. Five of his students are graduate level while the rest are seniors.

He walks to the window and looks down toward Washington Square Park. Although it stopped snowing yesterday, the park's circular hedges and walkways display a creative pattern from above. Lower rooftops, also sport a white coat.

He opens his briefcase and takes out a contact sheet that Ibrahim had given him. It's a list of eight names with phone numbers including his own. The name with an asterisk is the team leader, Mohammad Najjar, whom he knows well. He was told to contact him as soon as he arrived in New York. He punches his number and prepares to speak in Arabic.

"Hello, Mohammad?"

"Who is this?"

"I am Famir Masoud."

"What is your middle name?"

"Karim."

"Where did you study abroad?"

"The International Institute of Social Studies, at the Hague, in Holland."

"Good. Where are you now, Famir?"

"I just moved to a small apartment on 7th Street near the university. I will be teaching a class on Tuesdays and Thursdays."

"It's supposed to warm up tonight and tomorrow. I will text you with an outside meeting place. Please delete it after you see it, okay?"

"Okay. I look forward to seeing you again."

Just as Famir shuts the phone, a text shows up on the screen.

"Checking how U R. Hope all is well. Call me.—Fr. Stan"

He's excited to hear from Stan and he's about to respond, but holds back. He thinks that may not be a good idea. In spite of his inclination to stay close to him, he decides it's better not to communicate at this time, as too much is at risk. Besides, he would have to lie regarding his whereabouts.

Then, an email alert gets his attention. It's from Jim Winters.

"Hi, Famir. Thanks much for the thoughtful gift: tie clasp with a loon spread across it. How symbolic! Means more to me than you'll ever know. Merry Xmas to you! Hope all is well—when will you come back? Call or email soon."

The winter has brought not only snow and cold weather but rising casualties and infections from covid-19 around the world. Hospitals are filled to capacity. Non-covid medical emergencies must take a number and wait.

Retail stores and restaurants which were partially open a month ago now are ordered to shut down. And the economic toll is difficult to imagine after a year of shutdowns everywhere.

On this Friday morning, Famir wakes up with troubling thoughts. Fortunately, he has no class today, so he has a few days to sort out his concerns and adopt a position he can live with. He realizes Mohammad is here to determine his effectiveness regarding the big event of 2021. He's almost afraid to find out what it is as he's still unable to forget his minor role in the Jerusalem bombing that led to unintended moral consequences for him.

Like most revolutionaries who justify radical and violent incidents, Famir has always felt that limited participation in a just cause is acceptable within boundaries. To confront injustice that's created by powerful governments, you have few options with which to react. What he is beginning to fear is once you begin to right the wrongs with violent events, boundaries tend to disappear. The limited display of resistance now takes on a life of its own and many people die.

At times, he almost regrets his association with Stan. It has made him more sensitive to the subtleties of human life, the little lies and indiscretions that build into uncontrollable beasts. They add up to shape who you are.

He especially recalls the parish bulletin he received where Stan addressed wrong-doing and evil; how justifiable wrong-doing can be managed and self-explained. But when it breaks through the restraints, it enters the world of evil. And he believes indiscriminate killing of innocent life resides in evil's lair. He realizes his compatriots do not have this understanding.

Deep into examining his mixed feelings, he's interrupted by a text alert. It's from Mohammad.

"Meet-Lafayette Café-Outside Chalet 4:30 PM Mon-Bring Nothing."

Famir quickly deletes the text and makes a mental note of the information. He remembers seeing the café a couple blocks down 3rd Street. He's wondering what "Bring Nothing" means. Perhaps don't carry anything like a binder or briefcase.

Temperatures in the high 30s have melted most of the snow by Sunday morning. Famir walks toward Washington Square Park to the Judson Memorial Church for services. He climbs the front stairs and pulls the door open to enter into a wide space with a large draped table in front.

A young man appears with mic in hand. New Age music plays softly in the background while a large screen shows nature footage. There's a running brook through the woods, an idyllic view of a country road framed with weeping willows swaying to the breeze.

"A heartfelt welcome, to everybody," shouts a man in his 30s wearing a purple turtleneck. "I am Pastor Bruce to help prepare us to receive God's Grace and abundant love. Let us pray. In these times of fear and uncertainty where a world plague has us in its clutches, we look to you, Lord, to give us understanding and healing. If this scourge is an act of evil, we pray you destroy it as only you can. But if it is a divine act to punish us, then Lord, please be merciful.

"My dear friends," he continues with his homily, "there are angels in our midst. We can't see them, but they are here sitting next to us. They're not wearing a mask and they don't have to observe social distancing. They have come to calm our spirit and fill us with hope and confidence to face the adversity that's upon us. Let us close our eyes for a minute and pray silently to the angel next to us."

This type of social based worship is a new experience for Famir. For him, this service is not anything like the ceremonial rituals at All Saints Church. Fr. Stan, or course, adds his charismatic flavor to make services more engaging.

"And now," Pastor Bruce announces, "Rev. Dr. Thaddeus Bartell will speak to us on *Making the Right Decisions*."

"Thank you, Pastor Bruce. And thank all of you for joining us today to give glory to God. Thank you for wearing your mask and allowing extra room for your neighbors. We do this for health safety alone. You realize no matter how many masks you have on, the Lord knows who you are. And he understands that distancing is only temporary. And this state-mandated separation has complicated our own Christian mandate.

"Every week we implore our faithful to draw near and make a neighbor their friend. My friends, it's the most caring thing to do, to touch someone with kindness and empathize with problems they're facing; to feed someone who's hungry; to offer shelter to someone who has none—and the way things are happening in this country, you'll see a lot of need out there.

"The point is, you can still make a difference in someone's life without actually touching them. Please, remember, there are always other options! You can deliver clothing, food, money to them. If you have an extra car, lend it to someone who needs it more than you. You can talk to them on the phone and make them feel better. In these troubling times, the suicide rate has increased because of despair and hopelessness. Think of the lives you can save if you just say you care and are willing to help.

"It's all about making the right decision to achieve a good outcome. So, when you're up against a major decision, think it through carefully and avoid decisions that may place people in harm's way. Have a wonderful day, show kindness and be nice to everybody!"

Chapter 43

MANHATTAN PROJECT

The unseasonable thaw continues on Monday with streets and sidewalks dripping with slush and ice droppings. Famir turns the corner unto 3rd Street where he can actually see the vertical marquee sign *Lafayette Café*. He checks his phone: 4:15. He has a feeling he must be punctual and be prepared for yet another test. He walks favoring the curbside as icicles release from buildings and shatter on sidewalks below.

Approaching the café, he notices several outside greenhouse chalets lining the sidewalk. Each has a private A-frame type unit. As he gets closer, he sees patrons through the glass and the three chalets appear to be taken. He's trying to figure out where to go when a man stands near a table and waves through the glass for him to come in. There are others with him.

Famir enters the restaurant to get access to the greenhouse. He walks into a warm winter village atmosphere with hand-woven rugs, hanging snowflakes, alpaca furs and ski-style accents throughout. Five men sit around two tables joined together, a raging fireplace a few yards away. Famir figures Mohammad reserved this private chalet in the heart of Manhattan and brought the others to meet him.

"Greetings, Famir," Mohammad shouts in Arabic. They are all dressed like New Yorkers with jeans, turtlenecks, khakis and scarfs. They appear to be having a good time smiling and talking, an unexpected mood for Famir. It nevertheless, helps him relax.

"Please meet Bilal, Cairo, Dalil and Emann," pointing to each. "This is Famir!" They cordially bow their heads smiling.

At this time a server comes into the chalet with pad and pen and everyone stops talking.

"Good afternoon gentlemen, my name is Eduardo. What can I get you all to drink?"

"Eduardo," Mohammad takes charge looking right at him. "I want to place our order for everything now, served in platters, family style for six, okay? First endive salad. For entrees, grilled Arctic Char w/eggplant, mint & cucumber; and rotisserie chicken. Two bottles of Rose, one bottle of Chablis and cold water for everyone without ice. We want these items all at the same time.

"Edwardo, we like wine and salad with our meal. We would like one hour for us to enjoy the meal without interruption. Please don't rush in to ask if everything is alright. We expect everything to be alright. Then, bring us caramelized apples with vanilla ice cream and coffee. Are we clear?"

"Yes sir, very clear." Eduardo leaves and closes door.

Mohammad reaches into a bag and distributes cell phones to all.

"These have been calibrated and programmed on a separate frequency. It doesn't mean they can't be hacked. It's just more difficult. Gentlemen, we can't rest on that, so we will use codes for everything we talk about. For example, my name is Maine, like the state of Maine, Bilal is Boston, Cairo is California, Dalil is Denver, Emann is Elgin and Famir, you are Florida. These are our new names.

"We will not use our real names from now on. The event is *Manhattan Project*. The target is the U.N. Building, but we never mention it by its name, EVER in phone, spoken, written or text. Instead refer to the target as *The Park*. Any questions?"

"Moham...Sorry. Mr. Maine," Bilal asks, "Denver and I work at the Park. When will we get our..."

"Listen, we will have other meetings to discuss details about who does what. For now, let's be clear on our names, the project and the target. No slip ups, okay? For any communication about the project you will use the new phone—and use it ONLY for project business."

Famir gets Bilal's attention.

"Tell me, Boston, you work at the Park, right?"

"Yes, I'm in shipping and receiving docks, actually, in charge of receiving. I check all deliveries coming into the building."

"What about you, Denver, what do you do there?"

"I'm a security guard, Florida."

Mohammad gets everyone's attention again.

"Now take a couple minutes to program everyone's ID and number in your phone so you can call anyone of us with one click." He passes out six sheets with project names and numbers.

For the next few minutes they tap and punch on their phones while looking at the paper. When they finish, Mohammad collects the sheets, folds and pockets them. Moments later, the door opens to the chalet and several carts are rolled in. They put their phones away and remain silent while three servers quickly place platters on the table with a stack of dishes and glassware. Three bottles of wine are opened and placed in the middle along with two pitchers of water in ice buckets.

"We will return in an hour with dessert, gentlemen. Enjoy."

Mohammad is pleased and pulls out a crisp $20 bill, slips it in Eduardo's jacket pocket.

They serve themselves and begin talking in English about politics and the upcoming Super Bowl game. After a while, Mohammad raises his glass.

"Gentlemen," he says in Arabic, "We drink to a successful and glorious event."

"Fe Sahetek!" (Good Luck) they shout in unison.

"We set up the day before," Mohammad continues in a low tone, "Friday September 10, everything needs to be in place, ready to Boom!

He gestures with his hands expanding in the air. "Denver, that's your responsibility. And you have to ensure overnight security. We will discuss the details next meeting.

"All day Friday and Saturday the symposium will be going on with plenaries, group meetings, luncheon and dinner. On Saturday night, 9/11 it will happen during the banquet in the Grand Ballroom of the Millennium Hilton. Our final meeting will include Ibrahim El-Awad, hereafter to be named "The Chef." He's the director of this auspicious event and the person I answer to.

"Florida, I will just mention to you on a need-to-know basis that your phone is different from the others. Your phone has the activating program to set off the fireworks. You will get the password on the 10th, the day before and we will review and practice what you need to do."

"Mr. Maine, am I to activate the detonation?" Famir asks.

"Don't worry about that now. That's to be determined later. We have eight months, gentlemen. Until then, you are all to remain in the city. Do not make any major changes and stay under the radar. You will be notified of the next meeting. Please carry the special cell phone at all times, fully charged—and don't lose it or leave it anywhere! Even though you have a code for it, it can always be hacked."

Eduardo opens the door and conversations stop. He wheels in a cart with chafing dishes and a container of ice cream in an ice bucket. He personally prepares each plate with garnish. A large coffee container is brought in with cups and saucers. Once everyone is served, Eduardo leaves the check and he and an aide exit the chalet without saying a word.

Mohammad looks at the check total: $412. He reaches in his pocket and counts out five $100 bills and slips them under a sugar bowl. Then he walks to the fireplace with a sense of purpose. He takes out the contact sheets and releases them one at a time on the weakening embers, as he watches each sheet burst into flames and curl over the logs.

Chapter 44

LIFELINE FOR SURVIVAL

In addition to the pandemic that has overstayed its uninvited visit, a barely perceptible wealth transfer has also occurred in American society. On the one hand, the investment community, especially the stock market, has enjoyed unprecedented wealth gain while society as a whole has slipped into a painful recession. Among many casualties, a surprising one is the church—any church or house of worship!

It's no secret that unemployment levels are very high, people are shut in and going to worship service has become a remote option rarely exercised. It seems putting food on the table and staying healthy have taken center stage. As a result, the Archdiocese of the First Church of the Apostles has fallen in emergency mode for economic survival.

As a steward of the Archdiocese, Greg, along with the other ninety-nine stewards, has been summoned to New York to help resolve the financial woes of the church. They take their seats in the auditorium while the hierarchy sit at a dais on a small stage. Upon hearing the treasurer's report, Greg feels a chill go through him. The chair recognizes him as he stands to begin discussions.

"Your Eminence, esteemed stewards of the church, in view of the clear and present financial danger the church finds itself, I'd like to dispense with the long speeches and ruminations and make a motion: that each steward contribute $1 million in increments of $250,000. If we give 25% now, that's $25 million for us to get back on our feet and pledge the balance by the end of the year. By then, we hope maybe things would be back to normal."

"I second the motion" an older voice is barely heard. The secretary records the motion seconded by Mr. Arthur Gregory, board member of Dow Chemical.

"Look, ladies and gentlemen," asserts a man in a 3-piece suit. "Greg is right. Corporate America has made a killing this last year. And, let's be honest, we all made a lot of money. So, the church can't depend on the membership at this time for obvious reasons. It comes to us, to where the money is. Look around you. We have corporate executives here, industrialists, hedge fund managers and those from the ever profitable tech industry."

"Ditto, Mr. Gregory. I agree!" shouts a lady from the front row. Let's do this, people. We must make the right decision as we're out of time. I move we close discussion and pass Greg's motion."

The secretary reads the motion and asks for a verbal confirmation. It's unanimous!

At this point, Archbishop Philip rises and faces the stewards.

"My good people, thank you for your generosity. I am obligated to call to your attention other areas we can tap for funds so we can ride out this terrible scourge. In addition, we have the *Tax man* now looking over our shoulder. We need to restore continuous revenue to be self-reliant. And I'm hopeful that will come soon.

"For one, we have, as you know, two major properties: the orphanage and the retirement home in Westchester. A medical group offered $26 million for the orphanage. The Catholic Church offered $85 million for the retirement facility. In addition, we've been approached by foundations with grants to sustain our ministry."

A lot of commotion is created by the prospect of selling the church properties. At this time Bishop Anthony of New York stands to add to the discussion.

"First, let me say I am relieved to witness the generosity of our loyal stewards. Thank you! As for losing out tax exempt status, I fear it would mean the eventual demise of churches everywhere. Some of our legislators are saying that providing this exemption benefit to churches is unconstitutional because government is supporting religion.

"The truth is the U.S. Government debt has reached unprecedented levels. Last year was not only a disaster in federal revenue, but society and the economy were totally shut down. In recent months the only spendable income most people have is the so-called stimulus check from Washington and unemployment benefits. It's provided by the Federal Reserve, since the government really has no money.

"Further, these politicians allege that a tax exemption is a privilege, not a right and there is no such support for it in the constitution. Again, the point is, local and federal governments are scrambling for money and there is no stone they won't look under. My good people, that is why they are looking at the church because they have run out of things to tax. This is truly a problem affecting the survival of all churches in general. We must find a way to stop it in its tracks.

"Now, on another matter, I have been in fruitful discussions with the Catholic Cardinal Fitzsimmons here in New York with respect to cooperation and harmony among our faiths. At least that's how I perceived our understanding. However, in our last meeting, he clarified his position not as one of harmony but one of unity. He said, he has a green light from the Vatican to begin talks with our hierarchy and leaders on merging our faiths in the face of growing indifference to religion in this country. Also, the Islamic expansion is threatening our existence.

"In short, the Cardinal is convinced the Christian world would do well to establish a united front against those forces aimed at destroying the Christian Legacy; and mount a campaign to expose the growing secular/social godhead growing in America.

"Clearly, gentlemen, I believe we are quickly approaching a time in the Church's history when we must act...go on the offensive to educate, protect and preserve our Christian heritage.

A few quiet moments follow to digest the moral hazards that lie ahead for the Church. Finally, The chairman asks for a reading of the proposals on the floor. The secretary stands to recite the offers in question:

1. Offer for Orphanage	$26,000,000
2. Offer for Retirement Home	$85,000,000
3. Offer to unite w/Catholics	Discussion
4. Offer for foundation grants	Discussion

A young man in the middle of the group stands to be recognized.

"Hello, everyone, I'm George Hallagan. I think I speak for all here when I say to mobilize our forces against the evil of taxation. As for the two properties, the financials clearly show they are self-sustaining. So, why even think about selling good equity for cash that is depreciating?

"Personally, I think we're going to be fine. We have a sudden infusion of $25 million to keep the wolves away and the other $75 million will sustain us the rest of the year and maybe longer. I say we leave things as they are, accept whatever grants are legally available and ignore the other money offers."

"I agree with George," says a man who does not give a name, though everyone around him knows who he is. "But what about the Catholic offer for a Christian union?"

The chairman yields to Archbishop Philip who steps forward.

"It is true, the Catholics have been on a unity path with us for decades. Any discussion on this topic invariably leads to the question of who's in charge after unity occurs. His Grace Anthony and I have discussed the Cardinal's overtures. You see, uniting with the Catholic Church would historically put them in charge because any divestiture of authority from The First Church of the Apostles is an abdication of leadership. Canons clearly dictate the scepter of primacy would then shift to Rome.

"So, my friends there is an ecclesiastical reason they want to merge. Historical protocols dictate the succession of power."

"But what about the greater good, Your Eminence?" the anonymous speaker continues. "Is this only about power and control? Do you not think they are also concerned about the future of the Christian faith? Are we not of a mind to relinquish some authority to preserve the faith?"

"These are good questions and we need to talk about them. But we are not at the precipice of extinction yet. We're just having financial problems. Does that mean we have to give away a 2,000-year-old faith?"

The chairman comes forward to announce a break.

"Ladies and gentlemen, please leave your material here. We are going next door for a break. We will return in 20 minutes to discuss conditions of the other dioceses in the country."

Everyone stands to stretch and make their way to the hospitality room for coffee and refreshments. Greg is pleased at the generous outcome from the stewards. Also he has a good feeling about Bishop Mark who recently banked $1 million from his company to keep the diocese in financial health until this virus goes away.

Chapter 45

A Blessed Event

After her first trimester of pregnancy, Stacey took a six-month maternity leave. Her delivery schedule is around first week in May—that's in about five weeks. However, she needed to finish the last month of on-line teaching leading into Christmas.

This hiatus has been her opportunity to gather her thoughts on pedagogy and begin putting them on paper. As she's reading all her notes, her mind is racing at the thought of sharing her ideas on a more inclusive education of children. While at home, she's determined to do what she always dreamed of and just never got to do: write a book about it. And now, it's finally going to happen.

Her mind is exploding with ideas. In addition to teaching reading, writing and arithmetic her way, she will include valuable instruction in Emotional Development, Critical Thinking, Study Skills, Conflict Resolution, Spiritual Intelligence and Manners/Social Skills. The tentative title is *In the Realm of Holistic Learning.*

"These categories of Education were never on a subjects list or syllabus," she reads from her notes. "They were included within the instruction of the required subjects by erudite and dedicated educators who took seriously the responsibility of shaping a young person's total persona. Even my parents often talked about the moral and ethical framework of primary education years ago. And these ethical sidebars were reinforced at home during those years."

Stacey began jotting down strategies and ideas in a school tablet back in the fall of 2019 while reading Bennett's book. She continued recording her thoughts especially when Stan was busy writing his pamphlet. She felt that now is her turn to teach children not only subject matter, but also how to build character regardless of race or ethnicity. Unfortunately, the latter has mysteriously vanished from primary education in the public school system.

She adds the following to her text: *There is no teaching of human values in public schools. Culture dictates values. And they happen to be social based. Parents even lose sight of traditional values they grew up with. They get trained to understand the new dynamic and support it.*

She remembers what Stan told her:

Stacey! This is not about teaching any religious ideas. Ethics is all about how people treat one another. What parent would object to discussing Right and Wrong with children? It can help restore abandoned values of honesty and respect for authority. In short, it can re-direct children to appreciate our diverse culture, love of country and pride in being a part of the American fabric.

Deep in thought, she continues to write these revelations that come to her so she can shape the strategies into a book narrative: *Teaching Math, Logic and Critical Thinking skills would be useful in thinking through mathematical calculations, even for a third grader.*

...dealing with conflict between two people, a discussion of Right and Wrong may be used to resolve their differences. History shows us irreconcilable differences which lead to war and thousands are killed. Left unchecked, conditions can deteriorate to genocide where millions are killed. Of course, you won't discuss graphic details of violence and war, but you can talk about characteristics of Good and Evil without invoking any religious rule book or doctrine.

She recalls Stan telling her that when destructive plans and events acquire a life of their own beyond our control, they reach the level of

Evil...that religious people rush to prayer while the others close their eyes and hope for the best.

She takes a break from her education strategies and goes into the kitchen to prepare dinner. She looks down to see her expanded abdomen and marvels at the miracle of childbirth. She realizes the gift she's given to actually make a person. It's miraculous events in life like this that she feels people take for granted.

...maybe that's the reason Stan needs to go to nature; because he finds clarity and closure. But then, why does he have to go back again and again? Perhaps the enlightenment achieved is fleeting and the epiphany surrenders and quickly dissipates. As a result, the human condition requires continuous infusions of inspiration at regular intervals. Simply put, one has to reset and start from the beginning each time. Perhaps I'll confront my Loon in childbirth, or my book.

While deep in thought, she hears the front door open and shut and begins removing dishes from the oven to place over hot pads on the table.

"Hi, honey, I hope it's you."

"No, it isn't! Look out, I'm someone else! Did you feel up to cooking today or should we go out?"

"Oh, no, the table is all set and I made beef stew the way you like it with small onions."

Stan helps her bring the platters to the table and he puts his ear to her stomach as she stands still and quiet for a few moments.

"I feel movement..."

"Yes, yes, I do too! I think she knows we're listening."

They sit down and begin eating. Stacey can't wait to share her thoughts and ideas about her book.

"Stan, you know I've been collecting ideas about a book I want to write..."

"Yes, that's right! Are you into it yet?"

"Well, I pretty much filled a notebook of ideas I need to explore... but I did want to ask your thoughts about something I'm working on."

"Sure. What is it?"

"When you go to Saul's and enter the world of nature, you're able to re-charge your spiritual batteries so to speak...and experience a new vision."

"Yeah, I take my prayers there and the problems that weigh on me are somehow reduced in significance and simplified. Then I'm able to clarify and settle them. I really have to work at it, though. But you're right. It is a sort of conversion."

"So, what makes that process easier to do in that setting? Why can't that happen here, in Sycamore, or in All Saints Church?"

"I don't know if I can answer that, except to say that it's a different kind of meditation. Here, we reside in the world of the living and invoke God's blessings for redemption of wrongs committed toward one another; and yes, we invoke the Holy Spirit to light our way and help us understand that our neighbor is our brother."

"Okay, once you are inspired by the magical environment and you acquire this sixth sense to expeditiously resolve your concerns, why must you keep coming back?"

Stan helps himself to more stew and bread and thinks about the question. He is impressed by the depth of understanding Stacey has developed and rarely expressed. Also, he's realizing that women like Stacey have a great deal to offer in the struggle for awareness and reconciliation. And it's not restricted only to the realm of care.

"I suppose the sudden flash of enlightenment and wisdom," Stan continues, "has a short life and needs to be revitalized on a regular basis... Just like when you attend church. At the end of the service one is usually buoyed spiritually. By the time he drives home, the heights his spirit had reached begin to slowly crumble throughout the week; and he's obligated to come again next Sunday to recapture those heights again.

"Stacey, when you're at the sanctuary of nature, however, you behold God's complete creation, from the foliage, to the lakes, the frozen tundra, the animal life, sunlight, the stars and moon. It's no longer about human interaction, but about seeking a relationship with the entire cosmos. And when you achieve this, it is equally short-lived as well and you must come back and recapture the sensation. But, for a few days, you are on Pegasus, the white stallion, flying bareback into the horizon."

"Wow!"

"So, tell me, how is your book on primary education going to express such deep spiritual values for 3rd graders?"

"Well, that's my problem. I'm already committed to the notion that children do have the capacity to understand these things. The trick is to find a delivery structure they can relate to. So, to develop spiritual intelligence in children, I have to think about how to present this kind of material in a way they understand."

"Ah, yes, the delivery!" Stan emphasizes. "So much effort is spent on the substance of the message in instruction, whether in a school or a church; and so little time is allocated for discovering and applying the appropriate delivery system."

Stan thinks about this deeply while helping with the dishes. He's pleasantly engaged intellectually and spiritually by his own wife whose depth of character he had not witnessed in a long time. As Stacey is storing the food away, both quietly think about the question at hand.

Stan realizes his limitations regarding the education of children, even though he organized tutorial material for Sunday school education. He knows he's just not up to the psychology and dynamics of learning. They walk into the family room to catch the nightly news on TV.

This breaking story from Rochester, New York, Lab-Rinth Pharmaceuticals, one of three companies working on a vaccine, has announced that Phase III trials are showing great promise. An approved vaccine is scheduled for distribution in two to three months.

"Stacey! Stacey! I think I got it!"

"What are you talking about?"

"I have an idea that may work for you."

"What do you mean?"

"You need a new paradigm for children right?"

"Right."

"Balloons! Children love balloons. What if you begin with a story that everyone has a balloon attached to them all the time? And inside the balloon are all the good and wholesome things, love of God and country, family and friends, good feelings about good deeds and a general sense of happiness and well-being."

"Okay, I like that model. So, what happens next?"

"Well, because we all have flaws and are not made perfect, there is a tiny pinhole in everyone's balloon; and as we go about our activities, we begin to lose valuable content a little bit at a time. We encounter situations where we may not make sound decisions; we may hurt someone knowingly or unknowingly; we may be disrespectful or lie, even think of stealing something. For each such occurrence, a little more goodness seeps out until after a while, the balloon wrinkles and loses its shape. We begin to feel empty inside and start to regret the things we may have said or done..."

"That's when you need to re-inflate!" Stacey jumps in.

"Exactly! Each person needs to find out how to re-inflate their balloon and feel whole again. It may not be the same remedy for everyone. Here is where you can examine and discuss options. How does one regenerate?"

"Stan! That's a wonderful idea—and it's so understandable, even for adults. I know exactly how to lay this out now. Stanley Rybak, you are something else!"

She hugs him but can't get too close as their daughter gets in the way.

"By the way," he says, "We have to discuss a name for our daughter."

"Oh, that's already settled. Her name is Amanda, short for Adamandia, my grandmother's name."

"I love it! I think you better write what we talked about before you forget."

Stacey opens her laptop and begins to organize the material. She's thinking of opening with an introduction on the need for revamping primary education to include essential skills missing in the modern classroom. She envisions six sections to her book and a few chapters to explain details within each section. She can finally share them with Stan.

"Stan, let me tell you what I will cover. Listen to this! The first category is *Emotional Development* which deals with a healthy range of human feelings and emotions that many youngsters are afraid to discuss with anyone. They includes *Joy, Anger, Sadness, Fear, Surprise, Disgust, Betrayal* and others. Students will have opportunity to discuss and examine these feelings while others may want to share. Even if they are reluctant to express them, the teacher can surely cover the subject to make students aware that it's natural to feel these emotions.

"Then, we should follow with the subject of *Manners and Social Skills.* This topic speaks to how young people of all races and faiths treat one another. Respect, sensitivity, empathy, listening skills and cultivating a desire to please and understand other people. Again students have the option to relate their own experiences, or the teacher can offer examples.

"*Study Skills* should be taught to students. When they are given assignments and homework, they need to learn how to study, follow instructions and complete assignments. This section can be teacher-based with time management and practical examples. Too many students do badly academically because they simply don't know study strategies.

"*Critical Thinking* can be taught to young students to promote logical thinking and sound reasoning which lead to sound conclusions in various learning situations; especially in Math and argumentation. For too long we've been teaching children what to think instead of how to think. Argumentation is not arguing or yelling, but rather an exercise in logical progression of thought.

"*Conflict Resolution* is another category to help students resolve issues in a peaceful manner; a close examination of the original cause of conflict. Not everyone agrees on issues and it's important to teach ways of talking things out and arriving at a settlement both parties can accept: truly a valuable lesson for future negotiations.

"Finally, *Spiritual Intelligence* is a challenging area where students are taught that many things happen in life that we don't control or even understand. Students can be exposed to the existence of a higher design in life, that as they grow older they can explore its deeper meaning and purpose. Those who do can cultivate a sense of awe and appreciation for the mysterious phenomenon called human life."

"Stacey, you've covered all the areas that build character and a foundation for future spiritual awareness! I love it."

"Thanks, Stan. I'm confident this is a great outline to develop into book format and hopefully re-direct primary academics. I just need to find an acceptable fit for this valuable learning program into school curriculums—which means, convincing the education culture. That's the next challenge."

Chapter 46

CONVERGENCE AT DIOCESE

B ishop Mark comes out of his office holding a mug of coffee. He takes a sip and marches to Miriam's desk.

"At ten o'clock I'm expecting Father Stan, Greg and Jim Winters. Wait until they are all here and show them into my office."

"Very good, Your Grace."

Stan and Greg arrive and both are wondering what this visit is all about while they listen to Miriam tapping on her keyboard. Finally, Jim walks in and Miriam escorts them into the bishop's office.

"Miriam, hold all my calls the rest of the morning."

"Very well, Your Grace."

"Gentlemen, get comfortable and help yourselves to snacks and drinks. I called you here because we were all involved in the Famir case and you should know the whole story—and it isn't over yet!"

The three visitors grab a bottle of water each while Greg adds a couple pretzels. They sit and anxiously wait for the bishop to continue.

"It all began when we were in Nazareth last Easter. The group was taken to police headquarters for questioning and I received a message at the hotel to go to a nearby outdoor café to meet someone.

"Well, after a few minutes, a man came to the table, quietly introduced himself as Benjamin Morris, Deputy Director of Special Operations; and he gave me his card. My first thought was *what has he to do with me?* He proceeds to tell me about a dangerous Palestinian terrorist named Ibrahim El-Awad, that they tracked him many times to take him out, but he always slipped away.

"I was listening to this as though I was part of this special operation to assassinate a wanted terrorist. But I let him talk to see why this man is sharing such classified intelligence with me. Also, he confided that El-Awad has at least two doubles that look like him, and the only identifying mark that would give him away is a long burn scar on the inside of his left wrist."

Stan is listening intently, troubled with mixed feelings about Famir and apprehensive about attending the Symposium on World Religions for which the bishop has already signed him up. He's wondering when the next shoe will drop. Meanwhile, Greg, who has become the hero of the church, feels great guilt about his actions with the vaccine development. Jim, on the other hand, suspects Famir and always had doubts about Amira.

"My patience was wearing very thin by now," the bishop continues, "but who was I to object or complain to a special ops director in a foreign country? So, here's the connection. This El-Awad will attend the symposium in New York on 9/10 and 11 at the Millennium Hilton and I am supposed to sit next to him! He said I made the perfect finger man because I had every reason to attend the event as a bishop and that nobody would ever suspect me."

"What does he want you to do?" Greg bursts out.

"When I confirm the burn mark on his wrist, I am to signal a positive I.D. (and I don't know what the signal is yet) and a sniper positioned in a hidden area will kill him."

"My God! At the banquet?" shouts Stan, astonished.

"Yes, totally unexpected!"

"Okay, I give up," says Jim. "Your Grace, why would you ever agree to be part of something like this?"

The bishop adopts a more conciliar tone as though he was expecting the question. He stands and leans on his desk displaying the back of his hands. Stan notices his fingernails have lost their luster.

"You see, gentlemen, the reason Famir was acquitted, had to do with that sealed envelope Benjamin gave me to give to you, to ultimately give to the judge. Inside was an order to drop the case against him. No aspersions on your legal skills, Jim, but in cases like Famir's, only guilty verdicts are normally handed down. In addition, he promised that the Christian minority in Nazareth will enjoy freedom and safety."

"I wonder how long that will last," Greg pipes in.

"No, it's not just an empty verbal promise. He put it into the municipal operations record, whether he's in office or not. This is the most critical part of the arrangement. Nazareth is known as the Arab capital of Israel. It once was known as the birthplace of Christianity. So, don't you see? I had to go along with it. It secures the 1/3 Christian minority to maintain a sacred legacy alive. Besides, we also help in removing another dangerous terrorist!"

"Your Grace, this is still a dangerous situation you put yourself in..." says Stan.

"How, father? I'm in a room of hundreds of people. The sniper is trained to know the difference between a bishop and a terrorist. Besides, I'll try moving away once the I.D. is confirmed."

Greg appears confused about something he's going over in his mind. Finally it falls from his lips.

"Why is El-What's-his-name attending this symposium? Anybody hazard a guess?"

"Yeah," asks Jim. "Why would a terrorist attend a religious symposium?"

"Ben told me," the bishop asserts, "he will be there to supervise a bombing attack somewhere in New York. He said as we get closer to September, the intelligence will uncover the location and he'll let me know. Gentlemen, Ben has been in touch with me ever since our talk. I get updates from him all the time. I trust his guidance and I believe he's an honorable man trying to do his job."

"When will you know?" asks Stan.

"The attack site may not concern us, (and I don't even want to know) but the seating chart will be the last information I get from Ben—and it will be a text, probably the last minute even as I walk into the banquet hall. That's my only worry—the seating chart.

"I remember Ben saying El-Awad's handlers change locations all the time, especially the last minute. So, I'm thinking what if he's placed at another table the last minute? I can't see myself walking around tables checking people's wrists!"

"What would you do, then, Your Grace?" asked Greg.

"I don't know."

"See, that's the problem with these arbitrary arrangements," Jim asserts with great concern. "Things never go as planned and you find yourself in great danger. How do you know this guy doesn't have his own security people looking out for him, just like Father's there for you?"

"I'm afraid, I can't back out of this, gentlemen. I have to keep my word and do the right thing. If I don't show up, they may arrest Famir and we'll never see him again—even his family! And God knows what may happen in Nazareth."

Stan has another troubling question: "Forgive me for playing cloak and dagger here, but what if the final seating, places El-Awad at a table where a sniper can't get a clear shot?"

"I don't care about that. That's not our problem." the bishop points out. "My job is only to point him out, not to make sure he's assassinated! That's one reason I asked you to accompany me to this event. Between the two of us, we'll be able to get a fix on him."

The bishop passes out copies of El-Awad's photo. They all walk over to the table to get a drink and cookies. They're very quiet, unable to shake off the reality that this is a dangerous mission no matter how you look at it. Finally, Greg takes the floor.

"Your Grace, I have to tell you! I don't think you and Father Stan alone can deal with this. I believe Jim and I (looking at Jim) should also come with you. That will make four of us checking the place out—and we're talking about a huge banquet hall! We can be texting one another and checking what we see. What do you think?"

Stan looks at both Greg and Jim and smiles. Then he fixes on the bishop.

"Your Grace, I think that's a great idea. We'll need all the help we can get. As you get messages from Ben, forward them to us."

"You're adding to the tension and danger now with your participation," the bishop cautions. "You two are not cut out for this."

"What makes you think you're James Bond types?" Greg probes.

"One more thing, gentlemen," the bishop says, enjoying a brief humorous moment. "I want you to stare at that picture until you memorize the face, especially the eyes and don't let it out of your sight...just four months away!"

4 Months Later

Western Civilization, including America,
is very much oriented toward materialistic life.
The culture generates too much stress, anxiety and jealousy...
So, my number one commitment is to promote awareness of
our inner values.

From kindergarten onward, children should be taught about
taking care of destructive emotions in order to become more
calm, have more inner peace.

The 14th Dalai Lama,
Time Magazine Interview, May, 2010

Part 4

Chapter 47

THE FOUR HORSEMEN

September arrives much sooner than expected. Weather forecast calls for a warm weekend in the Big Apple. Bishop Mark, the Champion of the Faith; Jim Winters, the Intermediary; Greg, the Redemptioner; and Stan, the Seeker of Truth check in at the Millennium Hilton at U.N. Plaza, New York City. It is Thursday afternoon, September 9 and Stan stretches out in a huge double bed after unpacking. He thinks about all that's happened in the last few months.

Amanda is almost four months old and she is a wonderful baby, full of smiles, giggles, near guffaws; and she's always making strange sounds, trying to articulate what she hears. I think she is a gifted child. Then there's Stacey's book with the recently added sub-title Re-Lighting the Lamp of Learning, almost completed.

Then, he thinks about the seating arrangement circus that went on last week. Ben kept sending texts a few times a day as the seating of Ibrahim El-Awad kept changing. The bishop was told not to be concerned about it, that he will be placed next to him on the final change. As people file in the banquet hall, they can look at the giant screen for their table number.

Stan would like to take his mind off this frightening event of Saturday night and focus on the program. But he can't! He picks up the phone and punches Greg's room.

"Hello?"

"Greg, it's Stan!"

"Hi, Father. How are you adjusting to this weekend?"

"Not well. I can't get my mind off 9/11. How about you?"

"I'm not cut out for this! Let's go downstairs, I'll buy you a drink."

"Sounds like a plan," Stan says. "I can't even look at the program for tomorrow."

They take the elevator down to the lounge, and who do they see already there massaging their glasses with olives on the bottom? The bishop and Jim.

"Well, it took you two long enough to decide you need something to keep you together besides your strong faith!" shouts Jim.

"I just got another text from Ben," says the bishop softly, wiping away any trace of smiles or attempts to change the subject. "He said as of now, El-Awad is sitting at table 38 and I am at table 19. He said it's going to change again maybe several times and not to worry. I will be notified the last minute at seating time.

"He also said there is an unused circular balcony around the hall that will be kept dark. So, there will be no problem for the sniper to establish a direct line."

The bishop finishes his drink while the waiter brings two Martinis for Stan and Greg.

"On another subject," Bishop Mark continues, "Greg, tell us what's going on with the Catholics."

"Oh, yeah! Last month Cardinal Fitzsimmons of New York received a green light from the Vatican to contact Archbishop Philip and begin first round talks on *Understanding of Common Principles*. It is their new initiative for the eventual union of the two oldest churches of Christendom..."

"We've heard this before, Greg," says Jim. "Too much politics gets in the way with hierarchs protecting their own turf..."

"I know, Jim, but you have to give them credit for looking ahead. What hope of survival do we have in a growing secular world around us, not to speak of Islam's shadow of two billion people staring down the Christian world. Even though the Vatican may claim leadership, what's wrong with looking at the greater good?"

"What do you think, Your Grace?" asks Stan.

"The whole world is in turmoil, sloshing around in a swamp of corruption. Everyone is in terrible need of redemption. We are just beginning to recover from a world plague and are realizing the problems that will follow. Man's obsession for power and control will continue to make a mess of things. All countries boast of great charters, constitutions and human rights, but it's only beautiful words on paper. In reality, man cannot help but exploit his fellow man and make him subservient.

"But as for church unity with the Catholics, I see it as a first step to unite the whole Christian community. I believe Jesus would be pleased to see one Christian Church. This is how it was meant to be in the first century. So, here is how it has to work: every Christian Church ought to approach the Main Table and contribute its value. And when they have all come and given of their best, the bounty submitted represents the Christian Faith.

"The next step would be to invite all other faiths and do the same thing. And when all have contributed their value, therein will lie the Church of God and the faithful of the world would be finally united. Gentlemen, this is what God wanted us to do, not to split off and have different religions numbering well into the hundreds."

"Wow, Your Grace," says Greg, "that's funneling all worship into one pipeline, straight to God."

"That would be the quintessential church of all time, wouldn't it?" exclaims Stan.

"Exactly," says Jim. "The Faith would be One and would contain in its codex all the values and principles taught by Abraham, Moses, Jesus, Mohammad, Buddha and all the prophets throughout the millennia."

At this point of reviewing the last few months, Jim thinks of a problem that had become serious last year and tabled because of Covid-19.

"Greg, what's the latest on the tax exempt status of the church."

"Well, we had one phone conference about it, but the pandemic hit hard all year and the issue was tabled quietly. I suspect when things improve on the Covid-19 front, the government may revive the tax activity on the church. As I remember, Your Grace (looking at the bishop), our legal team in Washington said they felt they had a rock solid constitutional defense."

"Yes that's correct. Also, back in February when a cash shortfall faced us," adds the bishop, "during a financial meeting at the archdiocese, members of the council displayed great generosity. You were there when all the stewards pronounced resounding pledges."

On the Cusp of Peace

The next morning after breakfast, the program begins at nine o'clock covering several familiar topics for the four horsemen. For obvious reasons, none of them are that excited about attending these plenaries. They include *The State of Religion, Strong Headwinds of Relativism, Ethics on the Decline, Humanity: A Global Portrait.* These sessions are interspersed with a lunch, Q & A and a dinner at six o'clock.

They can pretty much predict the content where religious leaders will speak on the spiritual values of their faith and celebrate their outreach programs of unity and harmony among people. They've come to understand that no matter what gifted and inspired presenters say to lift the spirits of those in attendance, the fact remains they're "speaking to the choir." The guests not only heard all this before, they even preach these positions regularly. However, they know they're not talking to the people who need to reform.

"In these events, Jim says, "you notice the conspicuous absence of those who should be present but are not."

"Exactly right! Greg agrees. "Those in attendance should be not only religious people, theologians or clergy, but also the leaders of governments, industry, military, corporations and banks. These are the people who create havoc in the world; these are the ones who wage wars and fund projects of violence; these are the people who create poverty, hopelessness and despair; these are the people who need to listen to these talks and be inspired to change."

"You know, it's not every day you find yourself in a banquet hall environment," adds Stan, "where everyone is happy and enjoying the evening with great food and friends. Then, a terrorist is suddenly assassinated. And you know it's going to happen. And it isn't even a surprise to us!"

Chapter 48

AN EVIL EVENT

Ibrahim El-Awad, director	*Chef*
Mohammad Najjar, group leader	*Maine*
Bilal, shipping & receiving Mgr.	*Boston*
Cairo, electronics/communications	*California*
Dalil, security guard	*Denver*
Emann, demolitions	*Elgin*
Famir, trigger man	*Florida*

S ince the first meeting eight months ago, Mohammad Najjar and his team met another five times to successively move the details of the event forward and for everyone to know exactly what to do. Three of those meetings were by phone which also tested the communications quality of the special frequency.

The meetings were designed to clarify everyone's role to the point where it became second nature, like memorizing a script for a play. The members communicated frequently and tested themselves for any contingency that may arise. Even though Famir had one major responsibility, the others insisted he participate in all the exercises and dry runs.

On this Friday, September 10, they meet for a final time in Mohammad's suite at the Hampton Inn. The hotel is minutes away from Grand Central Station and UN building (The Park). They await the arrival of Ibrahim El-Awad for a final review of everyone's responsibilities. Mohammad checks his watch: 11 a.m. He phones room service and orders lunch for everyone.

"Okay, patriots, Boston, California, Denver, Florida and Elgin," says Mohammad. "Let's go over your overall stations and tasks before Ibrahim comes," he announces in Arabic. "Boston, you received truckloads of explosives in installments during the last two weeks. Tell us exactly what happened."

"I personally checked in four loads through the receiving underground platform. They came one at a time every third day and did not attract any attention from other departments. I and Denver took each load to the lower level and with Elgin's help, we distributed and secured the cases around the underground piles of the 39-story building..."

"What did the delivery manifest list as the items?"

"Pallets, boxes and shipping supplies."

At this point, there's a knock on the door and Mohammad lets Ibrahim inside. Everyone greets him with respect and praises. He wears a dark suit with a white scarf.

"The Chef is here, gentlemen," Mohammad announces. "We were just beginning to discuss everyone's job before you arrived."

"Please continue," says Ibrahim.

"As I was saying," Bilal continues "we distributed the cases around the piles of the third level below ground. Elgin, demolitions man, wired and tied the bundles into a series to a channel integrator switch. California, electronics/communications expert, programmed the circuit with the trigger phone."

"Have you tested the circuit?" the Chef asks.

"Over ten times!"

"Is the area secured? Who else knows about what you did?" the Chef fires back.

"Yes, the area is secured. The security manager, Denver, has the area locked and no, nobody knows what's down there. The three underground floors have shops, security offices, fire-fighting equipment,

271

warehouses, three-level parking, a petrol station and HVAC rooms. The parking area is not connected to the warehouse or storage rooms."

"Good! Are all the cases used?"

"Yes," Emann asserts. "We had several extra cases and we added them to the west side of building so when it goes off, the building will give way toward the west toward other buildings and a main road—for maximum results."

"Good work," says El-Awad. "Who has the trigger phone?"

"I do," says Famir with some hesitation.

"Have you double-checked the electronics, California? Does the phone work?"

"Yes, it has been tested many times," Cairo confirms. "You use the password to get access. Make sure you extend the little antenna, then to activate the circuit, press the speaker button. The phone is in a locker at Grand Central Station." He gives the key to Famir.

"Who has the password?" asks El-Awad.

"I do," says Mohammad. He gives it to Famir. Famir looks at it: *Jerusalem.*

Mohammad takes back the paper and tears it to pieces, throws it in the garbage. He then gets on the phone to add coffee and donuts to the order. He returns to the group.

"Okay! Here is how we do it. Pay close attention! All of us will have seats at the banquet. Once we know the Chef's table we will be watchful, all around him. We will do security detail because our esteemed 'Chef' is always under Israeli surveillance. They have been trying to kill him for years. We keep our eyes open around his table and watch for any unusual movement."

"I brought to a secure place 9mm guns for us," says El-Awad. "Once we pass through security, we will get them so we are armed. Everybody gets one before Florida. I'll explain why."

"Where are they, Chef?" asks Cairo.

"In the kitchen, of course!" says El-Awad with a slight grin. "Dinner will be served at 6:30. At that time I want you, Florida, to walk to Grand Central Station and get the phone from the locker. You have the key. You have plenty of time, so don't hurry; it's only a 10-minute walk.

"You walk back to the hotel, go through security again and go to the kitchen. Look deep inside the middle wall cabinet in the storage room, under towels, get your weapon and put it away immediately. Make sure nobody sees you. Then enter the banquet room and sit down to eat."

Mohammad now continues the instructions.

"At precisely 7:45 p.m. after dessert has been served, you will go outside and approach *The Park* within 50 yards to be well within range. You have to pass a memorial statue of Eleanor Roosevelt and then you are close enough.

"At 7:55 you will tap in the password and get access. You pull out the tiny antenna and at 8:00 sharp you press the speaker button once and hold it for two seconds. You will notice a red light blink once to indicate activation. Then you walk back to the hotel. There is a built-in two-minute delay, is that right, California?"

"Yes it is, Maine."

"Any questions, Florida?"

"No, we're good to go!" Famir responds trying to sound resolute.

"Okay, one final warning, Famir," Mohammad asserts. "*The Park* is approximately 600 feet from the hotel. That's about two football fields away. Walk away slowly toward the hotel. When you hear the blast begin the first cycle and the rumble that follows, come back to the hotel. I wouldn't worry about security at that time. There will be chaos all over. You need to show shock and alarm. Everyone will be running out of the hotel to see what's going on.

"Meantime the rest of you will stay close to the Chef and make sure we all exit safely with the other guests rushing to safety. We shall witness an evil symbol of colonialism finally collapse into rubble. It will be our message to the corrupt injustice over the years metered out by the big powers. Right will triumph over wrong and our cause will be heard around the world!"

There is a knock on the door. Two servers wheel in two carts of food. They set the table and serve everyone, leaving platters on the table. One of them uncorks two bottles of wine. They shout "Bon Appetit."

"We will return with coffee and sweets in one hour."

"Thank you," says Mohammad slipping them $20 each.

They sit around a large table and serve themselves a dinner that may likely be their last together. They joyfully pile on salmon and shrimp with artichokes and Mediterranean salad.

"Gentlemen, this is finally going to happen!" shouts El-Awad. "We will be victorious! Fe Sahetek! Raise your glasses and drink to a long awaited auspicious event. We will not be pushed around anymore. *The Park* has betrayed us for over 70 years. Now they have to build another facility so they can exploit other small nations."

Hour of Decision

Later in the afternoon, Famir goes to his room for some quiet time to collect his thoughts and address the pressure building inside him. Every minute that goes by, the realization of what he has to do continues to weigh heavily on his conscience. He can't help thinking about his own hypocrisy in betraying his own faith to serve a destructive political agenda.

The warm feelings that filled his heart from the caring people he met at All Saints the last couple years, remind him of a better life for him and his family, a life without fear, without guilt and continuous violence.

This is all he's been thinking about today during the final attack meeting. He knows he has to force himself to carry out his assignment, but he also knows the repercussions he and his family will suffer if he betrays the cause and doesn't act.

He calls Amira on his private phone and awakens her at midnight.

"Famir, are you okay? Where are you?"

"Amira, Amira! Listen! You have to get out of Nazareth. Tomorrow, go and buy airline tickets to New York. Pack only the essentials and leave the house. Take the kids and check into a hotel near the airport in Haifa; and take the earliest flight out. You still have active passport. Take all the money we have with you. I'm staying at the Hampton Inn now, but I have to leave this hotel because everyone's here. I will go to the Hilton Garden Inn..."

"Famir, what is going on? Why do I have to..."

"Listen, I am asked to do a terrible act tomorrow for the cause. I did not object, I have to cooperate with the plan. But, Amira, I don't know if I can do it! A few years ago at the West Bank, I got involved with what happened there—and I was okay with it, I just had a minor role. But I was a patriot then. Now they want me to be the point man to perform a horrific act..."

"What are you told to do?"

"I can't tell you now, but we can't go on like this anymore! Living in the States, I have realized our energies are wasted on violence and murder that never brings any positive results. I want us to be happy. And you know, we have not been happy. I'm worried about you and the kids.

"If I cannot act on this assignment, there will be hell to pay. That's why you have to leave. Don't worry about the house. Tomorrow, the word will go out and they may come for you. So, you have to get out. I am so sorry, but we have to secure a better life and future for us. Call me when you fly out. I will be at the Hilton Garden Inn, not the Hampton, okay?"

"Okay, Famir, please be safe. We will join each other soon."

Famir feels an enormous load is lifted from him with this decisive act to finally get his family to safety. He will now be free to do the right thing. He looks forward to settling in Elgin where his house will offer security and safety for everyone and a future for his children.

Amira knows full well when Famir was incarcerated, at least he was out of the plan for any hazardous event. But when she revealed that Famir had a chance to get out of prison with help from America, Palestinian money was brought in to help secure his release. She remembers taking money from Mohammad the same time she got a call that Jim was in town.

Chapter 49

SATURDAY, SEPTEMBER 11, 2021

The four accessories to an assassination arrive at the hotel restaurant for breakfast. They shuffle quietly viewing a long display of impressive selections, filling their plates as though it's their last meal.

"Any updates last night, Your Grace?" Stan breaks the silence.

"Yes, Father," the bishop grimaces, "several, including a disturbing one which kept me up half the night."

"What was it?" asks Greg with a worried look.

"Well, for one, Ben says it may be impossible to track El-Awad's location because of last minute changes. Ben's spotters reveal the three targets continue to shift and replace one another—like the magic cups-and-ball game. But he assured me, once they get a fix on the real target, I will be placed as close as possible. I asked him, what if he ends up at another table where I can't even see him let alone check his wrist? He said that's the best he can do unless something changes. I would have to handle it as best I can."

"So, is that what kept you up last night, Your Grace?" Jim finally asks.

"No, it was the last text I received around ten o'clock. Ben said current intelligence reveals four security guards will be on hand as Awad's protection team. And they don't know who they are or where they'll be. If he finds out in time I will be informed."

"This is just great!" Stan explodes. "Not only you may not sit next to him, you may not be at the same table. And there are four goons watching everything around him! And you're supposed to finger him and give a signal? I don't know, Your Grace, whatever can go wrong with this assignment, just did!"

They sit at a round table quietly and eat mechanically without any sensual response to the waffles, omelets, fruit or coffee. They consume nervously, facing their food. Finally, Greg lifts up.

"What are we going to do?"

The bishop looks up and adopts a stoic pose only he can do.

"Gentlemen, we shall proceed as planned and work with what we have. Let's keep alert, and between the four of us, maybe the real target will reveal himself. We apply common sense and reason as much as possible and then we treat the unknown with prayer."

Gala Banquet

The two-day Symposium on World's Religions ended with a heart-warming presentation by Pastor Elizabeth Powell from St. Matthew's Episcopal Church, in New York City. Her message of fellowship, peace and understanding through an unwavering fidelity to Christian teachings, embodied the values that everyone seeks, no matter their race or nationality. It truly touched everybody—well, almost everybody.

Around five o'clock guests leave their meeting rooms following the breakout discussion sessions from the Saturday speakers. They gather around the elevators talking, sharing ideas and generally nodding their approval to the week-end's events. Most take the elevator to the 4th floor banquet hall while others take the stairs. Two large rooms are joined together to accommodate the 400 guests of the conference.

They file in the hall leisurely, many approaching several portable bars in service for a drink. A giant monitor on the wall displays the fifty table numbers and their location. The bishop and his group are enjoying a drink with ever restless eyes, looking for the target. The bishop checks his phone for recent texts, but there is nothing. He sends a text to Ben asking for the latest information on the target. Moments later, a text displays:

"You are still at table 39–so is target, but as I said before–can change. Coming to hotel—We have people on it. Will advise."

Stan brings the bishop a bottle of water. "Should we sit?" he asks.

"We may as well."

They walk over to table #39 and take their seats; the bishop at 6 o'clock and Stan at 3 o'clock for a different view of the table. Fortunately, no one else had arrived yet, so they can do this. The bishop gets another text.

"Arrived at balcony. Our people lost fix on target. The 2 doubles switched places with target in crowd. Not sure if real one is still at #39. Sorry, use own initiative to achieve I.D. Let me know. Good luck!"

He shows Stan the message and laughing to suggest they're looking at some picture. Stan raises his shoulders and smiles. Just now, three people holding drinks come to fill the table at 7, 9 and 10 o'clock side. Three seats are still vacant, 12, 2 and 5 o'clock. The hall now is full and most of the guests are still milling around talking.

"Would everyone kindly take your seats please," a voice calls through the speakers, "so we can get started?"

Within minutes, three men in dark suits come to table #39. One sits at 12 o'clock wearing a white silk scarf while the other two take seats 2 and 5 o'clock. This completes the table of eight. The bishop is eyeing #12 over his glasses while Stan finds himself between two of the target's bodyguards. Bilal and Cairo notice Stan in his priestly suit between them, but see no problem.

Two tables over is #14 where Greg sits facing the target from the side. And one table over on #23, is Jim who can see his group from the rear.

"Ladies and gentlemen," a voice penetrates the air space, "my name is Ted Mitchell, your host for this evening. On behalf of the 2021 Symposium Committee, I thank you for attending this year's conference and I hope it has been a meaningful experience."

The bishop notices the possible target twist his left wrist to see the time on his diamond-studded Rolex facing inside. He could not see any burn scar. He looks at Stan who shakes his head.

"At this time," the host continues, "I call on Pastor Elizabeth Powell for the invocation."

The Episcopal priest stands, looks around at all the people who saw value in coming to share religious beliefs in peace and tolerance. With white collar under a black vest, she sports a red jacket and black skirt. She smiles broadly and brings the mic to her chin.

"Good evening my good friends. Thank you for coming to listen to a variety of spiritual topics that bind us all together. Let us pray: Lord, we thank you for shedding your grace over this symposium. We also thank you for guiding us toward deeper understanding and peace. May this event enlighten us and open the door to achieve renewal in a meaningful and lasting way. We ask your blessing for the nourishment we're about to receive, for you are Holy and ever-present, now and forever. Amen. Enjoy the evening!"

"Amen," the bishop whispers and crosses himself to close the prayer. He checks the time: 6:30. Heated food warmers are rolled out onto the floor where servers begin passing out the soup. At the other end of the hall, Famir stands, leaves his napkin on his chair and mechanically heads for the nearest exit as though guided by a force he's unable to resist. A part of him still feels in control as he's done nothing wrong...yet.

The bishop gets a sudden text from Ben. "The other target is at table #23! Do what you can with your people. Find the right one! Sorry, no more info. Let me know!"

He looks over at #23 and spots a target. He's astonished how similar these three look. The bishop texts Stan near him, asks him to go to #23 and tell Jim to check the target at 9 o'clock on his left. If that's the right target, it's up to Jim to send the signal.

Servers are collecting soup bowls and begin distributing salad dishes with three types of dressing. Meantime, Stan gets up, waves to table #23 from a distance and walks over to Jim. He leans over him and whispers loudly while smiling and pointing away.

"We think the target is here to your left. Confirm and let us know. Wait a few minutes before you start looking him over—Good to see you," he shouts over the noisy hall.

He taps Jim on the shoulder and returns to his table laughing. Jim's heart is racing like never before. No courtroom drama has ever been half as stressful as this. He looks around at his table and smiles. At 9 o'clock to his left is the rumored target with a white scarf. Another man with the same look sits near the target along with two older gentlemen to fill that side of the table. Jim can't tell the real one, with scarf or without.

Immediately on Jim's right and just across from the target, a young couple is flirting and having a good time. Jim notices a diamond ring she's flashing around while he's showing her photographs on his I-phone. It looks to Jim they must have been recently engaged. He smiles at them hoping they may offer a temporary respite from the pressure building inside him.

"Let me guess," Jim announces. "You just got engaged!"

"Yes," she responds. "Does it show?"

"In more ways than one. Congratulations!"

"Thank you!" they say in unison.

By now, Famir is returning from the Grand Central Station with the special phone. He checks the battery life: 92%. He enters the hotel, passes through security, takes the elevator to banquet floor and makes his way to the kitchen. He now understands why he didn't get his weapon earlier. He bypasses the main prep table, passes two workers and enters the storage room. Searching in the middle cabinet, he finds a 9mm weapon under towels. He stares at the heavy weapon for a moment and quickly tucks it away.

"Can I help you, sir?" a kitchen attendant startles Famir.

"Oh, sorry! Just need a towel. I spilled my drink on the table. Thank you."

Famir feels an enormous burden carrying the two instruments of violence and mayhem. He walks back to his table totting several towels. The kitchen aid watches him with a confused look.

Salad plates are now being gathered while a string ensemble plays soft elevator music, hardly the appropriate accompaniment for the building tension among a handful of people. Heated food warmers are rolled out again with the entrée of the evening: creamy herb chicken with mashed potato and green beans almandine.

Ted Mitchell approaches the mic again.

"Ladies and gentlemen, may I remind all that a video of the weekend's program is available at a table outside the hall for only $10. The committee hopes to do a 2nd Annual event next year. You will receive more information as it becomes available. Make sure you enter your name and contact information. At this time, I'd like to ask all of you for a minute of silence in observance of the 20th Anniversary of 9/11, 2001."

A hush comes over the hall as everyone bows their head respectfully—well, almost everyone.

"The committee thanks the presenters for a thought-provoking program. Enjoy your dinner and the rest of the evening. Thank you!"

The target's men are still positioned around him and find no visible threats. Benjamin is on the balcony looking down through his field glass. He has spotted the three targets but still awaits the real one to be exposed. He receives a text from the bishop:

"Target not at #39. We think #23—we have man stationed there –will advise."

With great trepidation, Jim is touched with a flash of genius. He texts the bishop: "I think I know which 1, but must get closer 2 make sure. Will take I-phone camera from couple next 2 me, go behind target & take picture. If I confirm target, will snap picture. Flash is signal!"

The bishop reads it and gives Jim a thumbs up from a distance. A surge of fear runs through the bishop like an electric current to signal the presence of evil. For a moment he envisions the icon of St. George. The imposing image of the fearless saint on horseback gains detailed clarity in his mind as the holy warrior prepares to drive his spear through the menacing beast.

Bishop Mark sees himself in a front row seat to witness the extermination of evil incarnate as he awaits the fatal thrust. He quickly reaches for his amulet by following the chain loop into his vest pocket. He removes it and clutches it tightly, his hand shaking. He then forwards Jim's text to Ben. All eyes now converge on table #23.

A clatter of dishes fills the hall as the dinner plates are picked up and tables are cleared for dessert. Famir looks at his watch: 7:40. He's unable to finish the last piece of chicken, wipes his hands and lays down the napkin. He stands and walks out to the hallway, into an elevator to the main floor...then out of the hotel.

Back at table #23, Jim turns to the young man next to him.

"Would you like a picture of you and your bride to be?"

"Oh, could you? That would be wonderful."

He gives Jim the I-phone under the watchful eyes of the target's men. Jim walks slowly around the table and approaches behind the suspected target to the alarm of his protectors.

"Excuse me sir, I'll just be a minute to take a picture of the soon to be newlyweds across the table, okay?"

The bodyguards from several tables slip their hand inside their coat while El-Awad nods with a smile. He even lifts his wine glass to toast them. The bodyguards relax. While pretending to examine the phone camera, Jim's searching eyes over the target's shoulder pore over his arm with the speed of a digital scanner. Luckily, the target reaches for the breadbasket with his left hand while holding his wine glass with his right. Jim gets a quick glimpse of a long jagged burn scar exposed on his inside wrist. Being the object of intense scrutiny, he's surprised at his own composure; and can't believe this task fell on him.

Recognition of the target invites a fleeting moment when the noise and chatter around him magically subside. Now, Jim can only hear the distant dulcet melody of Offenbach's "Barcarolle" from the string quartet led by the calming accompaniment of the viola da gamba; a soothing combination that expands his emotional range—from the barbaric to the sublime.

Outside the hotel, Famir walks across the plaza passed the Eleanor Roosevelt statue and takes out his special phone. He pauses for a while and does not move. He then starts punching *Jerusa...* but he's overcome by a raging conflict erupting inside him.

Renewed guidance quickly filters into his consciousness to reset his course. He now turns toward the east side of the building and walks decisively, toward the wharf. When he reaches the pier, he clutches the phone tightly and looks up facing the bright moonlight. Moments later, he extends his arm back and flings the I-phone in the air with all his might, releasing the loudest scream. It surprises him and also draws the attention of two lovers walking on the distant boardwalk. He waits to hear it plunge in the water.

Back at table #23, Jim stands immediately behind the target, under the clear view of Ben and the sniper. He looks through the camera, makes a hand gesture for the couple to move closer to each other. The sniper above, moves in position with crosshairs on El-Awad's chest while the latter is smiling, wineglass in hand. The target checks the time: 7:55.

"In a few minutes it will be over," he whispers. He raises his glass again toward the couple, but actually toasting the impending disaster to follow. Jim steadies as best he can and clicks the button. It sounded like a trigger's fatal snap. He waits for the flash to follow as the music gets louder and floods his mind. He knows it should take only but a second, but it seems like an eternity. Finally, a splash of white light covers the table like a flash of lightening, forcing everyone to protect their eyes. Then Jim quickly rushes out of the way, around and back to his seat.

This abrupt move alerts the protectors who reach for their weapons. El-Awad checks his watch: 8:00. The scene freezes and time stands still for Jim. He knows the sequence of events is unleashed and there's no stopping it now.

A thump-like sound repeats twice, barely heard among the celebration revelry on the floor. But the bishop hears an unmistakable sound: a piercing screech from the dragon when two deadly shells penetrate El-Awad's chest. First he's thrust back into his chair, then falls face down on his dessert.

"Ya Lahwi!" (Oh, my God!) The bodyguards scream almost in unison.

"Hnak fi Alshurifa," (Up there, in the balcony!) yells Dalil.

For a few seconds, they are stunned to see their leader's face in a pool of blood soaking through the silk scarf and tablecloth. They scream in Arabic and begin shooting at the balcony gallery indiscriminately, but the sniper takes them out. The other bodyguards and doubles flee from nearby tables.

Famir starts walking back from the plaza feeling 100 pounds lighter. He knows the time has long passed and nothing's happened. He also realizes this is the end for him and his family. As he's nearing the hotel, he expects his partners in crime to be running out looking for him with guns blazing. Instead, he sees people rushing out of the hotel screaming and yelling. He has no idea what is going on, but he pulls out his weapon for protection as he expects the group to be after him. He rushes into the chaotic hallway and stops someone running out.

"Hey! What happened?"

"Someone shot upstairs at the banquet hall...then two more people killed. There's a man shooting at people from the balcony..." Famir

285

hears the wailing and screaming as guests rush out of the hotel, some of them falling and being trampled.

Meantime, security people on duty spill into the hotel from all directions. Famir rushes into the hall as everybody is running out. He is astonished to see El-Awad lying still with head on the table as if asleep, hands hanging down.

"Famir!" shouts Stan. "My God! What are you doing here? Why... you holding a gun?"

"Oh, Father, it's a long story..." he mumbles, eyes fixed on El-Awad.

At that moment another shot is heard and Famir feels a stinging pain in his arm. The gun falls from his hand. A security guard with weapon drawn approaches ready with cuffs to arrest him. Disoriented, Famir collapses in a nearby chair as he's ready to pass out. Stan hears the call to action and does some fast thinking.

"Officer, officer! He's with our group," Stan shouts, "assigned to the bishop's security. There's the man you want to make sure is dead," pointing to El-Awad. The officer checks Famir's wound in his upper arm. He ties it with a table napkin. "It's a flesh wound, sir. You'll be fine. Ambulance is on the way. Just stand by."

Soon, police arrive and tape the crime scene as the officer begins to question Famir and Stan. At that moment the bishop, Jim and Greg arrive with Benjamin, who shows his credentials to the officer.

"This is a special sting operation. We've been tracking this man for three years. He is the mastermind responsible for planning bombings and attacks in the West Bank in Israel. He came here to supervise a terrorist attack somewhere in the city. Were any of his people apprehended?"

"Yes," the officer looks at his pad. "A man called Bilal and another named Cairo. They will be questioned. We lost one in the crowd. The other two...Emann and a Dalil were killed here."

"El-Awad also had two doubles who dressed and looked like him. Any sign of them?"

"No, Mr. Morris—but the others! They will talk. We have their phones which will reveal the whole plan."

The bishop approaches Famir and hugs him as the latter holds his shoulder.

"I feel someone needs to explain what happened here," the bishop announces with a sense of relief.

"Yes...and there's no need to worry about a terrorist attack here because I can explain the other side of the story," Famir asserts cryptically, almost out of breath.

The bishop and the group look at Famir wondering what he could possibly mean. The investigators and forensic people soon pour in to do their job on the crime scene. The detective in charge questions and gets statements from everyone.

"Not to worry," Benjamin reassures the group. "I'll stay here to support your position and make sure they get the story right. Thanks for all you did. You all handled yourselves with control and bravery. We would not have succeeded without your help..." he looks at Jim, "and you! What a master stroke of genius! How did you think of taking a picture of the young couple—a perfect motive to get behind the target! Great ingenuity and bravery. We can use your skills in Israel."

After paramedics tend to Famir's shoulder, he and Stan ask for permission to get some air. They walk slowly downstairs and out into the plaza. The imposing 39-story structure before them, they stand in awe, a full moon next to it. Arm in a sling, Famir faces the whole compound as he explains what happened.

"Father, I had the trigger! With the push of a button, I could have become a hero in their eyes. But I would have destroyed this whole complex and hundreds of people along with it—my hands were shaking when I held the trigger phone. I just could not do it.

"What makes anybody think that I would willfully destroy and kill, unless my mind is so trained and twisted as to render the act essential at all costs? But I had to participate and play the deadly game. Totally, frightening!"

"Yes, that's right, Famir! More than frightening! The word we're looking for is *Evil*. You could have unleashed chaos in untold property damage and loss of life. But you must always remember! You didn't do it! Instead, you performed an impossible task—and crossed over to the side of righteousness to ward off evil in its tracks. And you did this knowing you would sacrifice yourself and your family—because you knew what would happen to all of you."

"Such a thin line between me and a horrific act! It's all about misguided passions, isn't it, Father?"

"Yes, when Good becomes foggy and Evil acquires clarity!"

Stan puts his arm around him as they behold the symbol of international peaceful cooperation among nations illuminated by a pale moon; a symbol that may have prevented mankind from destroying itself many times during the past 75 years.

Chapter 50

IN THE CLEARING

The view from the cabin looks out onto tranquil Long Lake at Saul's Fishing Resort. Greg, Jim and Stacey relax in comfortable chairs in the screened porch just before the dinner bell. They stare hypnotically at an orange glow slowly developing on the calm surface as the October sun stretches to touch the horizon. The distant echo of a loon signals with back-to-back yodels the decline of this day and the promise of re-birth tomorrow. All life here knows that unlike tenuous human promises, nature can be trusted to deliver.

They also watch Stan and Famir sit on the bench at the large pier, as they quietly check in with nature. This cabin, *Tymothy I*, is one of the biggest on the grounds with three bedrooms upstairs and extra rooms in the lower level. Stan made the late October reservation two months ago for a reunion of the group following the New York event. Fortunately, a sudden cancelation made possible to book Timothy I cabin to accommodate everyone. He just had a sense somehow things would turn out alright.

The pandemic that changed life on earth in 2020, spilled into 2021, but halfway through the year, many countries' casualty and infection numbers improved. However, by autumn, schools, businesses and institutions re-imposed the use of masks as variant strains took hold again, while restaurants kept the plastic shield between booths. Many feel that's likely to become a permanent fixture as confusion about masking is likely to remain for a while.

"Famir, I'm so glad you were able to come. I wanted to bring you here last year, but I knew you had to go home. By the way, see that buoy over there?"

"Yeah, what about it?"

"That's my buoy! It bears my name!"

"Really! How so?"

"Three years ago, I caught a big musky right at that spot—a real beauty! And I got on the leader board that day." Since then, they call it *Stan's Buoy.*"

"How about that!" Famir smiles. "You know, Father, I never thought that I would feel this good about myself, my family and our future. Thanks for allowing a family in need to use my house in my absence. Last month Amira and the children moved to Elgin. Our home is here, now. We really had no life over there..."

"Was that because of your divided allegiance to the church...and to the cause?"

"Precisely! Ever since I headed the Arab/Christian Cultural Center, I always believed that human values can eclipse cultural, religious and racial divides; that all people, deep down, want the same things: peace and security..."

"That's true. I believe that also. Remember the Buddhist monk Samsara two years ago? He said that just a handful of troublemakers can suck up all the oxygen and claim attention on behalf of a whole body of people—when most people do not subscribe to violence as the only option. Famir, somewhere in the evil cycle, courageous people must step forward, stop returning violence and examine peaceful alternatives."

Just then, a loud dinner bell sounds and all eyes turn toward the main lodge. They begin walking up the hill to the familiar building. Along the way, the other three join them from the cabin. A young fawn approaches Stacey and fumbles with her shoulder bag with its snout. She pets the delicate, almost fragile head but has nothing to offer the young buck except kindness. She can't help feeling that they approach us not only for food.

They walk up the terrace steps and enter through the side door, passed the soft-serve machine and approach the "Rybak" table. Stacey carries Amanda while Stan feels a rumble in his side pocket. He picks up to see a long text from the bishop.

Greetings, Father. Hope you're getting well-deserved rest up north. Something for U to think about while there. Tom Parish in Rockford retires at year end. I want you to take top spot at Holy Trinity Cathedral. You have a priest and deacon on staff. 400 families. Need answer by week-end.

Everyone takes their seat as Amanda lies comfortably in a carrier. Stan shows the message to Stacey and watches her light up. She reads it again, hugs Stan and yells out.

"Hey everybody! Great news! Stan just got a big promotion. The bishop is transferring him to Rockford."

"That's wonderful," Greg says. "Bigger city, bigger church? Bigger paycheck?"

"Holy Trinity Cathedral! Impressive!" says Famir. "We may have to move to Rockford."

"You will take the assignment, right Father?" asks Jim.

"We didn't discuss it yet, but I don't see why I wouldn't. I'll just miss some people who may not follow me."

The server comes to the table and places three platters of food: Ribs, baked potato and peas along with a basket of rolls. The chalkboard shows apple pie with ice cream will follow for dessert. Stan reaches in a bag and pulls out two bottles of wine. The server uncorks them and pours into everyone's glass.

"I'd like to make a toast," Stan announces. "To Greg Elliot, whose efforts in producing a vaccine ahead of schedule, led the industry last year and people today have been already vaccinated across the country. Congratulations Greg!"

"Thank you everyone," Greg replies with relief. "The vaccine development was the pressure cooker of all time. Thankfully, it turned out great. We've all had quite a year in 2020."

"Yes, we did!" says Stacey, "and 2021 is even better!" She raises her glass facing her group.

"A toast to all of you for your bravery and skill in helping to take down a known terrorist and diffusing an international tragedy." She holds up the New York Times front page with bold headline: *Church Group Outsmarts, Exposes Terrorist Plot at U.N. Plaza.* Guests from other tables realize the group they saw interviewed on CNN is right here. They stand and applaud with shouts of accolades."

"But the most courageous of all," Stan asserts loudly, "is a Palestinian Christian and member of my church, named Famir Masoud. Please stand, Famir. This man, at the risk of his own life and the lives of his family, single-handedly saved hundreds of lives and billions of dollars in potential damage by aborting a horrific terrorist attack. Ladies and gentlemen, he is the true hero! In fact, a ceremony will take place next month in Albany, N.Y. where the governor will present the *Medal of Valor* to Famir Karim Masoud."

More applause follows for Famir. Everyone settles down to eat when a man comes over to Famir from another table with his son.

"David," his father says, looking at Famir. "Meet a real hero!"

They shake hands as Famir looks at the youth.

"Son, remember, the person next to you loves you and protects you. Do not take this love and care for granted. Appreciate it and make sure you live up to it and be worthy of it. When you grow up do not become distracted, keep your eye on the right path and learn to always do the right thing. Sometimes it's hard to identify the right thing. Your father knows what I mean! Listen to your parents! Many children are not as lucky as you."

After the dishes are removed, they go up to the dessert bar and bring back plates of apple pie. They get in line to add the soft-serve and sit down next to the hot coffee.

"Father, I forgot to ask you: how is the pamphlet doing?" inquires Greg.

"Quite well, Greg. Tony over at Temple Graphics has been working with me in printing it in various languages. Then they ship them to our mailing house for distribution. It's really done well. Many donations have come in to sustain the publication and generate a little revenue to boot."

The rest of the evening is spent at the family room talking and reminiscing in front of the fireplace, and at the cabin.

The following morning, a pontoon boat arrives at the dock with a guide/driver. Stan ordered it for the day. He thought it best for everyone to be together and try their luck at fishing more comfortably. After breakfast, they walk down the pier and step onto the pontoon boat with their fishing gear. They sit in captain chairs though Stan prefers to stand. Amanda is taken to a neighbor in another cabin. Leah, a long-time friend, agreed to take care of her until they come back.

The sunny morning gradually gives way to darker clouds moving in.

"Dark clouds are good for fishing," Clyde, the guide shouts. "I'll take you for Walleye, I know just the spot."

The boat glides down Long Lake along the shoreline for about 10 minutes when it stops at a familiar drop-off point. They begin casting toward the shore, letting the bait sink toward the 20-foot drop. Greg and Stacey stand and cast into the depth, retrieve and cast again.

"Father tells me you're writing a book," Greg says as he's retrieving his bait.

"Yes, I'm almost finished. I have two readers looking at it."

"What is it about?"

"It's called *In the Realm of Holistic Learning.* It's about teaching primary school children traditional values at an early age along with the three R's, something that schools have abandoned decades ago."

"That's very interesting! Do you think schools will consider..."

"Whoa! I think I got a hit," she screams. Then everybody hears the drag tick loudly.

"Let it run, honey," yells Stan. "You got a nice one. When he stops, tighten the drag a little and start reeling him in slowly. I can't believe it! She rarely fishes!"

"I know what you mean, Greg," she says as the reeling gets more labored. "I may have a problem convincing districts to approve it, except that I can prove there is no religion or faith-based teaching involved. It's strictly moral lessons of right and wrong and respect for one another—nothing to do with religion or race."

Stan comes over and tries to help reel in, but stops. He reaches for the line and pulls it taught. He feels a jerky pull and stops.

"You still have your catch. It could be a lake trout. He's just sitting there, maybe wants you think your bait is stuck on a rock."

"What should I do, honey?"

"Wait him out. He'll start moving again."

"I have an idea for you," Greg says getting back to her book. "Don't waste time with school districts about a moral-based model."

"What do you mean, Greg?"

"Hey, I got one," yells Jim on the other side. He sets the hook and starts reeling in with not much effort. In a few minutes, he pulls up a baby Walleye. He returns it back in the water. "I want your daddy or uncle," Jim yells.

"Well," Greg continues, "school districts are too political and besides, in the past few years, schools are instilling in children more diversity, skepticism and an 'anything goes' system in a general non-moral framework. Also, some school districts have already introduced the subject of racial inequities to children. For sure, they are not as concerned about real education and permanent values, you know that!"

"So, what's your idea?"

"Stacey, I go to New York a lot. I have a friend at Shearson, you know, the educational publishers. His name is Vince Hampton. I think he might be interested in your take in restoring basic values in primary education. We had several conversations on the subject over lunch. But as you may suspect, nothing really changes. As publishers, they usually go with what the school districts want. My point is..."

Stacey's fish is on the move again. The ticking continues as it pulls most of the line in her reel. Stan comes over to help her.

"Don't let him take all the line...cause then he'll break it. This is a smart fish."

"Just my luck to hook onto a smart fish!"

Now, Clyde comes over to help Stacey bring in her catch. He takes her rod and begins reeling in real fast, then slow, then fast again. Then, lets him run a little, but keeps the line tight.

"The object is to tire him out so he stops fighting. Eventually he'll know he met his match and give up."

Clyde starts reeling in with some resistance. When the fish relaxes, he reels in faster. After a ten-minute struggle, he pulls him toward the boat.

"There he is! A beautiful Walleye. He must be near 30-inches. Take a picture!"

Excited, Stacey gets her I-phone and takes a couple pictures while Clyde releases the fish. He now starts heading back to the dock, where sure enough, the lunch bell rings.

Today's fare is two kinds of pizza with salad and coleslaw. For dessert, a variety of puddings and fruit. And, of course, the always available soft-serve. As they're enjoying lunch, Stacey remembers to ask Greg to continue about his idea.

"Oh, yes! I was going to suggest I put you in touch with Vince. He just might be interested in using your model to re-orient primary education material. From what he said, this sort of thing happens every generation.

"I don't think you're going to have any luck going to school districts with this," Greg cautions. "But if a publisher like Shearson decides to reawaken the educational community and even embarrass existing models, this work can be their poster child for the next 20 years. More important, it would be great for their book business."

"That's a great idea, Greg, I never thought of it that way."

"I don't have his card with me, but when I get back, I'll call him and explain what you're doing. If he shows interest, which I think he will, I'll get you in touch with him."

"Thank you so much, Greg."

The afternoon schedule has Stan, Stacey and Greg staying at the cabin. Greg has the lower level. He decides to shower and take a nap. Meantime, Stacey explains to Stan Greg's idea about her book.

"That's wonderful, honey. I can go with you to New York if you want."

"Well, we'll have to do it before your new assignment. Let's see if that guy, Vince, is interested. We have three months."

They kind of kick back in front of the fireplace. She is so excited about Stan's new assignment and a new direction her book can take. Stan hasn't seen her this happy since their wedding.

"I'm so glad things are working out for both of us," she says as her eyes are getting heavy from a very active day.

"Not entirely for me! I'm afraid I'm not batting 1,000."

"What do you mean?"

"There's one person I couldn't help."

"Who?"

"Tony! I just couldn't get him to open up totally. There's still something about him...I sense he's still carrying a heavy load. I just hope and pray he comes around soon before he's conquered...wish I could have brought him up here."

"Stan, I know he thinks the world of you. You've done the ground work on him. He will need more time, but I think he is strong and has the courage to cross over soon."

Stan and Stacey too, submit to an afternoon nap.

Meantime, Famir and Jim have a drink of moonshine that Jim brought in a flask. After catching their breath, they go outside to the crisp October afternoon wearing light blazers.

"Let's walk down this trail," Jim said. "You up for it?"

"Sure, Jim, I love to walk."

They pass a row of bright yellow honey locusts with interspersed dogwoods darkening to more orange and red. Then around the bend, the sugar maples add their rust colors to nature's tapestry, deliberately and predictably.

"Famir, I don't think we had time to talk...about what happened at Nazareth."

"You did a great job and got me off. I'd still be locked up over there!"

They kick and crush the large dried leaves as they walk.

"That's just the point! Do you remember I had this sealed letter that I gave the judge before the hearing?"

"Yeah, what was that?"

"Inside that envelope was an order from Benjamin to dismiss your case. All I had to do is present a good defense, which I did. That just made the case for acquittal more obvious."

"I don't understand, Jim...why was my case dismissed?"

Now, the red oaks that have been here for God knows how long, showcase their presence purposely, releasing their signature leaves by their feet.

"The bishop made a deal with Benjamin," Jim continues. "In return for your acquittal, he was to finger El-Awad at the banquet. Well, the target happened to be at my table and I had to do it. He also promised security for the Christian minority in Nazareth. The point is, the bishop stuck his neck out for you. He negotiated your release!—I want to make sure you know that. You owe him some gratitude."

"Jim, I didn't know! I owe him more than gratitude. I owe him my life!"

"That's true, you do. Most people charged with crimes over there never get out! By the way, I always meant to ask you, what were you doing at the banquet in New York? Weren't you at home in Nazareth with your family?"

"Jim, I had to participate in the terrorist plot. I didn't want to be part of it, but I knew my family was in jeopardy if I didn't assist."

"Oh, my God, you've been living a double life all along! We suspected something was up with you when you never came back."

"But this time, I moved my family out of Nazareth to safety. Jim, I...I had the switch in my hands! Hundreds could have died!"

"Yeah! I don't know how you pulled it off."

"Imagine, Jim," Famir begins in a pensive tone, "if the bishop did not intervene, you would not have come to defend me, there would be no order for acquittal and I would still be in jail now."

"Yes, and someone else would have punched the trigger phone— and there would be no U.N. building today! Who knows, it could have started a war."

The return trail to the lodge, takes them by water's edge. They walk quietly thinking about what might have happened. They pass by the river birches with their peeling bark, the scarlet black gum trees and the ever golden-brown hickories, all living a consummate existence, barely noticed.

Jim savors the surroundings and imagines how much better life would be if there was this kind of order; if people only lived the way they're supposed to. His mind now wanders back to April of last year when the judge threw out the case against Continental and his team basked in material triumph. He remembers the glint in Morrison's eyes, like a child who stole candy and got away with it.

Funny how things work out, he beams. *Last year, the new administration in Washington shut down all pipeline projects and furloughed thousands in the energy sector. I wonder how Continental is doing now.*

When they arrive at the cabin, all is quiet upstairs and downstairs. The dinner bell sounds again and everyone slowly enters the dining room. Tonight, the menu includes roast beef with mashed potatoes and broccoli. And for dessert? Assorted pastries. They take their seats and the server comes with the platters. Stacey invited Leah to join them and thanked her for looking after Amanda.

"Oh, she was no trouble at all! Very well behaved and observant. I have to tell you, when she wasn't asleep, she watched everything I did. I could see her mind working as she observed my actions with the widest smile."

"Leah, tell us something. We got friendly with one of the loons the last time we were here. I know it sounds strange, but have you had any experience with them?"

"Funny you mention loons," she smiles. "Yesterday when you all were fishing, I took Amanda out for a little sun down by the pier. We were sitting there enjoying the warm sun and water when a loon landed near the pier. I didn't pay much attention to it, but it began wailing loudly. I think it was talking to Amanda.

"The funny part was, the baby began howling right back—and they were having a grand old time yelling at each other. I really think they were communicating!"

"I believe it," says Stan. "It might have been the Adviser!"

The group now settles down to enjoy food and fellowship. Peace and tranquility reign over the tables at the dining room. Everyone is quietly reminded of their origin, at a place where human problems are brought and untangled. It's the mystical landscape where many come to fish and in the process, experience a personal reset.

Stan pauses to fix on everyone, trying to tame the tensions and passions from a complex world of a fast-paced life. He's convinced they're unwittingly seeking refuge from a world of diminishing values, a condition fraught with fear and uncertainty. He's learned to read it in their faces—and his own, as well.

For Stan, revitalization begins with a look at a willow branch bathing near the shoreline, a nearby loon thrashing with excitement, or a young fawn nipping at his pockets. Encounters like these help repair his inner workings and inspire his ministry. Almost like arriving with a soiled shirt and before long, it's magically dry-cleaned.

Once again, the recurring question comes to mind: *What's the difference between a Christian and a moral person?* But now, he's able to finally settle this.

> *For one, both share a similar moral platform to guide their life. However, the Christian has the advantage of 2,000 years of Holy Tradition and Church history with volumes of sacred writings to verify and validate the person of Jesus and His short, but enduring ministry. Also, the Christian has a Church to attend to authenticate a body of faith for continuing support; to keep lit a beacon to guide him through troubled straights in life. On the moral side, he invokes Polonius' advice to his son Laertes in Shakespeare's HAMLET—"This above all: to thine own self be true."*

An awful awareness settles in the consciousness of guests, as well; either from a jolting bolt of lightning or a daily dose of enlightenment. They realize that, human flaws notwithstanding, the struggle toward renewal must continue. They've come to understand that failure to connect to a higher self does not mean they should stop trying and accept a morally compromised life. Even individuals conquered by the *New Normal* find inspiration to join those reaching out in a continuum toward hallowed levels of human excellence.

Moreover, they're able to view their place within the cosmic spectacle. They see clearly the right/wrong fork ahead with refreshed instincts to make the right choice. Clearly, the obscure and dark tunnel in which they found themselves only a few days ago, gradually acquires the brightest light at the other end. But...what about the rest of the world?

About the Authors

PAUL FRANKS

Originally from the Chicago area, Paul earned his college degree that attracted him to Big Pharma. As he built a 35-year career in Sales and Marketing, he also developed a life-long stewardship in religious education of young people through several church communities. His focus celebrated traditional moral values as a necessary foundation toward a well-balanced life. While retired, his weekly volunteer service continues at the county food bank for the needy. Paul enjoys reading, fishing, golf and bocce. He resides in Geneva, Illinois with his wife.

S. P. STAMATIS

Born in Europe and raised in Chicago, Steve took his dad's advice to learn English seriously. He developed a love for the language and later earned a Master at DePaul University. Following a 40-year career in the printing industry, he enjoyed early retirement years teaching English at area colleges. He's written two other novels, several screenplays and a volume of poetry. Many insist we evolve from profound life-altering events. This may be true, but Steve believes it's the subtleties in life that shape who we are. He lives with his wife in Addison, Illinois.

CPSIA information can be obtained
at www.ICGtesting.com
Printed in the USA
LVHW050757050222
710353LV00029B/647